I0762958

BUT WON'T I MISS ME

HARPERVIA

An Imprint of HarperCollins*Publishers*

BUT WON'T I MISS ME

a novel

TIFFANY TSAO

HarperCollins books may be purchased for educational, business, or sales promotional use. For information, please email the Special Markets Department at SPsales@harpercollins.com.

hc.com

FIRST EDITION

Designed by Yvonne Chan

Title page art © dule964/stock.adobe.com

Library of Congress Cataloging-in-Publication Data has been applied for.

ISBN 978-0-06-344849-0

Printed in the United States of America

26 27 28 29 30 LBC 5 4 3 2 1

For my mother, and the mother figures in my life

And for my two little clouds

“Therefore, since we are surrounded by such a great cloud of witnesses . . .”

—Hebrews 12:1

I.

VIVI

i.

The shock was not sudden but creeping, like sitting in a bathtub of warm water turning cold. My stomach had been bubbling with hope when Acek had turned the key and opened the front door. But as I wandered through the new house, an invisible weight descended. My head began to ache. Cloud felt heavy in my arms.

Acek pulled open the curtains to let in more light. Disturbed, they released a dry shower of dust and the faint scent of mold.

"Can't rent a place in the city this size for this price," he observed in his gravelly monotone.

"Never," I murmured, trying to sound appreciative. Which I was. Genuinely. What would I have done if it weren't for Acek? Where would Cloud and I have gone?

Cloud began to squirm, and my bad shoulder twinged. I set him down on the mud-colored tiles to let him crawl around as I further sized up the place we'd call home.

Weeks beforehand, Acek had told me over the phone that this place came partially furnished. At the time, I took it as a plus and told him to say yes. Now, I wondered if Acek had been trying to warn me. The puke-yellow sofa was pimpled in gray lint and sagged. The kitchen cabinets and drawers were stocked with chipped crockery, five forks, and a melted silicone spatula. There was a broken-down wardrobe in the bedroom. In the other room sat a black desk coated in gummy residue to which roach and rat droppings had become stuck. But Acek's expression showed no sign of disgust or dismay, and I recalled what my sister had said once—about how Gabe had spoiled me. And I felt, guiltily, how she must have been right. Splitting up with Gabe meant leaving all that. This was my life now.

Cloud made it to Acek's foot and, clutching at Acek's trouser leg, pulled himself up to standing. I saw a look of uncertainty cross Acek's face as his calloused hands hovered above Cloud's little head, unsure of what to do. I swooped in—at least, as much as I was capable of swooping in—and picked Cloud up, noticing how dirty his hands and knees were from that briefest of crawls.

"Well, I'd better get going," said Acek, running his hand through his thinning hair and glancing at his trusty Casio watch.

His niece, Nina, had driven us. She was still waiting in the car.

"Thank you so much, Acek," I said, reminding myself of all the things he had done to help me in this new stage of my life. He'd given me back my old job. He'd helped me find this place. Out of his own time and pocket, he'd even installed essential appliances—fridge, cooktop, washer, phone—so everything would be ready when Cloud and I arrived. There was a new mattress in the bedroom, too, as well as some basic food items in the pantry and fridge.

As we stood together, the sunlight muscling through the filthy windowpanes, I felt the sudden urge to hug him, or pat his shoulder, or squeeze his hand, or something of the sort. This wasn't necessarily strange, given he was the closest thing to an uncle I had. But we rarely showed affection that way. And something about his demeanor stopped me.

"I'll call you later about Monday," he said finally. "Take the weekend to rest and settle in."

I nodded. Monday was when I'd start work. He'd already mentioned there was an employee carpool. Nina would pick me up. Then he said goodbye and left.

I studied the bus timetables Acek had stuck to the fridge. Cloud plucked off a magnet and tried to pop it in his mouth. I pried it from his fingers and bent down to pick up the fallen timetable, but my thighs were too weak to lift us back up. We sank to the floor. Unfazed, Cloud crawled off my lap to explore the kitchen. Kneeling, I stared into the blankness of the fridge door. And the most horrible feeling flashed through me, though I couldn't name it then. Or now.

That was more than a year ago. I've grown used to everything. The dust and grime has never gone away, no matter how much I clean, but it's become familiar after living here so long. It's our dust now. Our grime. Our sticky dropping-studded desk, which I've draped in a plastic tablecloth and piled with the two empty suitcases so I never have to be reminded of its surface. Our broken-down wardrobe, which is only a little more broken-down than many other items of furniture I've acquired over the past year. Our pimply sofa, where I sit every night after putting Cloud to bed, just like I'm doing now, gathering the energy, which will never come, to fold laundry, to put away dishes, to clean the bathroom, to tidy up the toys.

I've even grown accustomed to Acek's aloofness, which I thought I was imagining that day.

You can get used to anything, I tell myself, half bitterly, half in encouragement.

The memory surfaces, as it does from time to time. A memory of a memory. Of waking up after my rebirth. Of soft morning sun streaming through the trees, casting shadows on the private hospital lawn.

"Hey." It's Gabe's voice—soft and cool as the pillow against my cheek.

I roll my head away from the window to face my husband. He is sitting by my bed, eating yogurt and berries from a bowl. Probably from the café downstairs. Spending the night in the hospital has only accentuated his effortless good looks, his thick black hair more tousled than usual, light stubble throwing his chiseled but boyish features into relief.

"How do you feel?" he asks, taking my hand.

I think before answering. "Good. I feel good." It's actually true.

A fleck of purple-stained yogurt flies from his laughing lips. "See? Told you you'd be fine."

"Where's the baby?" I ask. I haven't named Cloud yet.

Gabe presses the call button. "They'll bring him, now that you're awake."

"How long did it take?" I ask.

"An hour and twenty minutes."

I stare. "That's it?"

Gabe laughs again. That easy, disarming chuckle of his. "You were a hungry girl."

I don't know why I'm so surprised. Everyone told me it would be this way. Quick, with no recollection of pain. As if I'd simply fallen asleep and woken up refreshed.

Even the terror I felt before losing consciousness has a fuzzy, faraway quality to it—the fear that spiked when my muscles began to slacken, and the midwife pulled the baby I'd just birthed from my arms.

"No, no, no," I mumbled, the words coming out in a slurry, the midwife gently pressing my head into the pillow, my body into the bed.

"*Ssshh*. It'll be over before you know it," she said. "You won't feel a thing."

Gabe appeared, his face hovering over mine. He kissed my forehead.

"You'll be fine, Viv," he told me.

I tried to scream, but blacked out instead.

Now I've woken up to the sun and the lawn and my loving husband. The nurse brings the baby in for his first breastfeed, and the world is complete.

I'm tingling with joy as my son begins to suckle. It must be joy. What else could it be?

The nurse beams with approval. "A perfect latch."

Gabe kisses my cheek and gazes at our child.

I pick at my top molars with my free hand. There's something lodged there. It's flat and jagged. I yank it out and examine it: a shard of bone, sheathed partially in gooey flesh.

The nurse holds out a small metal tray for me to drop the bone into.

"We try to clean you new mothers up as best we can," she laughs. "But it's no easy task."

My eyes run to my nails, the undersides of their white tips caked with dried blood. I feel myself start to shake, but with great effort, it passes. The tingle remains. A constant thrum.

See, I reflect, from my ugly sofa in the new life I've made for myself. *You can get used to anything.* And like back then, I sit quietly, and will myself to be calm.

I have the time and space to do this alone at night. Tomorrow, a new day begins.

ii.

I burst out of the house into the cool dark morning, backpack slung over my right shoulder, Cloud's socks and shoes clutched in one hand. Cloud himself is tucked under my left arm—barely. I am holding him horizontally, by his middle, and he is screaming in rage. My co-worker Zoe sees my plight from inside the car and opens her door. I heave Cloud and his shoes in and clutch my left shoulder, which is on fire. Zoe helps again by shutting the door, trapping him inside. I run around to the other side and get in. The sound of my panting fills the air.

Lina turns around from the front passenger seat. "Good morning, Vivian," she says in her educated Malaysian accent, which has a British-posh ring to it. She's the most proper of all us employees. I don't think I've ever seen her in anything less dressy than a blouse. You'd think she worked at a desk, not a hobbler's bench.

"Morning," I mumble, strapping Cloud into his car seat.

Meanwhile, Zoe tickles his feet as she puts on his socks. He giggles, the white-hot tantrum of a few seconds ago already forgotten. That was why he was crying in the first place: he wanted to go out barefoot.

"*We must wear socks and shoes when we go outside,*" sings Zoe, Velcroing his little sneakers on.

I said almost the exact same thing earlier when pleading with Cloud, but never mind. It's different coming from Zoe, the kind of person children love. She's in her early twenties and had four younger siblings growing up in Vietnam, so she's great with kids. She wears tiny tees and baggy jeans to work, and always throws in fun jewelry. Today she's wearing a sparkly fruit-bat pendant, which Cloud is fingering in awe.

I open my backpack and take out our hastily packed breakfast: for me, a slice of bread spread with peanut butter and folded in half, for him a plain slice. We didn't have time to eat before leaving the house.

"Plain bread again?" asks Lina, who has taken the trouble to turn around once more, this time to inspect our food.

"He likes it that way," I say, mouth full of peanut butter.

She looks doubtful. "Doesn't he need protein?"

I know I could try to explain that Cloud only started hating peanut butter two weeks ago. That he now protests at even the thinnest smear. That I try to feed him protein in other ways. But Cloud woke up an hour earlier than usual and getting everything packed and ready with an almost-two-year-old grabbing my legs, demanding my attention, is really hard (physically carrying him screaming and struggling out to the car being the final straw), so, I do not have the energy to defend my decision to Lina, the most annoying of my co-workers, who herself was once a new mother but whose son is now grown and whose rebirth went without a hitch, as all rebirths do, my case being the exception, so she will never understand.

Stop being so negative, Vi. I remind myself she's just trying to help. It's not her fault she has lapsed into judgmentalism. People always find my state difficult to comprehend.

Despite my silence, Lina persists. "Have you tried making peanut butter pancakes? You could mix the peanut butter *into* the batter."

It's just as well that she's sitting in front. Otherwise, I'd strangle her.

From the driver's seat, Nina observes in her low voice, "I'm sure Cloud will be fine."

And then, Lina actually shuts up. I'm pleased—and surprised. Nina rarely says anything. She's a lot like her uncle, Acek, in this respect.

We reach the main road and Nina guns it to 45 kilometers per hour. It's the fastest we can go on the modified petrol they sell to waste-era vehicles. They want drivers to switch to newer energy-efficient models, insofar as they want anyone to drive at all. But Acek's done the calculations, and replacing either of our ancient vehicles—this rusty sedan or the company van—would be far more expensive than making do with the current state of affairs.

The sky has lightened to a cornflower blue by the time we pull up to work at the corrugated steel shed behind the run-down house where Acek and Nina live. In the summer, we start early to save electricity and take full advantage of the natural light.

As we spill out of the car, we greet Libby, who prefers to cycle to work. Like Zoe, she's a student who works for Acek part-time. Libby's bike is already resting against the shed wall next to our sign, *Arvin's Hobbling Services*. She's taken off her helmet and is fluffing her pink-streaked blond bob. Her full name is Liberation. She's the only one of us who isn't Chinese, though Acek swears he didn't take race into account when hiring. "It just happened," he claims.

I believe him. We once swapped recruitment stories during lunch. Everyone except his niece and me was hired via a flyer on the Chinese supermarket community bulletin board. Libby shops there too—a fact which made Lina's eyes nearly pop out of her head.

Though we're all ethnic Chinese, except for Libby, we're also quite the international bunch. Acek, Nina, and I are Chinese from Indonesia—Medan, specifically; Zoe's Chinese (a.k.a. Hoa) from Vietnam; and Lina's Chinese from Malaysia.

These are fine distinctions that don't matter to most people in the area, and they've dubbed us "the Chinese hobblers." They think we don't know, but we do. But today, we're leaning in to our nickname. It's Chinese New Year's Eve. We're celebrating together, as if we're one big family. Plus, tomorrow, the first day of the lunar year, Acek is giving us the day off.

We five employees trickle in through the wide roll-up door, me bringing up the rear, holding Cloud's hand. But instead of heading to their benches, everyone who enters the shed makes an immediate detour to the left. Once Cloud and I enter, I see why. A waste-era electric generator sits next to two squat silver cylinders of propane gas—a compact trio of highly illegal items. In the meantime, Acek comes through, parting our little crowd, carrying a metal tripod trailing two tubes. He sets it down with a grunt beside the cylinders, and I realize it's some sort of cooking setup, with a burner and valves and connectors for gas. It looks like he made it himself.

Hands on hips, he surveys the items with pride.

"Is this for tonight?" asks Lina. She manages to sound excited and disapproving at the same time.

Acek fixes us all with a deadpan gaze. "Don't tell the cops or you'll all lose your jobs."

Everyone laughs nervously, not just because of the joke-threat of unemployment. There's a certain thrill about a celebration so energy-lavish that it defies the law.

The mood changes tangibly. In anticipation of tonight's dinner, there's a lightness to everyone's movements as they settle down to work. Even I feel buoyant. I lead Cloud to his playpen next to my bench. My goal is to finish the toaster oven. Finally. With this goal in mind, I survey Cloud's toys like a warrior assessing her arsenal of weapons.

The play kitchen generally keeps him occupied the longest, but he used it a lot yesterday. There's the chance he'll weary of it too quickly, or worse, for good. The train set keeps him absorbed, too, but requires more frequent intervention if something goes wrong. The xylophone is useless, as is the pull-along duck on wheels—they've become non-entities as far as he's concerned. *Loved one day, discarded the next,* I reflect in passing.

After more deliberation, I select the imitation Hot Wheels cars with their broken but still serviceable plastic track.

"They can race," I say in as excited a tone as I can muster, placing them in a corner of the pen.

He looks doubtful, but I maintain my smile. To my relief, he takes the suggestion and toddles over to play. The clock starts now, not just for the cars, but for me: I estimate fifteen minutes before he calls for my attention or assistance. I scatter a few more vehicles on the other side of the pen, on the off chance they buy me extra time.

My left shoulder still aches too much from this morning's battle, so I pry open the toaster oven's side panel with my right hand. I fire up my sluggish brain to recall where I left off yesterday. The new inverter's already installed. Now I test it for efficiency. Not great, but it's the best we can do. More importantly, it passes official state requirements, albeit by a hair.

All I need to do now is replace the plug. I've just gone across the shed to rummage through the plugs and connectors box when I hear someone hollering my name. It's Lina. She's pointing frantically in Cloud's direction. I rush back to the playpen.

He comes into view, little eyebrows knitted in concentration as he fiddles with two pieces of track. My immediate happiness at seeing him alive and unhurt gives way to irritation. Why has Lina called me over?

"He's having trouble with the tracks," she explains loudly in a tone I know well. It's the one that seasoned, older mothers often use to speak with me whenever I'm with Cloud, which is all the time. The tone that even mothers my age or younger use once they realize I'm faulty, and therefore, how much I require their insight and intervention.

"Thanks," I mutter.

Lina is often oblivious, but she picks up on my sarcasm. "I'm just trying to help," she explains. "I know your condition makes it hard to sense these sorts of things."

"Then why don't *you* do something about it?" I ask.

She looks genuinely aghast.

"But you're the mother," she says. "I'd never dream of doing that!"

I close my eyes and take a deep breath. I understand what she's saying. If I were a normal new mother, I would never let someone else attend to my child. Her way of assisting is to stand on the sidelines, trying to get me to operate normally. It doesn't occur to her to lower the standards for normal operation; my health may be poor, but Cloud's needs haven't changed.

I enter the pen to help Cloud, who is getting increasingly frustrated, as Lina has anticipated. He wants to attach the track to another, incompatible one. I try to show him how they don't fit together, ashamed that even someone whose mothering abilities have long since faded has keener maternal senses than I do. But the more I demonstrate, the more incensed Cloud becomes. He screams and bangs the offending track pieces against the playmat, then hurls them out of the pen where they clatter against the concrete floor.

I glance at the clock on the wall above the entrance. Two tantrums today, and it's barely seven-thirty. I want to hide. I want to leave. I want to sleep. Instead, I lower myself with great effort into a cross-legged position and pull Cloud into my lap.

A change comes over me, as it sometimes does in such situations, and always beyond my control. *Machine mode*, I've come to call it. My eyes dim. My hearing grows more muffled. My emotions retract like snail antennae, shrinking from the exterior world. "There, there," I say, my voice modulating to a gentle register. My hands press his little head into the crook of my neck and pat his back. "I know," I hear myself say soothingly. "I know."

Except, I don't know. Not at all. I don't know how two pieces of orange plastic can infuriate anyone so. I don't know why, despite my best efforts to defuse these situations, they persist in exploding. I don't know what I can do to make everything better. I don't know why I am missing all the skills that I require to improve the situation. Cloud and I have been thrown into a deep pit, and I lack the ability to get either of us out. We will die in this pit, but everyone dies at some point, so if I can just postpone our deaths, it will be okay.

Cloud has calmed down, but not quite enough to be left alone in the pen again without making a fuss. I lift my body to its feet and sit Cloud on my right forearm, taking care to favor my left shoulder as much as I can. I walk back to the box of plugs and connectors. I set him down, and we both sift through. I select three possibilities and lead him by the hand back to my bench. He's chosen something too. My hope is that it will keep him occupied while I try to compare plugs and make a fit. Instead, he drops his choice and reaches for the three I've set on the bench.

"Those are Mama's," I say, pushing them out of reach. He lunges for the toaster oven's disembodied dials, and I push those away too.

"Wa," he yells in frustration. "Wa" means "want."

"No," I say softly but firmly. My fingers close gently around his wrists.

"How is the toaster oven?"

I glance up. Acek is watching us, sipping coffee from his thermal mug. It's the first time he's acknowledged my presence today. Even now, it's really the toaster oven he's acknowledging. This is normal behavior for him these days, and yet it still stings.

"Pretty much done. Just a bit of rewiring, and I think she's good to go."

My approval-seeking tone surprises me. It's the voice of a bygone era. It reminds me of when I first started working for Acek as a teenager, enthusiastic and eager to please.

Acek's expression remains neutral. "I told the client how much the repairs will cost. It's more than she thought. She said if we can sell it for her, she'd prefer that instead."

Out of the corner of my eye, I spy Cloud making a grab for the toaster oven frame. I haul him into my lap to restrain him. My left shoulder smolders.

"Okay, Acek," I reply in that same strangely peppy voice. "I'll give it a good clean too."

"You set the price, Vi."

I nod as Cloud struggles to break free of my grasp. "Wa," he insists.

At this last "wa," Acek seems to realize I could do with some help. He crouches down, the paunch beneath his gray striped polo shirt compressing into a ball.

"Come to Akong," he says affectionately, patting his knees.

Cloud toddles into his arms.

As they walk away, I pretend not to see the jellybean he slips into Cloud's mouth. Or think about the jellybeans he feeds Cloud in a surreptitious trickle when he thinks I'm not looking. Cloud probably gets at least thirty over the course of an average workday. I suppose I should be grateful that Acek is affectionate to Cloud, even if he's no longer warm toward me. Trying not to care, I return to the toaster oven. I now have added incentive. It's been Acek's new system since moving the business out here: for any item we end up reselling, 10 percent of the net profit goes to the employee who fixed it up. If the item comes from a customer—as in this case—they too get 10 percent commission, like selling on consignment.

Acek's always been savvy at the business side of things. It's how he turns a decent profit, though you'd hardly know it from the way he dresses and lives—the same cheap polo shirts and polyester trousers on rotation, the same secondhand furniture he salvaged from the streets and through migrant community networks when he arrived in this country in his late twenties, before I was born. Acek only buys something if it's on discount or cheaper in bulk. Even the jellybeans he feeds Cloud are from two human-torso-sized jars under his desk. I bet WholeSale had a deal: more jellybeans than any single person could consume in their lifetime, two for one. But to his credit, Acek's not a cheapskate where it matters. He treats us employees well, and our wages are fair.

Employees, plural. That's taken getting used to. Back in the city, it was just him and me. There are more customers out here. The cost of living's lower, but so are incomes, and even now, the cost of even the simplest RDC-compatible appliance is an investment that your average below-average household can't take lightly, if at all. Twenty years ago, when the shift from alternating current to revolutionary direct current was announced, the government assured everyone that more affordable appliances were being developed. *Technology evolves quickly to meet consumer demand*, they assured the public. But RDC machines are still expensive, and people out here still prefer to hobble old AC ones to fit the new grid.

Free of Cloud, I fit the new plug in no time. I bring the toaster oven to the testing station and turn the dial. I check my watch. At the three-minute mark, the heating element begins emitting an orange glow. I bring my hand close to feel how warm it is. For the final test, I'll have to ask Acek if he has any bread.

Acek is alone at his desk, doing paperwork. I ask first about Cloud's whereabouts, then about the bread. The answers to both questions lie in the house. I exit the shed and enter through the back door, passing through the kitchen to the lounge room, where Cloud sits in Nina's lap on the rattan-frame sofa watching TV. The blue curtains are closed—though the fabric is worn so thin they hardly keep out any sun at all. He's watching *The Wiggles* on DVD. As with most hobbled TVs, the screen flickers, but

Cloud remains mesmerized nonetheless. I wonder if he remembers the TV we used to watch—the latest in RDC technology; giant flat-screen; crystal-clear images. So energy efficient that we never had to worry about exceeding our household quota, not that we ever had to worry if we did. Those were the luxuries of being married to Gabe.

"So we'll pay the fine." Gabe would always say, letting the episode we'd just finished slide into the next, his arm drawing me closer to him on our sofa, his cheek nuzzling mine.

My chest aches at the memory, my body missing the sensation of being held and loved by someone my size. From this angle, in this light, Cloud's resemblance to Gabe is undeniable—the slope of his nose, the shape of his eyes, the way his little lips break into a smile.

Nina's startled to see me standing in the doorway.

"Acek asked if I could mind Cloud for a bit," she explains. "He had something to do."

Nina and I both call Acek "Acek," but in her case, he's her actual biological uncle—her father's younger brother. Her parents died in a car crash three years ago and left her the house. It's the main reason Acek moved out here, so his niece wouldn't be alone.

I met Nina for the first time last year. She came with Acek to pick Cloud and me up at the station. Truth be told, I'm not sure I know her any better than I did back then. She's quiet, though I wouldn't call her shy. Reserved, more like it. She keeps a certain distance, even when she does speak, even when she's standing right next to you. And she wears heavy makeup but pairs it with stretched out tees, ill-fitting jeans, ugly hoodies—streetwear, but without the style. The total effect is jarring. Somehow, you're not sure where to look.

I catch myself. *Don't be such a bitch, Vi. She lost her parents.*

As someone whose mother died young, I should be more sympathetic. Who cares what she wants to put on her face or what clothes she wants to wear? Not like I'm fashionable myself.

"Do you have any bread?" I ask. "I need to test a toaster oven."

Nina slides Cloud off her lap and heads to the fridge. I plunk down next to Cloud and squeeze his little thigh.

"Having fun, sweetie?" I ask, putting on my widest smile.

He answers with an abstracted nod, then returns to the blissful world of full-grown men and women prancing and singing in brightly-colored outfits. The settings keep changing. One minute they're in a forest, the next minute they're rowing a boat on a lake. It reminds me of the old Chinese music video DVDs that Pa would watch: a singer on a green riverbank, then at a famous landmark, then on a beach, the song itself rolling relentlessly on. Though he's happy, I feel guilty that he's having so much screen time. Twenty minutes per day is the recommendation for children under five, as Gabe was fond of reminding me.

When I remember this about Gabe, the ache in my chest goes away.

"Be good for Aie Nina, okay? Mama has just one more thing to do. Then we'll have lunch."

This time, Cloud doesn't even bother to respond.

I head to the kitchen, where Nina's taking out a slice of white bread.

"It won't be much longer," I say apologetically. "I just want to get this toaster done."

She hands me the slice. "Take your time. I don't mind. Anyway, I'm in between jobs."

"By the way, thanks for this morning," I add, to make up for my mean thoughts about her fashion sense.

She looks confused.

"In the car. When Lina was being Lina."

"Oh, that." Nina cracks a faint smile. "No worries."

She looks like she's about to say something else, but shuts her mouth instead.

*

The bread takes fourteen minutes to brown—not too bad for this kind of model. I do some calculations to come up with a price, then give the toaster a good clean. Some stains can't be removed, but overall, it looks pretty good. I return to the lounge room to retrieve Cloud. He's still glued to the TV, still in Nina's lap.

"Come, darling," I say in my sweetest voice. "Time to change nappy. Then, when you're nice and dry, we can have lunch."

He eyes me with suspicion. I wait one breath cycle, inflating, then deflating my lungs. I pull my lips into yet another smile and hold out my arms, keeping them at waist level for my shoulder's sake. "Mama made your favorite. Pasta."

A gleam of interest shines through. He's a fish eyeing the hook.

I add a further enticement: "There's a bikkie for dessert."

"Bikkie!" he cries, toddling over.

There's no way I can carry him. Instead, I lower my arms and lead him by the hand back into the shed.

As I change Cloud, I remember how overwhelming I once found the business of nappies. Inserts, liners, boosters. Cotton versus bamboo. All-in-ones versus all-in-twos versus pockets. Prefolds and flats. It had never occurred to me, pre-motherhood, that it *could* be so complicated. Then again, if I were a normal mother, it would have been easy from day one.

But things are getting better, I tell myself. No, not tell—*remind.*

Because it's a truth that I must remember, even though I don't feel or see it. It's what will get Cloud and me through. I try to list how things are getting better. For example, he is approaching the age where my rebirth complications won't matter as much; all new mothers revert back to their normal abilities five years after rebirth, and though I'm sicklier than my pre-rebirth self, the difference between other mothers and me won't be as pronounced. He can walk now, thank God—he no longer needs to be carried everywhere and all the time. He wakes up only once a night and goes right back to sleep. He's started talking, so my inability to sense his emotions isn't as much of a hindrance. In a few years, he'll start school. Imagine: five days a week he'll be cared for by competent professionals who will be able to properly nurture his little body and mind.

I dump the wet-bag of soiled nappies and wipes beside my backpack, disinfect my hands, and get out the boxes containing Cloud's lunch and mine. My stomach churns with faint anxiety about whether he will detect the mashed lentil puree I stuffed inside the penne tubes this morning and whether he will deign to eat them or refuse. Leaving no tube unstuffed was a calculated gamble: if there's no alternative, he has to eat them, right? A line pops into my head from the booklet from the Mothering Made Simple course, which Gabe signed me up for when Cloud was less than six weeks old. *Lentils are an excellent source of environmentally sustainable non-animal protein. Nutritious and delicious. Children love them.*

Just because he rejected lentil puree spectacularly last week and the week before and the week before that doesn't mean I should give up. *Persistence is key. Your child's nutritional well-being is at stake.*

We sit in his playpen together. I fasten Cloud's bib. I set the lunch box down in front of him. "Yum, yum. It's your favorite. Pasta."

I try to act nonchalant. *Eat, don't eat, it's up to you* is the vibe I seek to convey.

Cloud thrusts out his hands and devours two, double-fisted.

My stomach unclenches. Happiness rises.

Urgent hunger satiated, he slows down. His chewing becomes less eager. His forehead creases into a frown.

"No wa."

He drops the third pasta tube, half-eaten, back into the box.

I feign playful incredulity. "What? But you love plain pasta."

He meets my gaze. "No pay." Not plain. He's right.

"You ate two already. Weren't they yummy? Mmm."

I take his half-eaten tube and eat it myself.

"Mmm. Delicious." *Who are you fooling, Vi? You've never been a good cook.*

He laughs and offers me another, smashing it into my lips.

I eat it. "Yum! So good!"

He tries to feed me another.

"No, no. That one is for Cloud."

"No wa."

"Just try? If you finish your pasta, you get dessert, remember? There's a bikkie."

"Bikkie!"

"Bikkie later. If you finish lunch."

"Bikkie!"

"Two more pastas. Just eat two more for Mama, then you can have the bikkie."

We've devolved into the bargaining stage. I know it's all downhill from here, but it's too late. We're already bottom-bound.

"No wa! Bikkie!"

"Just one. Please? Eat it for Mama?"

"Bikkie!"

Just beyond the playpen barrier, Lina hurries into view. Is she coming to help? Did she take what I said earlier to heart?

She opens her mouth. "Mentioning the biscuit was a mistake. Nutritious food is its own reward."

The murder in my eyes sends her scuttling away. I turn back to Cloud.

"One more bite," I plead.

"No wa! No wa!"

Cloud kicks, sending the box flying. The tubes scatter all over the mat.

"No!" The word is out of my mouth before I can stop it. A loud boom. "NO!"

I crawl over and pick up the tubes, throwing them angrily back into the lunch box one by one. "Why did you do that?" I shout. Not that I expect an answer.

Cloud wails. Of course. His own mother is yelling at him. *Where's machine mode when I need it*, I think bitterly to myself, too angry to feel sympathy or remorse.

But I do feel shame. In it floods, filling my body, flushing my cheeks. I'm acutely aware that all eyes in the shed are either on us or trying very hard not to be on the mother gone wrong and her poor, poor son. His howls of anguish ring through the shed.

Zoe comes over. I can't even bear to meet her gaze. She touches my shoulder and the softness of the gesture makes me flinch.

"You must be tired, Chị. Have some lunch. I've eaten already. I can take him outside."

Zoe has the endearing habit of calling me "Chị" and Cloud

"Em"—"big sister" and "little sibling" in Vietnamese. The Vietnamese Chị and what I call my own big sister (Ci) are pronounced similarly, and the familiarity has a calming effect.

Zoe even opens my lunch box for me (filled also with pasta and lentils, but mixed together) and hands me my fork. Then she and Cloud are gone. I can hear her voice receding into the distance, telling him about how they're going into the wild to look for creatures. Then the shed is quiet.

I'm too embarrassed about my outburst to do anything but stay where I am, cross-legged in the playpen. An animal belongs in a cage. I eat my food. And as I stare at the fallen pasta tubes, my mind flits to another site of shame. The community center where the Mothering Made Simple class met every Wednesday morning for six weeks. Arched doorways and skylights. Meticulously maintained indoor hedges. Taupe and sage paint. Tasteful and elegant, like all the public spaces in our old neighborhood—the parks and playing fields, the pavilion and library, the green, the oval, the square.

I recall the week we learned about lentils and nutritional well-being. *Solids*, read the words on the whiteboard, as if *solids* could only ever refer to solid food for infants, and not, for example, geometrical solids, which had been my first thought. Another symptom of my rebirth gone wrong.

I try to remember what else I learned that day as I walked Cloud around the back of the room, bobbing and shushing him, notebook and pen abandoned on my chair. The plan had been for him to nap. The plan hadn't worked.

I could catch snippets of what the instructor was saying if I made a concerted effort to tune out Cloud's fussing. What solids were ideal for starting bub's food journey: sweet potatoes, bananas, carrots, oat porridge, Weetabix. What quantities were ideal at week twelve, and thirteen, fourteen, and so on. Such detail. I glanced at the other mothers, babies quiet in their arms, effortlessly committing to memory everything the instructor said. I wondered which one would be the most understanding if I asked her to write notes for me in my book.

The instructor proceeded to draw a color-coded wheel chart on the whiteboard suggesting different categories of foods to rotate among in three-day cycles, one-week cycles, two-week cycles, in differing combinations. Such an approach would assure the best nutritional outcomes. It would expand bub's palate and sensory intelligence. Even if bubba refused a food, it shouldn't be taken out of rotation. *Persistence is key. Your child's nutritional well-being is at stake.*

Yes, that's where I heard it. The instructor said it—before breaking off to address me by name.

"Vivian, is everything all right?"

She looked deeply concerned.

A dozen more concerned faces turned to stare at me. A mother unable to quiet her newborn? Unheard of.

"It's fine," I assured the whole room.

"A nappy change?" suggested the instructor.

"No, no. He's dry."

"You're welcome to breastfeed, of course."

I still remember the pause before my reply. "I know."

It wasn't long afterwards that I made my move, grabbing my diaper bag and striding briskly away with Cloud in my arms. Two floors up I found an empty function room carpeted in mauve, stacks of chairs and folded tables stored neatly to one side. I remember how swiftly I worked, even though I had only one hand free to pour, measure, and shake. One eye I kept on the door, as if the other mothers from my class were bound to burst in at any time.

But they didn't. No one did. I popped the teat in Cloud's mouth and angled the bottle to slow the flow. How peaceful it was, on the carpet in that empty room. *I could stay here forever*, I thought. The cool cloudy-day sun shone through the windows as Cloud's lips and cheeks moved in a satisfying suckle motion, his tiny eyelids drooping gently down. Once he was asleep, I packed everything up with my free hand, careful not to wake him. Solids awaited. I returned to class. In hindsight, I should have stayed put.

*

Once I'm done with lunch, I clean up the rest of the scattered penne and head outside in search of Zoe and Cloud. I feel calmer. Better. I resolve to stay this way.

Zoe and Cloud are crouching under a tree on the far side of the property, examining the base of its trunk. They must be hunting for the "creatures" Zoe promised. Maybe they've found something. As I get closer, I see he is holding something in one hand. It appears to be a half-eaten boiled egg.

"It's mine. I hope you don't mind," says Zoe in a rush, probably because of the look on my face, which must be something like anger or shock. "He's not allergic, is he?"

"No," I manage. "It's just that . . . he doesn't like eggs."

"Oh," she says.

We both stare at him eating.

"Have you tried before?" she ventures.

I regulate my tone as best I can. "Yes. That's how I know he doesn't like them." It still rises slightly at the "them."

"Well, we peeled and salted it together," Zoe says sunnily. "Maybe that made it more fun. And I told him there was a special treat inside. A *golden* treat. Right, Em?"

Cloud beams at me, lips fringed in crumbs of yolk. "Eh! Eh!"

Is he repeating her "Em" or is he saying "Egg"? I can't tell.

Zoe shifts from one foot to another, unsure of how to interpret my silence. "Well, Chi," she says at last. "I'd better get back to work."

I feel awful for making her feel bad. I'm genuinely grateful that she stepped in back there. Unlike Lina, she actually helped me. I summon the energy to put her at ease.

"Thank you, Zoe. Really. I needed that break." It's working. How warm and appreciative I sound. "Thank you *so* much."

She smiles—and high-fives Cloud before she goes, leaving him and me alone.

I crouch down. There's some energy left from thanking Zoe. I squeeze it out, like toothpaste. "Mama's so happy you like eggs now!"

Cloud responds with a smile and pops the last bit into his mouth.

"Well done!" I exclaim, pulling him into a hug. And the hug becomes real. I *am* happy he likes eggs. Who cares if it was thanks to someone else? *Your child's nutritional well-being is at stake.*

I start to pick him up, but my shoulder twinges. The situation unearths another glittering gem from the class. "Modeling and Encouraging Good Habits" in Week 4: *a can-do attitude is one of the greatest gifts you can give your child.*

"Why don't you show Mama how strong your legs are?"

I point across the grass to the shed—not far for an older child, but enough of a distance for Cloud that I would usually carry him for efficiency's sake.

I hold his hand at first, but because my shoulder objects to stooping, I release my hold at around the halfway mark. He's slowing down.

I walk ahead, turn, and crouch.

"Come to Mama," I extend my arms as much as I can and brighten my eyes, widen my smile.

As he advances, I retreat.

"Mama harry," he calls, holding out his arms for me to carry him.

"Are you a strong boy? Yes, you are!"

Miraculously, we're almost at the shed. I crouch down in the shade of its wall and keep cheering him on.

He rallies and runs the last ten or so meters into my chest. I tip gently backward against the wall and extend my legs. I'm exhausted, but I manage to bounce him a little on my thighs. I let him play with my fingers and I play with his. I hum us a song. These are the moments that will save us. *If I can postpone our deaths, it will be okay.* I kiss his pillowy cheek and press it to mine until he squirms away. I pluck a long, broad stalk and present it to him as if it were a bouquet.

A breeze blows low, rippling the green blades. Overhead, wisps of cloud drift, dappling the field in shadow and light. In an attempt to stretch out this moment and make it last for as long as possible, I slow my breath, my senses, my thoughts. I imagine pulling each ticking second into a long, fine thread. I don't want to go forward in time to meet my next failure. I want us to stay here, now, with my best self.

It's not to be. A few seconds later, a white van screeches onto the property. It looks like our white van, except it's brand-new and reads *Billy's Boys, Premium Hobbling Services* on the side. They're the other hobbling business in the area, but people don't call them "the Anglo hobblers" or "the white hobblers," they just call them "Billy's Boys." I have enough maternal instinct to tighten my grip on Cloud.

The man who gets out is literally Billy's boy—Billy's son Jerome. You can see the veins in his forehead and neck, even from here. Acek's already jogging out to intercept him. My mind turns immediately to the propane cylinders and the gas-powered items just inside the shed entrance. I know that the others are thinking of them too. We could roll down the shed door, but would that attract even more attention? What can he see from where he's stalking up the dirt drive?

As my mind races through possible strategies, I see the others emerging from the shed and standing in a cluster to block the contraband from sight, trying to look like they've merely come out for a gawk at Jerome.

"Fuck you, Arvin!" screams Jerome, slowing to a halt. "Dirty chinks. How can a man make a decent living?"

"What's the matter, Jerome?" asks Acek, unflinching, voice even. In the meantime, even as he continues walking, he shifts course to Jerome's left. It's as if Jerome is in the center of a large circle and Acek is following its tangent. Jerome has to turn away from the shed to keep Acek in his sights.

"Don't you fuckin' pretend you don't know."

"This about Green Springs?"

"You fuckin' know it's about fuckin' Green Springs."

Green Springs is a motel an hour's drive away from us. But, by the looks of their new van, Billy's Boys could make it in half the time. Shame then, that we got the job and not them.

"We won the contract fair and square," replies Acek, but not in a taunting way. His hands are stretched out in front of him, palms facing down, a gesture meant to pacify.

"Fuckin' fair and square, my eye. Manager told me your bid. How's a man to make a decent living, let me ask you that? Fuckin' ching-chongs. Just 'cause you're willin' to work dirt-cheap an' we're not. We got too much dignity for that."

Acek nods gravely at this nonsense, even at this last declaration about Jerome's dignity. "Yes, I can see that, Jerome. I'm sorry."

"What do you know, fuckin' chinaman?"

Suddenly, he lifts his head and swings round to look at the rest of us—the others at the shed door, me and Cloud to the right.

"All girls, too. Coincidence, I suppose? Whatcha runnin'? Hobblers by day, brothel by night?"

"Hey!" someone yells from the shed. To my surprise, it's Lina. She steps forward and stabs a scolding finger in the air.

"Stop that! Stop it now! You are engaging in inappropriate and racist behavior! We will call the police!"

Jerome looks surprised too. "Fuck you," he yells at Lina once he's recovered.

"No, fuck *you*," retorts Lina. "*You* should be ashamed of yourself. You'd better go before the police get here. We've already called them, in fact."

"Don't believe you," Jerome snarls as another car chugs into the drive—a rusty red pickup truck. Jerome's dad, Billy, gets out, makes straight for Jerome and cuffs him on the side of his head.

"Whadja think you're doin'?" yells Billy, sparse white hairs waving in the wind. He tries to cuff Jerome again, but his son blocks the blow.

"They stole the Green Springs job, Dad! I'm givin' them a piece of my mind!"

"You don't have any extra to give," Billy barks. "Get back to the workshop, *now*."

They exchange a long glare. Finally, the son stalks back to his van. Before getting in, he addresses Libby by way of a shout. "And *you*, missy! Best stick to your own kind!"

When Jerome's gone, Billy shakes his head, rearranging his hairs. "Sorry, Arvin. He's always had a temper."

He extends his hand for a conciliatory shake. Acek obliges but doesn't say a word.

Billy fills the silence. "Must say, though, we were surprised when the manager told us. How can you afford to bid so low? What's your secret?"

Perhaps it's the distance, perhaps it's the angle, but it seems like Billy's grip tightens.

Acek clears his throat. "Just business, eh, Billy? You have your secrets too."

At long last, Billy lets go of Acek's hand. "Yeah, yeah. Business. Of course."

Billy turns and trudges back to the pickup. Acek doesn't move. I can see that he's mulling something over.

"Billy!" he finally calls out.

Billy looks over his shoulder.

"Next motel job is yours."

This is Acek's way of making restitution—for working "cheap," which is apparently wrong.

Billy nods in acknowledgement but says nothing. Once he's back in the truck, he winds down the window.

"'Next motel job,' eh?" he sneers. "Who knows when that'll be?"

He reverses and drives away. As the red pickup putters out of sight, I let go of Cloud, thankful that he, too, sensed the gravity of the situation, that he held still for me to hold. I join the others, all of us laughing in relief.

"I didn't know you could be so fierce!" exclaims Zoe, giving Lina's shoulder an affectionate poke.

"I never thought I'd ever hear you say 'fuck'!" Libby cackles with glee.

Lina frowns. "Don't say that word."

"But you just—"

"It was an emergency," she snaps.

Meanwhile, Nina surveys the cylinder, the generator, the tripod—as if worried they've somehow sustained damage from Jerome's hate.

"Enough work for today," bellows Acek, trudging into the shed. "Let's party."

He's wiping his hands with a rag, as if he's just finished a dirty job.

He's right. It's a special night. We begin putting our tools away. We're not going to let those racist fuckers ruin our New Year's Eve.

*

Cloud and I stay outdoors while everyone else gets the ingredients and cooking supplies. Dinner will be in the house, but we'll prepare the meal in the shed. Cloud is searching for more ants like the ones he found earlier with Zoe. I check my watch. It's almost five. Since it's summer in the southern hemisphere, the light and warmth will last a few hours longer.

I suddenly remember what Pa said one Lunar New Year, shortly after we'd moved to Australia—him, me, and my sister, three years after Ma died.

"You know what they call Sin Cia in China? *Chun Jie*. Mandarin for 'Spring Festival.' The new year is meant to mark the end of winter and the beginning of spring."

At this point, he paused.

"Here, it's the opposite," he continued. "We're moving into winter."

Pa stared glumly into space, as if the world was getting colder before his very eyes. "Why are we even here?"

"Ann! Ann!" Cloud points to a lone ant scurrying down the tree trunk.

"Yeah, ant," I murmur.

I wonder if Cloud will grow up and remember me the way I remember Pa: sad.

From the shed, the gas-powered generator emits a steady growl. It's running a gargantuan waste-era rice cooker. I remember Acek and me buying it at a restaurant closing-down sale back in Sydney. Obviously, it's not cooking rice but "ryce"—rice's ecologically sustainable twin. Rice, up there with meat and dairy in contributing to global methane emissions, had to go. When ryce was developed—with its ability to flourish in dry soil rather than flooded fields—the switch was a no-brainer. People my age and younger are fine with it. Boomers like Pa and Acek still complain about the aftertaste.

A procession emerges from the house. Leading the way is Nina, bearing a chopping board, a cleaver, and a covered plate. Behind her, Lina carries a raw fish on a platter and a canister of vegetable oil. Acek is next, with a tray of assorted sauces and ingredients. Zoe and Libby bring up the rear with a wok lid, various cooking implements, a stack of empty serving platters, and some folded dishrags. It's better than a lion dance. Better than a dragon dance. The very air crackles with excitement.

When we get to the shed, everyone places their items on the rickety folding table we set up earlier. I gasp when Nina uncovers her plate. A cartoonishly massive slab of boiled pork belly. It can't be real.

"It's real," Lina affirms, too loudly, into my ear.

Its pale, creamy skin is studded with prick-holes and granules of salt. I lean closer and catch a whiff of vinegar too. In the meantime, Acek heads over to his tripod contraption and, with Zoe's help, connects the gas. A knob is twisted, then another, summoning a burst of flame. The wok is placed on the burner, and Acek pours in the oil.

In goes the belly, skin-down, with a tremendous sizzle and spatter. Acek covers it with a lid, but the aroma of frying pork escapes nonetheless. Any doubts I had about its authenticity are gone, replaced with an alarming onset of drool.

Cloud's spellbound. In fact, we all are, even Acek, whose usual impassive expression has been replaced with one of quiet intensity. He lifts the lid and flips the pork again. Then he lifts it out, slices it, and leaves it to marinate in a shallow lake of sauce. Once it's done marinating, Nina will place the pork slices into a ceramic bowl, cover it with a sauteed mushroom and mustard-green mixture, and take it to the electric pressure cooker—like the rice cooker, unhobbled and generator-driven—to finish it off.

In the meantime, Acek uses the wok to steam the fish and

stir-fry some bok choy. Then he removes the wok, wipes it down, and tests the burner flame a few times. By the light of each fiery eruption, I see the faint curve of a smile on his face. I can guess from the remaining ingredients what he's going to make next: kwetiau goreng. It's a dish he used to bring over sometimes when I was little, back when he and Pa were still friendly and on speaking terms.

After the oil, he throws in slivers of fishball and fat-speckled lap cheong—also the real deal from the smell of it, though much cheaper than fresh meat—followed by minced garlic, then the noodles and bean sprouts, all the while drizzling in various sauces and scattering salt. A bowlful of egg is poured into the middle and allowed to puddle on top of the kwetiau before being stirred and folded in. More flurries of soy sauce and salt. More scrapes and flicks of the spatula. Then he works the wok in a circular back and forth motion, the flames lapping at the rim and charring the airborne oiled noodles in flamboyant bursts.

"Learned this trick from a Malaysian friend," he declares, glancing at Lina because she's also Malaysian. "Gives the kwetiau a smoky taste. Didn't used to do it back at my parents' restaurant in Indonesia, but we got the taste from the charcoal. We were allowed to cook with charcoal back then."

This is the most I've heard Acek say all at once in a very long time. There's something besides intensity in his look now. It's happiness, simple and pure. He plates the kwetiau, turns off the gas, and disconnects the tripod. Before we know it, the khau bak is done too. We gather round as Acek inverts the bowl onto a plate, producing a neat circular mound of dark, glistening pork belly atop a bed of mushrooms and pickled greens.

We all pitch in to bring dishes and equipment back to the

house, making sure to lock up the shed. The food is arranged on the table. All adults get a tumbler of Victoria Bitter, except Lina, who doesn't drink. A previously unseen dish makes its appearance: a square leaf-wrapped bánh chưng, courtesy of Zoe, bought from a classmate's enterprising mother, who makes them at home to sell every Tet, the Lunar New Year in Vietnam.

We ration out the pork belly with great care, making sure everyone gets equal amounts. Cloud wolfs down his share so quickly, I'm worried he'll choke. He cries for more, so I give him most of mine and pop the remaining morsel into my mouth so I can at least have a taste. He even tries the fish, but isn't keen, so I get his portion. It all evens out. He says no to the kwetiau, but devours the individual strands of noodle and slivers of lap cheong that I pick out and feed him by chopstick. And, of course, he always says yes to ryce. He's eating so well, in fact, that I can pay attention to the conversation around us, which is focused, fittingly, on our feast.

Acek refuses to divulge how much he spent on the pork belly. Or where he got the propane gas. Or where he's been hiding the generator. Our effusive thank-yous are waved away, and he raises his glass.

"Just enjoy. Before I'm arrested tomorrow."

We all laugh and toast to the new year.

Acek waxes nostalgic about the khau bak his grandma used to make. He still can't get his to taste like hers. Zoe explains how the bánh chưng she brought is a Tet must. The filling is made from mung bean paste and mock pork. The signature Chinese New Year dish in Malaysia, Lina informs us, is yee sang, or yu sheng, or lo hei, depending on what dialect you speak. It used to have raw fish in it, but sustainable jellyfish has taken its place.

She leans over to explain to Libby. "In Chinese, the word for 'fish' sounds like the word for 'abundance.' That's why fish is an auspicious New Year food."

Libby nods. "Yeah. My Mandarin teacher told me."

Lina's stunned expression makes Zoe laugh-spray VB all over her plate.

"You're learning Mandarin?" Lina splutters.

Libby rolls her eyes. "Who are you, Jerome?"

"I am *not*. I'm just curious, that's all."

"I like learning new things," Libby says with a shrug.

The mention of Jerome shifts the conversation to what happened earlier. We retell the events, rendering them comical, stripping them of terror: Jerome barreling up the dirt drive, veins bulging, red as a tomato; Acek shrewdly steering him away from the shed; the look on Jerome's face when Lina stood up to him; how we should get a guard dog and train it to attack Billy and his boy so we won't have to worry about unwelcome visits anymore.

Acek starts out laughing with us, then goes quiet by degrees. His gaze is pensive, his forehead creased. I can tell he's thinking about what Jerome said. I'd reassure him, but he's on the other side of the table. Maybe I should go over, tell him in a low voice not to waste headspace on the nonsense, the utter garbage, that was spouted by Jerome. I've just resolved to do so, when his niece speaks up.

"It's rubbish, Acek. Everything he said. Don't think about it anymore."

The whole table erupts in agreement.

"Yes, of course!"

"Don't listen to him, Ông."

"'Brothel by night.' What a dickhead."

"Arvin, you're the best employer I've ever had. *Ever*. Hands down . . ."

"'Stick to your own kind.' What a Nazi."

"The *best* boss."

". . . I mean, I've only been employed once before, in my twenties. But no comparison! Now *that* man! What a sleaze . . ."

"The *kindest* boss."

"Jerome can get fucked."

"Haha, you said 'fuck' again!"

"He just makes me so angry!" Lina fumes. She downs the rest of her beer. Zoe, ever the queen of persuasion, coaxed her into changing her mind.

Acek clears his throat. "Okay, okay. No need to overdo it," he says, but from his faint smile, I can tell he's touched.

"Just out of curiosity," pipes Libby, "why *didn't* you hire any men?"

Zoe elbows her.

"Ow! What?"

Acek gives us all a thoughtful look. "I didn't do it on purpose," he says. "You just seemed like the best ones."

*

By the time dessert is served—store-bought peanut biscuits and kue keranjang—Lina is completely smashed. We've always known she has an ex-husband and a grown-up son. What we didn't know is that her ex is a lying, cheating parasite who drained her of the best years of her life before leaving her for someone younger, prettier, and stupid. Nor did we know that Lina's son refuses to see or talk to her because she's, in his words, "toxic and domineering and a negative influence on his life." She curls up on the couch and cries a little before passing out. Cloud eats seven biscuits and falls asleep in the crook of her arm.

The rest of us help clean up and pack everyone leftovers. In his capacity as our boss, Acek passes out angpao.

"Just a gesture. It's not much," he warns, handing me Cloud's red envelope, and Lina's too.

I tuck Lina's angpao into her purse, and we load up the vehicles. Nina takes me, Cloud, and Lina. Acek takes Zoe, Libby, and Libby's bike.

As the car glides along, I look over my shoulder at Lina and Cloud slumbering in the back.

"How much did she have to drink?" I wonder out loud.

"Two glasses?" Nina ventures.

Poor Lina, I think—for the first time ever. Loved one day, discarded the next.

When we reach Lina's home, a small granny flat she rents in someone's backyard, Nina and I each sling an arm round our shoulders and haul her in. We let ourselves in with the keys in her purse, slip off her shoes, and tuck her in bed.

On the way back to my house, it dawns on me just how much I've enjoyed this evening. I feel hopeful—the most hopeful I have in a long time. Cloud and I have started a new life. We're part of a community. And even if I'm no longer as close to Acek as I used to be, that's okay. Isn't that what life is? A perpetual moving on?

I glance sideways at Nina and recall how, earlier, she read her uncle's thoughts and got us all to reassure him. Yes, I felt a little jealous at the time, but now that I reflect, I'm glad he has his niece now. And more employees. He doesn't need me as much anymore.

I mean it. I really do, I reflect, full of meat, warm with beer. *I'm moving on.*

There's a season for everything. A season for Acek. A season for Gabe. A season to strike out on my own with my child.

I'm happy, I repeat to myself. *I really am.*

When we reach the house, Nina helps me with my stuff and opens the door. I have to carry Cloud in. My shoulder still hurts, but he's out like a light.

"Kiong hee for tomorrow, Vi," says Nina.

"Yeah, kiong hee," I wish back, wincing.

Once I've laid Cloud down on our mattress and taken off his shoes, I load our crummy hobbled washing machine with the day's soiled nappies so they'll be ready to wring out and dry by morning. I take out the angpaos Acek gave us. Five dollars each. He warned us, didn't he? *Just a gesture. It's not much.*

I'm just about to shower when the phone rings. It's probably my sister, but my guard is down, so I pick up the phone.

"Vi?"

Yep, it's her. "Hi, Ci."

"Oh good, you picked up. Happy Sa Cap Meh. We just finished dinner. Did you celebrate?"

"Yeah. Acek threw a party for all the employees."

"That's nice. How's Cloud?"

"Fine," I say.

"Good, good."

I begin to detect the impatience in her voice; she's not just calling because it's Sa Cap Meh. There's a point she wants this conversation to reach, but we have to get through the pleasantries first.

"How are Terry? And Matt? And Haze?" I ask. "Terry" is short for Theresa, "Matt" for Matthew, and "Haze" for Hazel—her children, ages eight, six, and three, or thereabouts.

"Yeah, yeah. They're fine. Terry's netball coach is leaving, which is a shame. Matt's loving violin lessons, to our relief. Haze has the sniffles, poor thing."

"How's Pa?" I ask.

"The same."

"James?"

"Good."

The small talk brakes. We've arrived.

"How are you feeling, Vi? Are you okay?"

"Why?" I ask.

She doesn't answer, so I ask again, suspicion rising. "Ci? How come?"

"You did get one, didn't you?"

"What are you talking about?"

"Mine came last week."

"*What* came last week?"

She's quiet.

"Ci," I press, "*what came last week*?"

When she finally responds, her voice is lower, gentler.

"Vivi. Did you check the mail?"

I hang up and fling myself out of the house again. After stumbling in the dark to the mailbox in my flip-flops, I return clutching a sheaf of envelopes and circulars. I fling them all onto the floor and sift through on my knees. An ivory envelope catches the light, shimmering like pearl. The gold wax seal is embossed with a leafy branch—a symbol of new growth or some meaningful shit like that.

I open the envelope.

Gabriel Mak and Leona Sau-Hoong Lim invite you to celebrate their joyful union . . .

My fingers grip the invitation so hard that it creases.

When the phone rings again, I lift the receiver and slam it down.

My hands shake as I rip the card into eighths and shove it, along with the envelope and RSVP form, into the bottom of the recycling bin. It's like I'm cramming myself down too, crumpling me deep inside my body, until I am small in the cavernous chamber that is my mind. *Forget showering. Go to bed, Vi.* I hoist the levers and send my body clanking into the bathroom, where my hands squeeze toothpaste onto toothbrush bristles and scrub the teeth in the mouth in my face. My body pulls on a drool-stained T-shirt and food-stained joggers and collapses on the mattress, next to Cloud.

Meanwhile, the man who was once my body's husband slumbers in his luxury apartment in Sydney next to, or perhaps spooning, the body of his soon-to-be new wife.

This was your choice, I remind myself. *You could have agreed. Then he'd still love you. Then you and Cloud would still be there, with him.*

As my body shifts, trying to find the most comfortable position for its aching shoulder, I ask myself whether I would have made the same choice if I could do it over. I know that I would.

A familiar image comes to mind: that my life is a long road down which I journey in my weary body, stepping step after step until I reach its end.

I shift my face close to Cloud's tiny, perfect nose. Even through the barrier of my body, I feel the sweet, steady breeze of his breath. I kiss the fat droop of his cheek. I remind myself, everyone dies at some point, but if I can just postpone death, everything will turn out okay.

iii.

I still remember when that image of a road slid into my head for the first time. I was standing at the bathroom sink. Gabe had already left for work. He liked to start the day early, whereas I preferred to start the day sitting like a lump at the dining table, coffee mug in hand, gradually waking up. But that morning, I had cut my usual ritual short to take a pregnancy test. My period was ten days late. I still remember those two lines materializing, parallel and pink. They reminded me of a section of road. I felt the road was my life and that I'd seen this milestone coming ever since I was a little girl. There had been other milestones along this straight road, too, of course, which I'd passed, as I had assumed I would. I'd finished school. I'd started working. I'd gotten married. Naturally, pregnancy and motherhood were next.

Now I had reached pregnancy, as expected, as desired—wasn't this what we'd been trying for? But I was also taken aback. I felt happy and yet unmoored, like a balloon set adrift, floating higher and higher into the sky.

I called Gabe's name, though I knew he wasn't there. Maybe I wished he were—to ground me. I even opened the door and padded out into our bedroom, then further still, through the corridor, past the open kitchen and dining area into the lounge room, as if exploring an unfamiliar place. The tranquil elegance of our apartment struck me afresh, its neutral hues and plain wooden surfaces against the backdrop of a breathtaking view of the city and sky. Did I really live here? I wondered in awe. Was this beautiful apartment really mine?

I thought about ringing Gabe's office, but I reasoned he would want to hear the good news in person. Gabe was that kind of guy. I would tell him later. I needed to digest the news properly myself. And I also had a train to catch.

I brushed my teeth and got dressed, marveling at how normal my body felt, as if it weren't in the process of growing two tiny new beings. It was as if nothing had changed, and yet everything had. A scene flashed through my mind—from the video I'd stumbled across weeks earlier on that blog. I'd watched it a few times over. That small moist blob on the concrete, gaining mass, taking form. I packed my lunch and water bottle and rushed down the stairs. If I missed the express, it would take more than an hour to get to the shop. I made my train with less than a minute to spare.

Gabe had been suggesting that I quit for a long time. He made more than enough money for the both of us. And compared to his salary, my wage was barely anything at all. In his opinion, it simply wasn't worth it, especially given the long commute. If I enjoyed working so much, I should just find something close by.

"But I've been working for Acek since I was a teenager," I'd protested when the subject came up yet again. Gabe and I had been making dinner. Or rather, I had been chopping things and setting the table while he did the making. We were supposed to take turns, but being the gourmand that he was, he often offered to cook out of turn so he could try a new recipe or satisfy a craving.

"Exactly," he said. "Don't you think it's time for a change?" He checked on the wild-caught sustainable salmon fillets poaching on our state-of-the-art induction cooktop. Everything in the apartment was state-of-the-art. Quiet luxury meets eco-tech.

I shook my head. "No one's looking for hobblers around here. It's too upscale."

"You could do something else entirely. Work in retail. Or at a café . . ."

"But I'm trained at hobbling. I'm good at it."

"Or you could take a course and become a proper electrician."

"I *am* a proper electrician. I have a license."

Gabe lifted out the pale fillets with a spatula. A delicate operation. "I meant you could re-train to work with new systems. You're only licensed to fix old stuff. Where's the future in that?"

I watched as he scattered fresh dill over the bars of fish flesh. It reminded me of mourners scattering petals on a grave.

"Besides," he continued. "When we have children, you'll have to stop working. If you ever go back to work, you'll be on track to more choices and higher pay if you know how to work with RDC tech."

I couldn't argue with that.

"Viv, I know you're comfortable at your job, but you have to think about the future."

The future. Now I was pregnant and living in it, I reflected, watching the passenger in front of me startle awake intermittently, his brown curly head against the window, leaving a greasy patch. I hadn't made any of the career changes Gabe had counseled. But that wasn't the problem. It was this pregnancy that made me uneasy. Not the baby, necessarily, but the other part of it—which I hadn't given much thought until we'd started trying in earnest. But is it any wonder I was caught off guard, given that no one talked about the other part much at all?

I only seriously began thinking about it because of the research I'd done in anticipation of getting pregnant. My sister had advised me against doing this.

"What if you have trouble getting pregnant and all your reading makes you sad?" she reasoned. "Then you'll have babies on the brain but no baby in you."

Vera had a point. But as usual, I didn't listen. I was always stubborn like that. I took advantage of the excellent library five blocks away and borrowed three books: *The Complete Guide to Pregnancy and Birth* (the sixth edition), *Childbirth, A Handbook*, and *The Biology of Being Born*.

I even began using the internet that Gabe had insisted on having installed when we (well, he) first bought the apartment. At the time, I had been against it. I'd told him the early 2000s weren't coming back. New government restrictions had made it too expensive. The environmental cost of growing internet usage—energy needs, rare-earth-element mining—had been proving too dear. But Gabe had gone ahead with installing it anyway, taking out a top-tier subscription for four hours of usage per week.

And wouldn't you know it? Defying expert predictions, the internet didn't waste away into nothing. On the contrary, it attained luxury status. If you browsed or blogged or bought things online, it meant you had money to burn. Three years married, and I was still adjusting to the fact that I, by extension, by being Gabe's extension, had access to that kind of cash. But once I'd started surfing the World Wide Web, I was grateful for Gabe's extravagance. I even exceeded our quota by twenty minutes and had to pay the extra charge. By which I mean Gabe paid it. He didn't mind. He'd even looked triumphant when I told him about it, a smug *I told you so, Viv* gleaming in his eye.

Sometimes I wonder how things would have turned out if Gabe had listened to me and not paid for internet. If I'd simply relied on the library to learn about rebirth. If I'd never come across that list of mummy blogs. I also wonder about the timing: what if I'd discovered Greta Wilde's site only after the video had been taken down?

Then again, not watching the video might not have made a difference. I may have ended up fixating on rebirth anyway. Wasn't that why I'd been drawn to the video in the first place, the fact of rebirth tugging at me, niggling at me in a way it didn't anybody else? No one seemed concerned about it. The opposite, in fact. When my sister was pregnant with her first, for example, I remember her deliberating between laughing gas, an epidural, or going "all natural." I remember her worrying about the pain of labor, practicing the special breathing required to manage it. But rebirth hardly came up, and if it did, only indirectly, as a good thing, when she would complain about pregnancy-related fatigue or discomfort. "That's one thing to look forward to—not needing sleep!" she'd say with a laugh. Or "I could use some of that new-mother superstrength right now." Or "Look at that woman's skin. I bet she's a new mum. I can't wait to have skin like that."

The books I'd borrowed portrayed rebirth in a positive light—what few lines they spent on the subject. From *Childbirth, A Handbook:*

> The third stage of labor is known as rebirth. The successful completion of this stage is vital to ensuring a mother's postpartum

well-being. After delivering the child, the mother's body will produce lunatonin, a hormone that causes the mother to enter a deep sleep. Only after this will the fetal mother detach itself and make her way out through the birth canal.

From *The Complete Guide to Pregnancy and Birth*, sixth edition:

Once outside the body, the new mother grows rapidly, attaining full maturity within minutes. Inwardly and outwardly, she is identical to her old self, possessing the same thoughts, memories, perceptions, et cetera, up to the onset of rebirth.

Next, the mother consumes her discarded body, which provides the nutrients she needs to care properly for herself and her child. For this reason, it is of key importance that she remain undisturbed. Incomplete consumption of the old body will severely impair the new mother's ability to function.

From *The Biology of Being Born*:

The natural world contains many examples of similar resourcefulness in other species. Reptiles and insects ingest their old skins after shedding. Non-primate mammals consume the placenta and umbilical cord after birth. Primates, including humans, merely take it to the next level. Rebirth is simply part of nature's plan to keep new mothers in tip-top shape.

There. Everything I needed to know about rebirth, described in clear language. What other information did I need?

As I looked out the window and watched the buildings whizz by, another scene from the video inserted itself: Greta's prologue, her earnest, radiant face. *We don't need to pretend it's all pretty with a big pink bow wrapped around it. Rebirth is what it is, and it's gorgeous.*

My stop caught me unawares, and I managed to hop off the train just in time. A day of close calls, it seemed. As I pushed through the turnstiles and made my way to the shop, it occurred to me that my fixation on rebirth was not unlike my insistence on working for Acek. What was wrong with taking up my highly paid husband's invitation to consider other avenues or stop work altogether and depend on him? By the same token, why dwell on a biological event that not only seemed to bother no one else, but was perceived as a desirable perk?

I quickened my pace and wondered why I was so intent on making life more difficult than it had to be. The foul stench from the stormwater drain outside Fred's Barber Shop wafted into my nostrils. Fred had already called it into the local council, as had Acek, and, I suspected, most of the tenants on the block. But nothing had been done. "They're smoking us out, but with sewer smells" had been Acek's wry comment on the matter. In Sydney, these rundown suburbs were on the chopping block for redevelopment. Energy-efficient, high-density towers were the way of the future, not crumbling two-story buildings like ours.

Before entering the shop, I took a rare glimpse upward at our no-frills sign—*Arvin's Hobbling Services* in blue capital letters on white background. Above that, at the overhang that had long ceased to provide effective shelter, the plywood too often drenched by rain and now rotting away. And even though I'd spent the entire train ride mulling about both pregnancy and work, my brain suddenly completed the circuit: I was pregnant; therefore, like it or not, I'd soon have to stop working. Again, that sensation—alone, adrift in the sky—as I pushed the door open and passed the front counter through to the back room.

Acek, alerted by the tinkling of the bells we had hot-glued to the door, greeted me with a nod. He opened shop at seven every weekday, though I didn't come in till eight-thirty. He did so to cater to commuters who lived in the area and might need to drop off a broken appliance before heading into work. Today, however, Acek informed me that no new jobs had come in yet. Not one.

He told me as he sorted through our box of sewing-machine motor parts—as if he were commenting on the weather, or recounting a bit of minor news. But I knew Acek better than I did my own father (a low bar, to be fair). The very fact that it warranted any utterance meant that he was, on some level, concerned.

"It's just one day," I offered.

He was quiet for a while. "It happened twice last week. I just didn't tell you. No jobs before nine."

"Maybe it's a sign you should sleep in," I joked weakly, though I knew the greater significance of what he was reporting. The bulk of our incoming jobs came from morning commuters, just as the bulk of pickups happened after five, on people's way home from the station.

Acek stopped sorting and gazed contemplatively into the distance. "It *is* a sign," he said. "Hobbling jobs are drying up. More people are making the switch." He sighed. "I suppose it was only a matter of time. If you can afford to live in Sydney at all, you can afford to buy RDC."

"Better move to the country, then," I joked again. "Cheaper houses, people can own cars. Maybe it won't be so bad."

He grunted before turning back to his task, leaving me to head to my bench and get to work.

It was just Acek and me back then. There wouldn't have been enough space for anyone else. The shop was narrow, cramped, dark. Bracket shelving filled every available inch of wall space, and each shelf was laden with boxes and stacks of every imaginable part and tool and piece of equipment. Not to mention various unrepairable items we'd salvaged from curbside junk piles or acquired at garage or closing-down sales, all of which waited patiently for a day yet unknown when we would need to strip them for parts. It was like being in a mechanical womb. But you got used to it. Or rather, you forgot about it once you started concentrating on the job at hand.

By the time I reached a good stopping place with the minifridge I'd been working on, it was past two. I wolfed down my sandwich and apple while standing at the sink. Then I set about brazing the compressor. I took only one more break after that—to explain to a customer picking up her food processor that the only setting that worked anymore was "pulse."

Before I knew it, the clock read five-thirty. It being winter, the sky was already dark. I'd been so immersed in my work that I'd almost forgotten I was pregnant. Or rather, I'd allowed the knowledge to perch outside the fringes of my consciousness, and now it had come swooping back in. I suddenly recalled my intention to share the good news with Acek.

I waited until he was done with another customer, a man who was upset about how much it had cost to hobble his microwave. ("I could have bought two RDC microwaves for the same price," I heard him complain. *What would he do with two microwaves*, I thought.) In the meantime, I swept the floor of wire snippets, bits of electrical tape, and stripped insulation sheaths. When the customer left, Acek donned his reading glasses and commenced the end-of-day closing, counting the day's takings, tallying receipts.

"Seeing the family tonight?" he asked.

"As usual," I replied. Thursdays were when I ate dinner with my sister's family and Pa.

"Send them my regards," he said, as always.

I nodded, though I wouldn't. Pa, especially, didn't want them.

I worked up the courage to tell him.

"I'm pregnant."

Acek looked up, eyebrows raised.

"Congratulations," he said.

"I took a test this morning," I explained, not wanting him to think I'd been keeping it from him all this time. "It might be wrong."

"How accurate are they?"

"Ninety-eight percent. Ninety-nine. Usually if they're wrong, it's a false negative, not a false positive."

His face softened into an expression I couldn't quite read.

"Congratulations," he repeated. "Gabriel must be happy."

Acek always referred to Gabe by his full name. When he referred to him at all. Though Acek tried his best to hide it, I knew he'd never been overly fond of Gabe.

"Gabe left early for work. I haven't told him yet."

Acek's eyes narrowed behind the lenses of his reading glasses. "Is this what *you* wanted, Vivi?"

I laughed. "Yes, of course! We've been trying for months."

His eyes narrowed further. I rolled my eyes in mock exasperation.

"*Yes*, Acek," I affirmed. "We *both* want a baby. Gabe *and* me."

I did want a baby. That much was true.

"Does your sister know yet? Or your father?"

"You're the first one."

Acek thought about this. "I'm honored," he said solemnly before giving a sudden bark of a laugh.

I still couldn't quite tell whether he was happy or sad.

"It might affect my work," I warned.

"'Might'?" He bark-laughed again.

"Well, it's still very early," I said. "Anything could happen."

He didn't respond right away. The silence gave the words an ominous air.

"I'm sure it will be fine," he said quietly, rising from his seat. He put both hands on my shoulders, studying my face with something like paternal pride or love. He really was much warmer toward me back then.

"You'll be fine, Vivi," he assured me. "If this is what you want, it's wonderful news."

I left shortly afterwards. Vera often complained about my lack of punctuality, despite Acek's shop being only a short walk away. But that was precisely why I hardly ever arrived on time: since it wouldn't take long to get there, I never felt like I had to hurry.

This evening was no different. I should have been ringing her doorbell by the time I left the shop. In the old days, I might have texted her on the cheap mobile phone she insisted I carry around when we first came to Australia: *Sorry 10min late*. But cheap tech and needless micro-communication were now things of the past. Only certain members of the corporate and professional elite carried mobiles these days. Sometimes I wondered if Vera and I would have a different relationship now if we were able to text or call wherever or whenever, like we used to back in school.

gd luck!, she might text if I had an exam. Or when she'd got her first part-time job: *i got it $$*, to which I'd responded, *ci! congrats!*

Then again, we were bound to drift apart once we grew up and began leading our own lives. We were never close in the way some sisters are. We loved each other, of course, but there was a top-down quality to our relationship. After Ma's death and Pa's deterioration, she assumed the role of parent in our family. She considered it her duty to make sure I was safe, fed, and doing well in school. She laid out strict rules about friends, acceptable social activities, and what time I had to be home. She mothered Pa too, taking charge of all the cooking, cleaning, and shopping. Even bill payments, government correspondence, and taxes became her responsibility after Pa and Acek's big fight.

As I scurried along the final stretch of street to her house, bracing my body against the night wind, I wondered how I would deliver the news. Should I tell Vera right away? Should I announce my pregnancy at the dining table so everyone could hear?

Right away, I decided, but my sister's admonishment upon opening the door threw me off.

"Late again!" she declared, thin lips pursed, bushy brows knitted—a look of disapproval so familiar it verged on comforting. She had raised me with it, after all. One hand was on her hip. The other held Haze, saddled against her small, lean frame.

"Sorry," I said, pulling off my sneakers. "I had to talk to Acek about something after work."

But before I could tell her what I'd talked to him about, Vera was striding away. Haze stared back at me over her mother's shoulder, gumming her teething biscuit. I followed Vera down the hall and pulled a funny face to make my niece laugh. As if channeling her mother's annoyance, Haze merely frowned in reply.

"Terry, Matt! Aie's here!" my sister sang out.

"Hi, Aie Vivi," I heard two well-mannered voices pipe back.

I started to take off my puffer jacket, but then thought better of it. In winter, it felt as cold in my sister's house as it did outside. That was Sydney for you; houses were only affordable if they were crumbling and drafty. Vera and James had plans to renovate, but they were still saving up. And of course, there was the mortgage to pay. And the cost of raising three kids. A lot to swing on James's systems engineer salary, as decent as it was. And any earnings from Vera would be out of the picture until Haze started school.

In the lounge room, Terry was doing homework at the coffee table, and Matt was on the carpet, building a Duplo-block castle.

"Where's your dad?" I asked.

"Watching the tennis at Uncle Malcolm's," answered Terry.

Malcolm was James's brother. James was often out when I came over for Thursday dinner. I didn't mind. It's not as if Gabe joined us very often, either. It was understood somehow that these weekly dinners were less for our husbands than they were for everyone else: Pa, Vera, me, and the kids.

"Vi, can you give me a hand?" my sister called from the kitchen.

I walked in to find her lifting the refrigerator with one hand, Haze still in her other arm.

"Can you pick up Haze's num-num stick? It rolled under the fridge."

With her bare foot, she pointed at the mushy teething biscuit.

"Bin it, please. Or we'll get roaches and rats again."

Once I'd followed her instructions, she set the fridge down and began ladling hot soup into a porcelain tureen.

"I can hold her," I offered. Now that I was pregnant, it occurred to me that I should practice.

"No, no. She's going through a phase. Only Mummy can hold her—isn't that right?"

This last part was addressed to Haze. As if to confirm, Haze tightened her grip on my sister and fixed me with a suspicious stare.

As Vera picked up the heavy soup-filled tureen with one hand—the same one she'd used to lift the fridge just moments before—I couldn't help but admire the compact musculature of her arms. Like many new mothers, she went sleeveless, even in winter. Increased strength, astonishing body-temperature regulation capabilities—I would have them too, after rebirth. Something to look forward to, I told myself, even as I was reminded of something else from the video: new Greta's bulging arms, engaged in the work of lifting, smashing, tearing, spattered with blood.

"Call Pa for dinner," commanded Vera, sailing out of the kitchen before singing out gaily, "Dinnertime, darlings!"

When I reached Pa's bedroom door, it was slightly ajar. I knocked anyway.

"Pa, dinner's ready," I called in Hokkien.

There was no reply. I poked my head in. "Pa?"

In the dark, I could make out my father in his armchair, the light from the TV flickering across his gaunt face. Despite my sister's utmost efforts, there seemed to be a little less of him each week, in both body and spirit.

I approached him and touched his shoulder—what I could feel of it under layer upon layer of blanket.

"Pa. Dinner's ready," I repeated. "Ci made your favorite soup."

This wasn't quite accurate. Even though my sister made it for him regularly because of its nourishing properties, Pa had never given any indication that he considered it a favorite.

Pa peered at me through his spectacles before pointing to the figures on the small screen. A pretty young woman in rich silk robes—Qing Dynasty? Tang Dynasty?—was sobbing piteously, and a handsome young man with his hair braided in a long queue was trying to console her.

It was a Mandarin-language drama, but there were Chinese subtitles for speakers of other dialects. Not that they were any help to me; my already atrophied knowledge of Hokkien was purely oral. Pa, on the other hand, had made a concerted effort to improve his Mandarin, which he now understood pretty well and could speak somewhat. This made him trilingual. He already knew Hokkien and Indonesian, being Chinese from Medan. But I never heard him speak Indonesian anymore. And I had the sense that, if he could swap it for fluency in Mandarin, he would.

Nowadays, he even tried to speak to us in Mandarin—our motherland's official language, he'd remind us. Never mind that none of us had ever set foot in China. Never mind that Hokkien was also a language spoken in China. He'd got it into his head that Hokkien—especially the Medanese variant we spoke—was inauthentic, impure. He'd only switch back to Hokkien when we indicated we didn't understand. Like now. He pointed to the screen and spoke. I stared blankly and shook my head.

Reluctantly, he repeated himself in Hokkien. "See? She's only pretending to cry. She's deceitful."

"Isn't everyone in these shows?" I joked.

The screen began to flicker.

"Happens all the time," he muttered.

"I can fix it," I told him, careful not to mention Acek, "if you let me bring it into the shop."

No response. I waited a few more seconds.

"Pa, come to dinner?"

His reply in Mandarin was close enough to Hokkien that I understood: he'd come along soon.

Vera and the kids had already started eating. My sister had made her usual variety of dishes. She always made sure that one of each child's favorite food was on the table, in addition to dishes that made the meal well-balanced and encouraged them to be more adventurous when it came to cuisine. I identified everything on the table accordingly: the lentil-bolognese pasta was for Matt; the mushroom-mince mapo tofu was for Terry; the Greek salad, quinoa patties, and chickpea-spinach curry were to encourage health and adventurousness; and the stir-fried bok choy and winter melon herbal soup were for Pa, in addition to the mapo tofu, since he only ate Chinese food nowadays.

Ryce for all. Naturally, Haze had her own plate, on which a suitable assortment of foods had been arranged: sweet potato cubes, plain pasta, plain tofu, plain chickpeas, and a single ball of ryce.

I silently added to the list of rebirth perks. Even I, with my pathetic culinary abilities, would be able to whip up daily buffets catering to every family member's taste and nutritional needs. Heightened efficiency, resourcefulness, organizational skills, a newfound hormone-driven interest in domestic chores—in less than forty weeks they would all be mine.

"Pa said he'll come soon," I said quickly when I saw the look of disappointment on my sister's face.

Conversation sunk into its usual pattern, with Vera launching polite inquiries at me between reminding, reprimanding, or complimenting my nieces and nephew on their eating and table manners. Occasionally, I myself would launch polite inquiries at Terry and Matt about their school or activities, or at my sister about James and Haze.

Eventually, Pa shuffled in. Wordlessly, Vera served him a bowl of soup and began putting food on his plate. If she didn't do this, he wouldn't eat.

"Hi, Akong," Terry and Matt chorused obediently.

He smiled wanly at them before turning his attention to his meal. Anyone would think he was eating alone, but it was always this way.

Conversation rolled on around him, with Terry and Matt finishing before the rest of us and excusing themselves to get ready for bed. My sister too excused herself, to oversee Terry and Matt, and to change Haze for the night. While she was gone, my father finished eating and shuffled back to his room without a word. I too finished eating and started to clear the dishes, but my sister stopped me when she returned. She was still holding Haze, who was now wearing a fleece onesie printed with sheep.

"Don't be silly," she said, taking the stack of plates from me as easily as if I were the baby's age. "What else is new-mother energy for?"

She whisked them away to the kitchen, then cleared the remaining dishes with shocking speed. I merely sat there and watched.

"You really don't feel tired at all?" I asked as she wiped down the table.

"The reverse. I almost can't bear to sit down."

"Is it hard to sleep?"

Vera thought about this. "Yes and no. I never fall into a deep sleep. I wake up every twenty minutes, and if Haze needs me, of course. But it's more than enough. I always feel recharged."

"How was Pa this week?" I asked.

"Not too bad," she said, wiping the table. "Apart from using up our household quota on those Chinese dramas." She laughed.

"Is he really?"

She shook her head. "Nah, I'm joking. Going heatless means he can watch as much as he likes on that tiny TV. On *really* cold nights, we use the electric blankets you hobbled for us."

"Yeah, those *actually* cold nights," I said wryly, pointing at my puffer jacket.

"Living in that fancy apartment has made you soft," she scoffed, turning her attention to Haze's food-smeared high chair.

Haze began to fuss, distracting us both. My sister undid her nursing bra and began to breastfeed while getting the broom. With her free hand, she swept the dinner debris into a small pile.

"Besides," she added belatedly, "Pa's sacrificed so much for us."

As I held the dustpan steady for her, I reflected on whether this was true. What sacrifice had he made, exactly, apart from the one abruptly and tragically demanded of us all? Hadn't he moved us out to Australia, away from the support of grandparents, aunts, uncles, cousins, out of romantic selfishness? Because *he* couldn't bear to keep living in a city, a country thick with memories of her?

And who had been the one to help us through the process? To pay the immigration lawyers and fees, to find us a place to live? Who had come up with a way to keep us from getting deported after Pa lost his job? Who had visited regularly and made sure Vera and I were doing all right? No one but Acek—on the strength of a childhood friendship that my father hadn't thought twice about throwing away in a fit of pique.

I emptied the dustpan in the kitchen bin and returned to the dining table. Vera finally sat down, though from the looks of things, Haze was already done. She detached from my sister's nipple, head lolled back, milk dribbling down her chin. Out like a light.

I'd never been the type to coo over babies. But as I watched Haze slumber peacefully in my sister's arms, I understood the urge for the first time. The yearning to stroke their tiny fingers and squeeze their plump cheeks. I remembered my news and decided it was now or never.

"I'm pregnant," I said. "I think."

She stared. "You *think* you're pregnant?"

"I took a test this morning. It came out positive."

"Vivi, for real?" She squealed with delight.

Her joy was infectious. For the first time that day, I felt genuinely happy, and at ease.

My sister quickly left for the bedroom to tuck Haze in. When she came back, her strong arms enveloped me in a bone-crushing hug.

"What did Gabe say?" she asked, releasing me.

"He doesn't know yet," I replied. Then, hastily, when I saw her look of surprise, "He left for work early. I want to tell him in person."

She swatted my shoulder. "Go home! Tell your husband he's going to be a father!"

I looked at the Duplo blocks scattered around the lounge room. "I'll help clean up. There's no hurry."

"*I'm* the one in a hurry," she laughed. "It's almost eight. I still have to read Matt and Terry their bedtime stories."

"More than one?"

"Of course. They're different ages, aren't they? They each get a story suitable for them. And they each need special one-on-one time with Mummy. The mothering guides recommend it. It's so they'll develop more confidence and independence as individuals."

She laughed again. "You'll learn all these things soon enough."

It was almost half past nine by the time I got home. Gabe had left a reusable Post-it note on the mirror above the foyer table: *Out for a run*.

I'd no idea what time he'd left, but I did know he might be a while. He was training for a marathon.

I took a shower and felt my middle for signs of a bump. Nothing. *It's too early. Don't be ridiculous, Vi.* As I towel-dried my hair, I opened the topmost drawer and took out the test, which I'd stashed before running out to catch the train. They were still there, the two parallel lines, now a dark dried-out pink that reminded me of pressed petals. There had been two tests in the box, so I took the remaining one just to make sure. Positive again. I placed one stick above the other on the bathroom counter, lining up the lines—two sections of road on a journey that billions of women had taken before me, and that, as long as the world didn't end, billions more would take after.

Gabe still hadn't returned. I logged on to our internet and visited Greta Wilde's blog in search of the video that I swore, after watching it four times in a row, to never watch again.

It was gone.

"Sorry, Wilde Gals!" read Greta's explanation. "The video was too long and I exceeded the maximum file upload size for my blogging tier! Oops! (Don't recommend, by the way. Phew, talk about a hefty extra charge!) Anyway, I'll make the video shorter and post an edited version soon. Keep watching this space!"

I logged out and sat back. Perhaps it was just as well. What was the point of playing it again? The whole recording was burned into my brain, anyway, from start to grisly end. As the screensaver came on, color-changing prisms bouncing back and forth across the monitor, I set the whole video rolling in my head.

*

Greta adjusts the recording device from where she's sitting on the sofa. She looks stunning in her signature easy-breezy way. Dewy skinned. Fresh faced. She's wearing a cropped tie-dye tank top that accentuates her washboard abs and sculpted arms.

"Hi, Wilde Gals! Greta here. Sorry for my très long absence! As you know from the photos, last week, I had my third—little Nora. (Ssshhh. She's napping in the next room.) For those of you who already have kids, you know what a whirlwind the first few days can be! The massive energy spike, not needing any sleep . . . it's like being on speed, am I right? Haha, I'm just kidding. I've never taken speed. And you shouldn't either. PSA: don't do speed."

She wags her finger in mock disapproval.

"Aaanyway, as you all know"—here she clasps her hands together—"I am a big advocate of at-home birth. We did it with our second, little Greg Junior, and it was such a WONDERFUL experience that when we found out little Nora was on the way, there was no question. I told Greg we just HAD to do it again.

"So, exactly the same setup: same midwife, same rooms, same inflatable pool. Different music, though: I felt more Beyoncé, less Bruno this time round. But another BIG DIFF! I recorded the rebirth!

"Okay, okay. I can hear you all now: 'Greta. Girl. WHO records a rebirth? What about the BIRTH? Who wants to watch the credits when they can watch the movie?'

"But if you've been following this blog for a while, you'll know that I am a big fan of mothers embracing our identities as our mother selves. We're not just appendages of our kids. We are strong, amazing superhumans. And recognizing that will empower us to raise strong, amazing children and build a strong, amazing society. If children are the fruit, if society is the fruit, then mothers are the vine on which those fruits grow."

She flexes and winks at the camera.

"And, Wilde Gals, THAT is why I recorded my rebirth. We need to see with our own eyes where our strength comes from. We don't need to sanitize it. We don't need to pretend it's all pretty with a big pink bow wrapped around it. Rebirth is what it is, and it's . . ." (She throws her hands up and her large green eyes fill with tears), "gorgeous. Simply gorgeous. It's nature's way."

She dabs at her eyes, careful not to smear her mascara.

"So, without further ado, here's the recording. I hope you are as in AWE as I was when I played it back. Until next time. And remember, girls! Stay Wilde at heart!"

The video cuts to a dimly lit basement. Or at least, it's most likely a basement, judging from the wooden steps, lack of windows, and concrete floor. It's completely empty except for a purple yoga mat. Suddenly, a door creaks off-camera, and two figures carry an unconscious person down the stairs. The man must be Greta's husband, Greg, and the woman must be the midwife. The sleeping woman must be Greta. She's completely naked. Her middle is still ballooned from ten months of carrying the baby she just gave birth to. They lay her on the yoga mat and head back up the stairs. The door slams shut.

Twelve minutes pass. Nothing happens. Then, something crawls out from between her legs. Once it's a few meters away from Greta's body, it stops. It's about the size of a garden slug. Minutes pass, and it grows into a wriggling, puppy-sized lump. It gets bigger, takes on a more distinct shape. A baby. A child. Soon, it is identical to Greta herself, except for its bulging muscles and thick neck.

The new Greta wakes, stretching and yawning like a tiger. Her teeth also differ from those of the old Greta, who presumably doesn't have fangs. New Greta sniffs the air and locates her old self, who is still sound asleep. She bends down and, with one hand, seizes Greta by the throat and lifts her off the floor. Greta still doesn't move or wake. But her body twitches and crackles when new Greta crushes all the bones in her neck and smashes her skull against the wall.

New Greta repeats the action, seven, eight times, until the skull shatters into fragments and brains splatter everywhere. The head looks like an empty, bloody sack of skin and hair. Flinging the carcass onto the floor, she tears open the abdomen with a single swipe. A shower of blood. Organs spill out—which new Greta begins furiously cramming into her mouth. She consumes everything: innards, bones, skin, hair. She even laps up most of the blood. By now, she is less bulky, and her fangs have shrunk. She looks exactly like old Greta, but with a better bod. But what should we expect? She *is* Greta. Sated and drowsy, she curls up on the floor and closes her eyes until the midwife comes down the stairs with a towel and bucket to clean her client off.

*

The front door slammed, startling me into the present.

"Gabe?" I called out, heart pounding. "Is that you?"

What a silly question. Who else would it be, I thought as I heard the sound of trainers being deodorized and stored, the padding of my husband's socked feet coming down the hall.

Yet my heart was still racing as I swiveled the chair to catch him rounding the corner, sweaty and grinning, exuding endorphins.

"Hey," he said, giving me a peck on the cheek. "How was your day?"

"I'm pregnant," I blurted.

And like I knew it would, Gabe's face lit up. Lit up like the goddamn sun.

iv.

We've been on the motorway for an hour, but it feels like less with the broad sky above and the silver-green gum trees rushing past. Cloud snoozes in his car seat, barefoot—*oh, why not*, I thought this morning, sick of struggling over footwear. *Life is hard. We all deserve a break*. I spent the first part of the journey glancing over my shoulder, watching his eyelids gradually lower, then flutter open before descending again. At some point, they closed all the way. I stare at the sky and try to channel its blankness, try to appreciate this freedom, which has come like a gift after the news of Gabe's impending remarriage last night. I don't have to keep tabs on the full cup of Cloud's feelings while keeping mine from sloshing over. I don't have to feign interest or delight during interactions where I would rather be staring into space. I don't have to worry for his safety while yearning to bang my head against a wall until it bleeds. I'm not drawing up lists of what I must pack, prepare, and put away as I reflect on the seeming pointlessness of all my actions.

I can just sit. For at least a whole hour more. I try to keep perspective and hold on to the happiness I felt at dinner last night.

Cloud and I are part of a community here, even if things with Acek aren't the same as before.

I've never been gladder about Nina's tendency not to say much. I appreciate Nina in general for inviting Cloud and me on this mission to acquire parts. When Nina called at eight-fifteen, I was sitting on the sofa in my pajamas, intending to bathe and change Cloud, since I'd put him straight to bed the night before. I, too, wanted to get dressed and get us packed and ready to go so that we could use our day off to take the bus into town. Cloud could play in the playground. I could buy fresh fruits and vegetables, which we had run out of, except for a soft carrot, which I planned to slice into batons that Cloud would then refuse to eat. I was also intending to buy more eggs to encourage Cloud in his newfound egg-love. I made a mental note to add "eggs" to the running shopping list on the fridge in the kitchen. The phone rang.

"Acek got a call this morning from some guy in Kempsey," said Nina. "He has a box of parts he's looking to sell. Asked if we could drive up today to take a look. You and Cloud want to come?"

"Acek's not going?"

"Nah. He's got stuff to do around the house."

I was just about to express uncertainty—spending my day off taking my toddler on a long car ride for work didn't seem very appealing—when Nina added, "We could stop at the beach along the way. That's why I thought of you and Cloud." Then a pause. "Does Cloud like the beach?"

I recalled the very few times I'd had the energy to take him—after slipping into the long stream of my depression, only ever with Gabe. I recalled sitting Cloud down in the dry sand. I recalled sitting him down in the thin film of sea wave coating and re-coating the shore. I recalled Cloud older and able to crawl across the beach, with Gabe and me looking on. I recalled sitting on the beach towel, tired, and Gabe exclaiming, "See he likes it! You should take him here more." I recalled watching our son crawl farther and farther away until Gabe scrambled after him to bring him back.

I answered Nina's question. "I think he does." Cloud brought me his peek-a-boo book and butted the spine repeatedly against my knee. "Mama ree!"

"So you'll come?"

There was something hopeful in Nina's low voice, in the way she asked. It made me hopeful too.

"Yeah. Yeah, why not? We'll go."

So here we are, vrooming up the coast in the sedan, radio softly playing. Even though Nina seems comfortably silent, it occurs to me that I should at least attempt to make conversation to be polite.

"How did this guy get Acek's number?"

Nina shrugs.

"You've driven up here before?"

"Yeah. Once or twice."

So much for talking. But again, I don't mind.

We drive through a portion of road flanked by high rockface on either side.

"Wonder how much dynamite it took to blast through all this stone."

"Huh?" I ask.

"You know. So the road could go through."

"Oh. Right."

That's the extent of our conversation until we reach Kempsey. Nina then hands me directions on a scrap of paper, and I read them out loud—two blocks past the uniting church, turn left, and so on, until we reach number fifty-four, accurately described in the directions dictated to Acek as: *brick cube with windows, green gate.*

We roll down the windows so Cloud, still sleeping, has air. Then Nina cuts the engine, and we go knock at the front door.

The man is around Acek's age, graying and skinny.

"We're the hobblers," says Nina. "You rang us to take a look at some parts?"

He nods and disappears before coming back out with a midsize carton. At a glance, the contents look promising. He leads us to the driveway and sets it down.

"Sift through if you like."

Nina and I get to work, examining objects one by one and laying them on the concrete in batches. We use the categorization system Acek taught us and do the pricing in our heads. She and I work well together; we go through the whole box in no time. Then, in low voices, in Hokkien, we arrive at a combined estimate on how much everything is worth. Of course, how much they're worth differs from how much we'll offer.

Nina takes the lead in bargaining. Her assertiveness surprises me. I've never seen this side of her before.

"We can give you a hundred and sixty," she declares, poker-faced.

He gazes at us with cool disdain. "My mechanic friend took a look the other day. Said the whole lot's worth two hundred fifty at least."

Nina shakes her head. "Sorry. Some of them are outdated. Or too worn out. We can do a hundred seventy at most."

He's mulling it over.

"Your friend's welcome to them if he's willing to pay that much," she adds.

He scowls. "Two hundred."

"Hundred ninety."

"Two hundred, final offer."

"Fine."

Nina takes out her wallet and counts out two hundred in cash.

In the meantime, the man turns up an ear. He hears something.

"Oi, your little one's waking up."

Sure enough, I hear it: the tiny grunts and groans of Cloud waking from his slumber. I trot over to the car and retrieve him, bopping him up and down as I walk back to Nina and the man.

Now that the business part is done, the man's willing to be more friendly, as are we. "How old?" he asks, pointing his chin at Cloud.

"Almost two."

He breaks into a grin. "Wait here," he says. He goes into the house and comes back with an old plush toy. It's a lion. The brown fur is nubby and grayish, and the mane is matted and stiff.

He offers it to Cloud.

"Oh no, it's all right," I say hastily. But Cloud takes and hugs it, pressing it to his chest. It brushes against my cheek and makes me feel itchy all over.

"It was my daughter's. She died."

The itch evaporates. No one speaks until Cloud does.

"Ion. Rawr."

"Yeah, lion. That's right," the man says, his eyes going bright. He gives Cloud's chin a chuck.

"I'm sorry." I don't know what else to say.

"Yeah, well. It was a while ago," he replies, wiping his eyes. "My other daughter's coming to pick me up today. We're going back to country. My dad doesn't have long."

I realize he's Aboriginal.

"Sorry to hear it," Nina chimes in. "How old is he?"

"Seventy-nine."

"How far's the drive?"

"Far enough. Near Cowra. We're Wiradjuri. Where are you two from?"

I give the short answer for Nina and me. "Indonesia."

He raises his eyebrows in surprise. "Oh. You look Chinese."

"We are," I explain. "Our families migrated from China a long time ago."

"Ever think of going back?"

"To Indonesia?"

"To China."

I think of Pa and his newfound love for the motherland. My laugh comes out bitter. "Don't know anyone there."

"No family left?"

"There's an ancestral village somewhere. But I wouldn't know them. And they wouldn't know me."

"And your friend?"

He turns to Nina. She shrugs and shakes her head.

He's the one feeling sorry for us now.

"That's too bad," he says.

We get back in the car, and he waves us off. I feel guilty about not paying more for the parts—his mechanic friend was right.

*

We head to the beach Nina has in mind. It's back the way we came, but a short detour east from our southbound route. I realize Cloud hasn't eaten since breakfast and, as we walk, I feed him crackers from his snack box. Nina's brought some old towels. We lay them out, just after where the grass ends and drops into sand.

I strip Cloud—turns out he's wet anyway—and dress him in a blue whale-print swim nappy and rash guard. I slather his face and neck with sunscreen, which makes him struggle and scream. I top him with a bucket hat, which he promptly pulls off.

Nina merely waits patiently, then stretches out her hand to lead him to the sea, which he accepts. She swings him by the armpits, which my shoulder would never allow me to do, and dips his feet in the shallows. Then she shows him how to run from the lapping of the waves. I trail behind them and watch at a remove, hands on hips, pant hems rolled up. It occurs to me that I should, like Nina, have worn shorts.

We break for lunch at a picnic table just inland of the beach, on the grass. Nina's the one who packed the food. She offered, and we had run through Cloud's various likes and dislikes on the phone. There are boiled eggs, still in the shell, and a small container of salt (I'd told Nina how Zoe got Cloud to eat an egg). There's fishball fried ryce, made with leftovers from last night's feast. There is sambal. And crisp lettuce leaves, which Nina asked if Cloud likes, and to which I said, not since I last checked, but let's try. As she offers one to Cloud and he turns his face away, I think about how, when Nina had asked me if there was anything I liked to eat, I told her I didn't know.

Together, we crack the shell of Cloud's egg and help him peel and salt it, and to my great relief, he starts munching without a second thought. As if he's never not enjoyed boiled eggs. As if he's never regarded them with suspicion and contempt. As if he's never been outraged at the sight of one in any form—boiled and halved, scrambled, omeletted and cut into strips—on his plate. I reflect on how unhealthy it is to have my feelings so bound up with what my almost-two-year-old decides to consume. I reflect on how I feel this level of maternal concern is nevertheless expected of me. I reflect on how a healthy new mother would not think such concern unhealthy or engage in such reflection. I reflect on how, if Cloud is capable of eating eggs as if he's always eaten them, that if I die suddenly, he will in all likelihood be capable of loving another mother figure as if I had never existed at all. The thought is depressing and comforting at the same time.

I pull my thoughts away and study Nina instead, who is eating and glancing at Cloud between bites. She is wearing sunglasses and a hat, which leave only the bottom half of her face to observe, and I can't help but be amazed at how she really does have her uncle's jaw. I speculate that her father—Acek's brother—must have had it as well. I imagine what a big family portrait might look like—three generations, seated and standing in rows, of that jaw.

"How do you like living here?" I ask.

Her sunglasses make her expression hard to read, but the tilt of her head suggests confusion.

"I mean, when you had to move here from Melbourne."

She mulls the question over. "What did Acek tell you about what happened?" she asks finally. "I know he told you. I just want to know what he said."

"He said your parents died in a car accident," I say, my face growing warm for some reason. "And that they left the house to you, so you moved here. And he moved to live with you so you wouldn't have to be alone."

"Yeah," she says quietly. "Yeah. That's right."

I'm sorry I asked. It seems to have triggered some sadness. I'm about to apologize when she says, "It's not bad."

"What's not bad?"

"Living here. That's what you asked. How I like living here."

She's right. I'd forgotten my question. At the same time, we both break into a laugh, but abruptly, she stops.

I ask a follow-up. "How's living with Acek?"

There's a bitterness to my question that surprises even me. I wonder if she notices.

"It's fine. He's pretty self-sufficient for his generation, if that's what you mean. So we share the cooking and cleaning and all that."

"You must be sick of each other," I say, trying to joke. "Seeing each other all the time, at work and at home."

Again, she mulls. I imagine her words as gold coins in a drawstring bag. She peers inside, calculating how much to spend with her reply.

"Actually, it works out well," she says. "It's nice to have each other around. So I'm not lonely and neither is he."

She doesn't intend it to, but the last sentence feels like a slap in the face. *He wasn't lonely*, I want to say, but don't. If I'm honest with myself, I know she's right. I can see it for myself, the change in Acek since he left the city to move in with his niece. He's never been the cheerful, jolly sort, but he's certainly the closest to cheerful, the closest to jolly, that I've seen him in a while, the last time being my late teens and early twenties, before I married Gabe, when I spent almost all my time working at the shop.

I become aware that my face is frozen in a smile. Fortunately, there is a flurry of motion from Cloud, so I have an excuse to turn away. He's finished his egg—or rather, finished *with* it. He has detached what remains of the yolk and is stuffing it into the gap between the picnic table's wooden planks.

"But you must feel lonely. Without your family, raising Cloud by yourself."

I raise my eyes at Nina's remark. Now it's my turn to ask the same question she asked me. "What did Acek tell you?"

"Not much. He said you had health problems after giving birth. And that you split up with your husband and needed your old job back."

"That's all?"

Nina racks her brain for more information. "He said he knew your parents back in Medan."

I nod. I feel the bareness of her knowledge sweep over me. Like a wave, it washes me clean, reminding me of my place in Acek's life. Not a daughter. Not a niece, like Nina. Not even a niece or daughter figure. Just an ex-employee who needs help. Just an acquaintance's child.

"Yeah, I do feel lonely," I say, even as my reply omits my sudden realization—gears and springs finally clicking into place. I am lonely, but not because I left my family, or even because I left Gabe. I'm lonely because I thought that if I moved out here to work for Acek, I'd have Acek, and therefore wouldn't be alone. But I was wrong.

*

Shortly afterwards, we pack up the picnic things and, at Cloud's insistence, head back to the beach. This time, I make an effort to join in the fun. It's partially successful: I enjoy watching Cloud enjoy himself. I appreciate how his laughter reminds me of bubbles, how his grin lifts his cheeks and crinkles his little eyes and nose. This is mostly how I experience the joy of motherhood these days: secondhand. As if watching ourselves in a mirror, pleased at the reflection of our smiles.

Nina suggests one more activity before we drive back down: there's a cool-looking playground about ten minutes away. She drove past a few months back, and it made her think of Cloud. Why not, I say.

But as we pack up and drive toward the playground, as we park and cross the grass in the direction of the playground's turrets and rope structures—a fenced-in kingdom of play—all the reasons for why not come flooding back. They're the same reasons I stopped going to the playground near our apartment in the city, and the same reasons I carefully time our visits to the playground near where I do the shopping, going only at the least busy periods. These reasons are now spread out among the play equipment, assisting their children or keeping a watchful eye, or chatting in twos and threes because it's normal for other mothers of small children to have friends who are also mothers of small children.

Cloud breaks into a trot. In one hand, he clutches Ion the lion. Upon reuniting with it in the car, after the beach, he insisted on bringing it. Nina and I follow him, wading our way through the toned biceps and straight backs and radiant complexions, and with each passing second in their presence, I feel myself becoming increasingly loathsome. I feel like a cockroach scurrying between dark places, exposed mid-run by the sun.

"Sly!" yells Cloud, pointing Ion up a steep slope made of recycled tire rubber, which several mothers are scaling, upright and sure-footed, defiant of gravity, kids sitting easily in the crooks of their elbows. One mother carries twins—one in each arm, like squashes from a bounteous harvest. Upon attaining the summit, the women arrange their children on their laps and transform into human sleds, shooting down the high metal slide to the base, where they commence the climb all over again.

"Sly!" cries Cloud again, tugging at my hand.

But the slope is too much for me. I might be able to make it on my own, crawling with the aid of both hands, but with Cloud it's a struggle, and he's far too little to make it up by himself. I even convince him to pass the lion to Nina so I can piggyback him instead. But we're barely a quarter of the way up when I freeze, realizing my bad shoulder won't take it, trying not to collapse and send us both rolling down.

Spotting my distress, another mother from below catches up to us. Without a word, she tosses her girl from her left arm to her right, bends, and scoops up Cloud. She deposits him at the top, like a ski lift, and rides down the slide with her child.

I clamber back to the base and watch, wondering if Cloud will be able to slide down himself.

"Mama, hairy!" he calls.

The answer is no. "Hairy" is "scary" in Cloudspeak.

"Do you want me to go with him?" asks the mother who helped carry him up. She's standing beside me, about to head up again. Her look of concern irritates me to no end.

"No, I can do it," I say. My bad shoulder twinges and my abs and thighs are on fire, but I manage to attain the peak. I put him on my lap, and we whizz down. Upon reaching the bottom, Cloud springs up and squeals in delight, "Ahin! Mama, sly ahin!" Slide again, Mama.

"Coming down!" a voice warns from high up behind us. How can I go again if I don't even have the energy to scoot myself away from the bottom of the slide?

Then, all of a sudden, a hand reaches out to me. But it's not one of the other mothers; it's Nina. She helps me to my feet.

"I can take him," she says. "Have a rest."

Have a rest. The words sound so foreign to me. Who tells a new mother to rest?

Ion and I sit down on a low wall near the sandpit and watch from there, somewhat gratified that Nina doesn't find the climb completely effortless either. The slope was obviously designed with new mothers and nimble older children in mind. But Nina and Cloud make it. And do it four times over before another part of the playground catches Cloud's eye: the swings. He races over. I gasp as Nina grabs Cloud's shoulder just in time to prevent him from getting kicked in the head by an older kid mid-flight.

"I'll push him," I call, jogging over to help Cloud into the swing. I tag Nina out and hand her Ion. I'll need both arms. The swings for toddlers are heavier than the ones for bigger children, designed with a new mother's strength in mind.

I can't help but sneak a glance at the woman pushing her son next to me. She's even more dazzling than the others, with model features and a spandex-clad body to match.

"Too high!" her son yells.

"Oh! Sorry, darling." Her voice is amazing too: melodic and low. I watch as she modulates her arm movements to the gentlest of pushes, her thick, glossy ponytail swaying along. In the meantime, I'm giving it my all and covered in sweat, but I can only match half her loft.

"Higher, Mama!" pleads Cloud.

I try to oblige as I chuckle bitterly on the inside. Maybe he means "Hire Mama," and is demanding that a more able mother take my place.

In the meantime, the model mother turns and smiles.

"How old?" she asks in her beautiful voice. By which people mean, "How old is your child?"

"Almost two."

"Ah. Dylan's twenty-six months tomorrow."

So, our children are basically the same age.

"Is he your nephew?"

The question is lobbed so lightly and with such ease that I'm unprepared for the force of its blow. I wonder what aspect of my appearance most gives me away. My thinning hair? My bad posture? My saggy middle? The bags under my eyes?

"He's my son."

Her pretty features dissolve into shock.

"Rebirth complications," I add in a mumble.

"Oh. I'm sorry."

I keep silent. We continue pushing our respective children, me trying to maintain power and lift without looking tired or upset. I can't let her win, even though she already has.

Then, impossibly, it gets worse.

"You know," she tells me, her beautiful voice dropping so low and soft that it attains the quality of a vibration, a gentle electric current passing through me. "I had a sister-in-law. My brother's wife. She had rebirth complications too."

"Oh?"

"Yes, poor thing. She died. Both selves, I mean. But the baby's okay. Thank God."

She pauses for so long, I wonder if I am meant to thank God as well.

"They think her old self must have woken up and tried to interfere. Just awful. My brother was thinking of suing the hospital for malpractice, but his doctor friend said he'd never win. In the very rare cases something happens with rebirth, it means there's something wrong with the mother."

She turns to face me again, big eyes brimming with sympathetic tears. "Anyway, what I mean to say is: I'm sorry you had a difficult rebirth."

My head spins. The jarring combination of insensitivity and compassion disorients me. I force my arms to keep pushing, but Cloud's swing slows.

"Hire! Hire!" yells Cloud.

"What about a short break, darling?" By which I mean, *let's leave and never come back.*

"Wing!" he screams, kicking his legs. "Wing! No bake!"

"We can go back to the slides," I suggest, careful to keep my tone sprightly, though my voice is on the verge of breaking. "Or the seesaw? Please . . ."

Suddenly, the swing is empty. Nina stands in front of me, Cloud in her arms.

"There's ice cream, Cloud! Let's get ice cream!"

Before I know it, she is walking briskly away in the direction of a snack kiosk. She turns. "You coming, Vi?"

I leave the swing and follow, ignoring the model mother's attempt to say goodbye. Cloud gets a rainbow Paddle Pop. I get a Calippo. Nina opts for a Splice. Nina says it's her treat. We sit on a bench, Nina and Cloud in the middle, me and Ion on the ends. And because I'm too tired to help Cloud, and Nina doesn't know that Cloud needs help, the majority of his Paddle Pop drips and pools in his lap, a psychedelic pastel mess.

Who cares. I'll change him later. He's happy, and I'm grateful.

Despite my gratitude, my eyes fill with tears—like the model mother's, but different.

On the drive back, I fall asleep and don't wake up until we pull up to my house. Nina simply parks the car and waits, giving me time to fully come to. When my eyes blink open, the late afternoon sun is falling through the leaves, dappling the dashboard in light. I stretch and yawn and turn to check on Cloud. He's fast asleep, again, the lion's head rising and falling gently on his small chest. It occurs to me to worry that excessive daytime sleep will wreak havoc on his night sleep, but I'm too exhausted. I place it at the bottom of the stack of matters I've just remembered to be anxious about: how I meant to stock up on groceries today but haven't; how I have to cook dinner; how I don't know what to cook for dinner; how I should have put the washing out to dry before leaving this morning to take advantage of the sunny day; the dirty nappies and ice-cream-soaked clothes in the wet-bag, which I have yet to wash; how Nina, who has done several hours of driving and must be tired herself, is waiting for me to wake my kid up and get out of her car.

I convert the last worry on the list into action.

"Do you want to come in for tea? Or coffee?"

Nina hesitates briefly before saying yes. Together we rouse Cloud and bring him and Ion and all the stuff in.

*

There's something about returning to the house that I always find depressing, especially on lovely days like this, which make the inside seem all the darker, all the more run-down and caked with grime. I become desensitized when Cloud and I are inside it, but when we leave and come back, its sorry state hits me afresh. It was the best I could afford to rent after leaving Gabe. I'd neglected to save much. Back when Pa, Vera, and I were still living together, I used my earnings to help with rent and household expenses. Then, when Vera got married, bought a house, and took Pa with her, I moved into a shared flat and spent most of my money on rent. And then, when I married Gabe and he started paying for everything, I contributed to Pa's upkeep. Then I had Cloud and stopped working, and all income stopped coming in.

Now, peering sidelong from the kitchen, waiting for my crappy electric kettle to boil, I observe Nina playing restaurant with Cloud, and I imagine seeing our living conditions through her eyes and am ashamed anew. Does she regard our pimply sofa with the same revulsion I used to? Does she feel the thin layer of hair and dried food debris beneath her socked feet? Is she appalled at the heap of clean but crumpled washing sitting on the coffee table like a centerpiece? Is she wondering how I can apparently spend every morning, evening, and weekend here and never feel the urge to put away any of my son's scattered toys?

"One pizza, please."

Cloud rushes to fill Nina's order, which is a matter of putting a faded plastic pizza slice in a wooden bowl and presenting it with pride.

"Delicious!" she exclaims, pretending to take a large bite.

I bring out some real food, which is barely more edible than what Cloud is serving: the flaccid carrot, in sticks, and the last of the plain crackers. I've attempted to fancy up both by fanning them out. I shift the crumpled clothes to make just enough room for the plate. Cloud immediately snatches up two crackers, one in each hand, and becomes a crumb factory, munching away.

"Sorry for the mess," I blurt.

Nina's expression is difficult to read, but when she speaks, she's sympathetic. "No one likes housekeeping," she observes.

"Yeah, but as you can see, I've taken it to the next level." I chuckle, trying to sound like I'm enjoying the good joke that is my life. "Oh, the tea!"

I head back to the kitchen to check the electric kettle's progress—it no longer turns off by itself. It's from a customer who told us to keep it upon hearing the prognosis. I've tried a few tricks to fix it, but none of them have worked. The loud hissing indicates it's close to boiling, so I wait until it does, then fill the teapot and thermos at the same time so I don't have to use the kettle if I need hot water later. I bring the teapot and cups out on a tray, with a small cup of soy milk for Cloud, and when I don't have anywhere to set them down, Nina transfers the clean laundry to the sofa's far side.

"You're good with kids," I observe as I offer Cloud some limp carrot. He refuses, understandably. I help him drink from his cup. He takes one sip and wanders away. "Have you thought about having any yourself?"

I don't think twice before asking the question—she looks slightly younger than me—but when she looks uncomfortable, I know I've made a mistake.

"Oh, I—I can't have children," she stammers, just as Cloud thrusts a plastic banana at her.

"Nana!" declares Cloud.

Nina tries to smile. "I love nanas! Can I have some grapes too?"

A cluster of plastic grapes lies on the floor, across the room. Cloud toddles away to retrieve them.

"I'm sorry," I say awkwardly. "I shouldn't have asked."

"Oh no, it's fine," she says, but in her voice is a fissure through which sadness bubbles.

We both sit in silence, sipping our tea.

A bunch of grapes, an orange juice carton, a can of beans, and a lamb chop later ("Not sure he knows what that is," I joke weakly when he hands her the chop), Nina excuses herself. She gives Cloud's hand a quick squeeze. I feel awful for being so insensitive, but I don't want to bring it up by apologizing again.

"Say 'Bye bye, Aie,'" I tell Cloud.

"Bye bye A Ee."

"See you tomorrow," she says, and in no time at all, she's slipped on her shoes and is gone.

A better host would slip on her own shoes and follow to say a proper goodbye, even wave her farewell until she's out of sight. Instead, I sit, sunk in the well of the sofa, turning over in my mind what I've learned about Nina, while my body receives Cloud's food items—now offered to me—and responds with enthusiastic comment. The new information colors the day's events a different hue: Nina thinking that Cloud might like the beach; Nina's desire to play with Cloud; Nina's abrupt departure. I put myself in her shoes. Not being able to have children. Wanting children. Wanting to be around children. Suddenly upset at being around what she can't have.

I think more about her sudden departure and wonder if I am to her what the model mother earlier today was to me: someone who is what the other isn't; someone to be envied. Me, of all people.

It's horrible, but it actually makes me feel better—reminds me I'm lucky to have Cloud, reminds me we're all just trying to survive in our own individual ways. Something else occurs to me as well: I didn't go into machine mode once today. Not even at the playground. I take the doughnut Cloud passes me and air-bite into it with relish, making sure to save the painted sprinkles for last.

V.

The knowledge of death is a funny thing. We learn about it when we're little and spend the rest of our lives knowing it will arrive. Yet we're able to behave as if death doesn't exist—as if we're not playing in its shadow, waiting for the great stone of it to drop. To put it another way, we always know we're going to die, yet we're able to carry on as if we aren't aware. Until it comes for us, we're still capable of experiencing optimism and joy.

I suppose, to me, rebirth became the equivalent of death. Unavoidable. Crouched at the foot of my body, waiting to smash in my skull and rip out my guts. Never mind that, rationally speaking, rebirth and death aren't comparable at all. Never mind that one is a new beginning and the other an end; logic didn't—doesn't—play a part in my fear. If it did, I wouldn't be in the mess I'm in now.

But if I were able to carry on in the face of rebirth as we do in the face of death, then maybe I would have been fine. The real problem was, once I got pregnant, I lost the ability to deal with rebirth as if it were death—to be happily preoccupied by the present without having my eyes riveted on the future end.

I suppressed my anxiety pretty well for the first trimester. But like the pregnancy, it was bound to show. At the fifteen-week mark (when the baby was pear-sized, according to my week-by-week pregnancy guide), I had a breakdown in public when Gabe and I were in a baby shop. It was Gabe who'd insisted on going in. We passed the shop every weekend on the way to and from the supermarket, and since learning I was pregnant, he'd been suggesting we look inside.

I'd tried to hold off, saying it was too early, that we should wait until the twelve-week mark, when the risk of miscarriage would drop significantly. Then twelve weeks passed, then thirteen, then fourteen, and I still made excuses. We still had lots of time; I wanted to find out first whether it was a boy or girl; I felt tired and nauseous and just wanted to get the grocery shopping done and return home. But he succeeded in persuading me. We didn't have to buy anything. We would just browse. Get some ideas. It would make me feel better. We could go straight home afterward, and he would come out again to do the supermarket shopping himself.

I relented as usual. Gabe was always so good humored and affable; it was difficult to keep saying no. And, for a while, amidst the racks of pastel-colored onesies and animal-print nappies and bibs, my anxiety melted like snow.

A shop assistant joined us. Could she help us? How exciting! Congratulations! When was bubba due? Oh, of course. She understood completely. It was important to look around and think carefully before making any decisions. Perhaps she could just show us certain essentials, so we could get a sense of the different options.

"It can be quite overwhelming," she warned with a laugh, leading us to the cots.

There were standalone ones and bedside ones. The latter attached to the mother's side of the bed, to make co-sleeping safe.

"Mum will have those heightened new mum senses, but Dad won't," she explained. "If you want to bring bubba into bed, then this will prevent Dad accidentally rolling over onto bub in his sleep."

We moved on to the baby transport section.

"Of course, Mum won't need help carrying baby the natural way. But if Dad is the hands-on type and plans to hold bub a lot too, then we have two options: ergonomic carriers or slings. The carriers are fiddlier, and to be honest, a lot of people end up returning them still new in the box. The new mum hormones kick in and, boom, they won't let bubba out of their arms." She laughed pleasantly again. "Can't fight nature, I suppose."

Gabe glanced over at the car seats. "We use a car-share sometimes. Do we need one of these?"

The woman beamed. "Absolutely. Even a new mum can't protect her baby in a car crash. They have ones just for infants, but if you want value for money, I'd suggest a convertible—you can take out the insert and adjust the height of the straps as bubba grows."

Gabe grinned. "Yeah, who wouldn't want a convertible?"

He and the shop assistant laughed, and out of nowhere, my heart began racing again. It had been happening every now and then, but I'd always been able to hide it. This time, my breathing grew short as well.

"Sorry," I gasped, breaking away. "I just need some fresh air."

But when the fresh air hit my face, tears began streaming down my cheeks. I moved two shops down and stood by a tree, wiping my eyes.

Gabe found me, took me by the shoulders, stooped a little so his gaze was level with mine.

"Viv, what's wrong?"

I told him how scared I was, and how I didn't know why.

He held me pressed against his chest for the longest time.

"It's okay, Viv. Don't be scared."

Like he promised, we went straight home after that.

*

Up until that point, Gabe had always had the magic ability to soothe me, to cheer me up, to draw me out or in. It was how we'd wound up going out in the first place, four years before. We'd met in his first apartment, at his twenty-seventh birthday party. I hardly went to parties at all, but Gabe was James's old friend from school, and Vera had asked if I could come. Much later, I found out that she'd pleaded—apparently, she was trying to encourage her little sister to stop being so anti-social, to get out and meet people instead of tinkering all the time with old machines.

Pleading hadn't been necessary. The party was a casual affair at the two-bedroom city apartment he was sharing with someone else. Even then, on his first salary, he could afford to rent somewhere smaller on his own, but he liked the company a housemate provided—which showed you what kind of guy Gabe was. Outgoing. Friendly. Easygoing. Genuinely warm. Gabe liked people, and everyone liked Gabe.

He made me feel welcome from the minute I stepped into his apartment, trailing shyly after Vera and James, a party-sized bag of chips in hand. It was one of his pleasures: coaxing people from their shells, finding the right conversation topic to make them glow, to make them enjoy themselves, to reveal what a special, wonderful person they were. Tipped off by what Vera had told him, he started by asking me about my job.

"How'd you get into your line of work?"

I shrugged. "Just liked it. A friend of Dad's saw I had potential. Offered to apprentice me and pay for the courses and license too."

Gabe got me talking so much, someone had to remind him they should sing "Happy Birthday" and cut the cake.

Everything always glided like butter with Gabe. Within weeks, we were a couple. Within a year, we were engaged. His friends expressed surprise. They didn't expect him to go for the mousy type. My sister worried he was out of my league, and therefore, unfeasible in the long run. But James assured us that despite his charm and good looks, Gabe was a solid guy—faithful, reliable, and steady.

Looking back, perhaps the ease of it was the warning sign. Or to put it in electrical terms, better several short spikes than a single, long surge. But who could have anticipated the blow-out? All I knew was that love had never been so effortless and natural, light-years apart from the one-way crushes I'd had in high school, or my "relationship" with the guy from Electrotechnology Essentials, which consisted of silent coffees at the TAFE café.

I'd never met anyone who had such a healthy attitude when it came to, well, everything. His family, for example: two parents and five siblings, whom he felt close to, even though they lived sixteen hours away by train. When I asked him if he felt isolated being so far from them, he merely laughed.

"Family's family," he said, a remark so confident in its self-evidence that it bordered on meaningless. To understand, you had to understand.

But sure enough, on the few and far between occasions they'd call each other long-distance, Gabe would chuckle and chatter with each of them as if he were talking to a good friend, getting updates on how his parents' farm was doing, bantering about sport with his dad and brothers, about local gossip with his mum and sister. They'd rib him about his suit-wearing, high-rise life. He'd grin and take it on the chin. My relationship with Pa was just the opposite, I reflected: I saw him every week and we barely spoke. And though I considered my relationship with Vera pretty good, we'd never really been on chatty terms. When I observed as much to Gabe, though, he took it in his stride—as if it were his to take.

"Don't worry about your family, Viv," he said kindly, lightly, and drew me in to kiss the top of my head.

No reason why not to worry. No elaborations or explanations. It was so simple. And as a result, it felt simple. Life didn't have to be as complicated as one made it out to be.

Even Gabe's complex family history was no match for his sunny disposition. When I'd first learned his last name, Mak, which was Cantonese, I'd made the initial assumption that his family was from Hong Kong. Turned out that his father's side was Chinese from New Guinea and his mother's side was Chinese from India. His father's parents were from Rabaul, his mother's side from Darjeeling, and their families had emigrated to Australia, respectively, after World War II and the Sino-Indian War.

The subject came up on our second date, which was dinner at his place. The last time I'd been there was his birthday party, and in the absence of a crowd, I could fully appreciate how truly nice his apartment was. Natural paint. Eco-flooring. Discreet cabinetry. Even the lighting was inexplicably wonderful—bright yet soft around the edges. The whole place looked like something out of the home design magazines that Vera started collecting after she and James bought the house. Gabe seemed unaware of my admiration.

"Sorry about the mess," he piped from the open kitchen, where he was pan-toasting hazelnuts. I wandered over. Only one piece of hobbled equipment in sight: a vintage jaffle sandwich maker.

"That's Kevin's." Kevin was his roommate. "Belonged to his Nana. Says it made the best jaffles. Won't part with it for the world."

"Well, are they the best?"

"Not bad. But worth half-an-hour's wait—fifteen to warm up, fifteen to toast?" He shot me a wink and shook his head. "Nah. Give me a new one any day. Sorry, Kevin's Nan."

As we ate, I looked over the photos on the sideboard. Some were obviously Kevin's (he was white), and some were Gabe's. One faded picture caught my eye.

"My dad's side," explained Gabe. "That was back in New Guinea." He brought the photo over and set it between us. "That's my granddad on the right," he said, pointing to a slouching boy in front. "The other kids are his brothers and sisters. And those are my great-grandparents."

"What's in the background?"

"Their provisions shop."

Then he told me their story. How Australia, in charge of administering New Guinea at the time, evacuated all the European women and children in Rabaul, but left the European men and all the Chinese behind. How the whole family fled inland on foot when the Japanese invaded. How one of his grandfather's brothers died on the way.

"If you think that's wild, you should hear about my mum's side," he said, a storyteller's glint in his eye.

His mother's family used to live in India. They owned a shoe shop in Darjeeling. One day, out of the blue, when his mum was three, all the Chinese were rounded up and taken to a camp in the desert, where they had to live for five years in harsh conditions. When they were finally released, someone else had taken over their house, and all their stuff was gone.

"But why?"

"Sino-Indian War. 1962. Border battle between India and China. It didn't last long, but India felt they couldn't trust the Chinese anymore. Even deported a bunch of them to China too—people who'd never set foot there their whole life!"

"So how'd your parents meet?"

"Here in Australia."

"So, you're, like . . . Indian-New-Guinean-Chinese-Australian."

Gabe laughed. "Too many hyphens. Just Chinese-Aussie. If people really want to know, like you, they can get the full story."

It amazed me, how he could tell such heavy stories so lightly. As if it were no big deal.

"Your background's pretty interesting, too, if I remember correctly," he remarked. "I think James mentioned your family's Chinese from Indonesia."

"Yeah, that's right. From Medan, in Sumatra."

"When did you move here?"

"Ages ago, in 2000."

Gabe thought a bit. "Weren't there anti-Chinese riots around that time? Something like that?"

"Yeah, around then. In 1998."

"Is that why you moved?"

"No. Yes. I mean, maybe it was a reason, but not the main one." I allowed myself time to chew and swallow. "My mum died in 1997, the year before the riots. She was cycling home and got hit in the head by a rock. My brother-in-law didn't tell you?"

Gabe's smile vanished. "No, he didn't. That's awful. I'm sorry."

"It's okay. I mean, it's not okay, but it happened a long time ago. I don't even remember much about it. I was five. Vera was eleven."

I put down my fork. Not because I was upset or anything. This kind of thing happened every time I thought about my mother, which wasn't even much at all. It was like a barrier in the road that you had to wait to lift. Like a lump of food sitting in your stomach, waiting to be digested.

"Are you okay?" Gabe asked.

"I'm fine."

It was the truth, but nonetheless, he reached over and placed his warm hand on mine.

"Don't be sad."

He smiled, which made me smile. Who knew it was as simple as that?

"They endured what they did so we could be here," he reflected. "We owe it to them to move on."

I thought of digestion again: the lump in my stomach being processed, being absorbed into my body, transforming into fresh cells, growing my nails and hair.

I supposed he was right. This was the best way to think about such things. The healthy way. We resumed eating, and I'd never felt so light.

Don't be sad, he'd said that night. And there he was, four years later, holding me outside the baby shop, saying almost the same thing: "Don't be scared."

But this time it didn't work, and that's when I realized it. Gabe's spell had lost its power. I could no longer see the world as he did, with such simplicity. And this terrified me almost as much as the small me inside me that would grow to kill me and take my place.

*

After the baby shop incident, I tried various tactics to soothe my fears. Gabe couldn't help me anymore. I'd have to find another way. I mentioned my anxiety to my sister when I was over one weekend, but she just laughed.

"You're worrying about the wrong part!" exclaimed Vera, mashing potatoes with her free hand, Haze in one arm. "Worry about the birth! Now *that* was awful. Especially Terry's." She laughed. "Cheeky little monkey didn't want to come out!"

"Tell the story!" pleaded Terry from the kitchen table where she and Matt were picking stones from lentils. They were making sheep-friendly shepherd's pie—part of the kids' culinary education.

From my sister's smile, I guessed the tale was a favorite.

"*Well*," she began, her face taking on the expressiveness of a comic actor, her voice slipping into the rhythm of what must have been familiar lines, "Terry was meant to be born ten days earlier! But she must have been so warm and cozy in there, she wanted to stay put!"

Both Terry and Matt giggled away.

"And when she did decide to join us out here, she took her own sweet time getting out!"

As the giggles continued, I revisited my own memories of that night—James calling from the hospital, anxious. Eighteen hours and nowhere close to full dilation. My sister in agony. Baby facing the wrong way, its spine to my sister's—they called it "sunny side up."

"Then, guess what? You finally started making your way through the birth canal, but stopped halfway. Maybe you found something in the corridor that caught your fancy. Hmm." My sister looked faux-quizzical and tapped on her chin. "What do you think it could have been?"

"A lolly!" suggested Terry.

"Lolly lolly," echoed Matt gleefully, following his older sister's cue.

My sister laughed. "Well, whatever it was, you wouldn't budge! Then the midwife said we couldn't wait any longer, we needed to get you out."

"Then they got the scissors?"

Vera nodded. "Exactly right, my darling. Then they got the scissors. And they made the door wider so they could help you through."

I almost choked at the word "door." She mimed a pair of scissors with her mash-covered hand as she said this, slashing through the air.

"It didn't hurt, right?" asked Terry, though surely she knew the answer by now.

"Of course not, darling. They gave me a special medicine to take away the pain. I didn't feel a thing."

Terry looked pensively down at her own body. I wondered if, despite hearing the story countless times over, there was something about it she was processing only now.

"Then they sewed it up?"

"No," my sister explained gently. "There was no need. Mummies have very special powers. We heal ourselves after having a baby. We get strong new bodies so we can do a good job taking care of you."

My sister turned her attention to the boiled potato in her hand. With a squeeze, she turned it to pulp. After that, at the request of her audience, she told Matt's birth story too.

On the train home, I reflected on the enjoyment my sister took in making her children laugh. It was a side of her I'd never seen before she became a mother. And I recalled my niece and nephew's mirthful faces. Surely that kind of joy was worth something, but how much?

I imagined my sister's body, legs splayed, the raw slit between them no one had bothered to mend. And emerging from the wound, the wet, wriggling lump that would finish her off.

*

Whenever panic surged, which was frequently the more pregnant I became, I would launch into the breathing exercises my midwife taught me. They were to calm me during labor but were proving helpful in the here and now. Don't get me wrong. Every new baby item we acquired (we had to start eventually), every new week on the baby progress calendar affixed to our fridge, every punch and roll of Baby himself inside me sparked happiness, of course. But dread would quickly follow—and shame, at being so fixated on myself, and a trivial matter at that, instead of the new life I would soon bring into the world.

And so, I entered the final trimester of pregnancy still plagued by fear. The only effective distraction so far was work. I rarely missed a day, though my growing belly made Acek nervous. He began suggesting constantly that I sit down or take a break. But

I refused to let up. Despite the dwindling number of jobs, I kept myself occupied. I reorganized the back room. I repainted the shopfront. I hauled out items we'd bought for cheap at closing-down and estate sales and began dismantling or attempting to fix those.

One afternoon, I was kneeling on the floor, wrestling with a bulky electric foot massager. The only way to reach the motor compartment was from an odd angle, and I'd been at it for a while, grunting and cursing, my belly in the way. Acek snuck up to stand at my side.

"Vi, you're pregnant," he said quietly.

"I know," I snapped.

He let a few seconds pass.

"Vivi."

That's all he said, but it was all it took to make me cry.

He sat down on the floor next to me and let me sob to my heart's content. I couldn't even bear to look him in the eye.

"You don't want the baby, Vivi?" he asked at last, wonderingly, almost woefully.

I managed to hiccup, "I do. I just don't want to die."

He didn't ask what I meant, merely nodded, and occasionally rubbed my back.

When I looked up at last, I could see he was greatly troubled.

"No one wants to die," he agreed.

It was nearly closing time, but because it was summer, the light outside refused to fade.

*

Soon it was time for my thirty-week ultrasound, or more specifically, my thirty-week expensive, cutting-edge holosonogram.

Gabe had booked it to be helpful. He knew how anxious I still was, and though he couldn't understand why, he didn't like to see me in such a state. He thought viewing the baby in 4D would help shift my focus, make the prospect of motherhood more appealing and real. What he either forgot or didn't seem to realize was that it would also be the first sighting of my new self.

I still remember how queasy I felt when I gave my name to the receptionist. As I waited, I tried to read a magazine, but I was too agitated to make sense of any sentence I read. There were a few other women there, two of them with partners. It puzzled me, how serene they looked as my heart thumped in my chest, and my stomach roiled, and a little limb stretched and swept across my insides.

In the room, the ultrasound technician asked a series of questions in a perfunctory manner, ticking a box on her computer screen for each of my replies. Then it was time.

I lay down. First, she measured my belly. Then she flicked off the light and turned the projector on. As the wand glided over my skin, a bright red blob materialized in the middle of the room.

She began to move the wand as if my abdomen were a coloring book she was filling in. Limbs appeared, scrunched around a torso, followed by the outlines of a head. Then a nose, a pair of lips, a pair of shut eyes. For a brief moment, I was enchanted. My baby. The image continued to fill out, continued to rotate: tiny fingers and toes, tiny buttocks, a tiny penis and scrotum, the cord connecting him to me, supplying nutrients and oxygen, as if he were a scarlet astronaut hovering in dark space. Was he dreaming, I wondered, or thinking? When your whole life experience is the inside of a uterus, what exactly do you think or dream?

"That's all of him," said the technician, sounding faintly bored. I didn't blame her. How many holosonograms did she do a day?

But she wasn't finished. The wand kept circling, scribbling, arcing wider and pressing harder into my abdomen.

"And . . . there!" she crowed with more enthusiasm. "There you are."

Just below the baby, a blue blob came into view, prawn-sized and prawn-shaped.

The technician stopped speaking. From the sound of the mouse clicks and key clacks, I guessed she was absorbed in taking measurements for the report. I stared at the blob, which I knew from my extensive reading, was still an embryo. Its brain had just started to form. I made an effort to engage with it in the same way I did with the baby: what was it thinking? What was it dreaming? I thought of how it would soon have all my memories, be an exact replica of me. Did that mean it was, on some level, thinking what I was thinking now? That it had dreamt what I'd dreamt last night? I stared harder, trying to make myself out, and couldn't. *That's me? Impossible.*

Without warning, the technician zoomed in, swelling the projection of my future self to an intimidating size.

"Technology these days," she murmured appreciatively before lapsing into silent concentration as she took down measurements.

The creature's image continued to rotate. I took in the lumps that were its limbs, the ridged hunch of its spine, the dark mass of its gut, the smaller dark spots that were its eyes.

The urge to laugh welled up inside me, like an urge to vomit. I quickly suppressed it. How funny it would be if I woke up to discover I'd imagined this whole reality—mothers giving birth to mothers, mothers eating themselves. Must be a joke.

I recalled having this same thought when Gabe and I took the maternity-ward tour the week prior—entering a rebirth room, windowless and bare, tiled in lavender, the floor sloping gently toward a grate where the blood and bits would drain. I stared down the grate. *Must be a joke. An enormous joke.* I'd blinked hard, but everything was still there.

The lights flicked on, and the projector shut off.

"Everything seems to be on track," said the technician, "but your ob-gyn will contact you with any concerns. You can collect your album and flash drive at the front desk."

As I sat on the bus home (Acek had insisted I take the whole day off), album in lap, I tried to work up the desire to flip through. I did manage it. Thankfully, the photos were mostly of the baby—full-body shots and close-ups of his face, framed by his little hands.

I could already imagine Gabe's excitement at seeing these. Again it came, an unexpected moment of joy, followed by a flurry of feather light kicks to boot. *I'll see you soon*, I said silently, then affirmed, *Yes, it will be me. Only better. Are you listening, me? You won't even feel like it's not you.*

It's strange now, funny even. I thought the worst thing that could happen was that rebirth would go smoothly. It never even crossed my mind that something more terrible might happen: that I'd go through rebirth and it would go wrong.

VI.

We're in the hospital canteen waiting for an update on Acek—by "we," I mean Zoe, Libby, Cloud, and me. Nina's not with us because she's with Acek—they took the car and left first; the rest of us followed in the company van. Lina isn't here because someone had to go back and the rest of us don't know how to drive. Zoe couldn't remember if she'd unplugged the iron she'd been working on when Acek collapsed, and we all agreed that Acek, if he survives, would be really pissed off if the shed burned down.

We split a banana bread—Cloud eats most of it—while waiting for Nina to arrive with news. It made sense for her to stay with Acek, given she's his niece. We swap origin stories about how we started hobbling in the first place. Libby got into it in high school, just a few years ago; she took an extracurricular course in mechanical repair and liked it. Her teacher did hobbling on the side, and took Libby under her wing.

Zoe's story is more intense. Her mentor was her own mother, who taught herself hobbling to support the family. It was after Zoe's father's business partner fled with all the money, leaving Zoe's father a broken man. Her mother rose to the challenge and started a business much like Acek has now, with several employees. She even saved enough money to send Zoe here on a student visa. Zoe's mother-mandated mission is to get her graduate certificate in finance, find a job that will sponsor her work visa, then bring her parents and younger siblings here to join her. Her mother grew up in the eighties, when it wasn't a good time to be Chinese in Vietnam, and has traumatic memories of being bullied mercilessly at school, and her family's shop getting repossessed by the government.

Zoe turns to me. "How about you, Chị?"

Keeping one eye on Cloud—he's been playing with Ion the Lion, but I can tell he's getting antsy sitting too long in one place—I tell them how Acek was the one who taught me, when I was little. He and my father were friends. I don't go into further detail.

Libby's eyebrows lift in surprise. "You've known Arvin for that long? I couldn't tell."

"Me neither," exclaims Zoe. "In that case, you must be so worried about him."

I imagine Zoe and Libby wearing boxing gloves, each in turn delivering a punch to my gut.

Yes, no one can tell how close I once was to Acek, how I've known him since I was a kid. Yes, I'm extremely worried, despite being hurt enough by the distance he keeps that I want not to care, which I wish would somehow hurt him back.

Zoe and Libby have started their own conversation; they're both young and still studying, so it's natural that they have more in common with each other than with me. They talk about the classes they're taking, their favorite music, easy late-night snack hacks.

Using Cloud as pretext, I excuse myself: I'm taking Cloud for a walk; if Nina brings news, we're just outside. My feelings are a buzz in my ears, like a chainsaw, as Cloud toddles beneath the gum trees hunting for ants. Three weeks after Zoe introduced him to them on Chinese New Year's Eve, they're still his new favorite thing—along with Ion, who enjoys eating the ants that Cloud finds.

As my eyes track Cloud's wanderings, my brain also wanders, back to what I told Libby and Zoe, then backtracking further—to the moment I was telling them about, the evening I discovered the magic of electricity, thanks to Acek. The same way, perhaps, Cloud, thanks to Zoe, has discovered the magic of ants. It was after Pa got fired from his restaurant manager job—the one that sponsored his work visa so we could come to Australia in the first place. Later, Pa would claim the whole move was Acek's idea (though various things Acek would say after Pa stopped speaking to him implied that Pa was the one desperate to leave Medan after what happened to Ma).

On paper, it was straightforward: the restaurant paid the fees and took care of the documents associated with Pa's visa. In reality, it was more complex. Sponsoring people wanting to migrate here was a side business for the restaurant. They deducted an overblown fee for this service from Pa's salary, which was lower than reported on paper. But the plan was to grin and bear it until we got permanent residency. Once we got that, Pa could find a better (and non-illegal) situation. In the meantime, Acek helped us out. He'd come here earlier, at the age of twenty-nine, and knew the ins and outs of Sydney migrant life. Through his connections, he found us a place with cheap rent, advised us on where and how to find good deals, and, as I later found out, slipped Pa a small amount every few weeks "to help out with the kids."

But Pa's condition had continued deteriorating after the move that was meant to cure it—to the point where his employer decided that the labor he was providing wasn't even worth underpaying. Pa began spacing out on the job, or hiding in the office or toilet, or leaving for long spells to "run errands." The staff he was supposed to manage resorted to managing themselves, with disastrous results. Pa got fired, but Acek, who knew the shady guy who ran this enterprise, persuaded him to continue keeping real life separate from what was on paper. The guy agreed to keep Pa on the books—for the same fee, of course.

It was during the long period of Pa's unemployment, which became permanent, that we began seeing even more of Acek than usual. He used to come over every so often (he lived around the corner), but now he stopped by after work every day. It wasn't as if he wasn't busy. He was completing his apprenticeship to become a licensed electrician, while still taking odd jobs with the city's main water company—mostly night work. He'd finish for the day, come over to our place for dinner, often contributing end-of-the-day discounted takeaway, then head back home for a shower and quick nap before setting out again. If he didn't have night work, he'd bring something home-cooked.

It was clear that he was worried about us. Over dinner, he would ask strategic questions aimed at discerning the actual situation. What had our father done today? How was school going for Vera and me? What did we eat for breakfast? Anything new happen? If he sifted through our replies, he could find the information he actually wanted: how was Pa's job search going? Had he even called the numbers Acek gave him? How were we kids managing? Did we have enough food? Were there bills we couldn't pay?

As the weeks of Pa's joblessness dragged on, he started replying to Acek's questions with single words or grunts. Then came his sharp drop into sullen silence, and he stopped answering at all. Undaunted, Acek began conversing solely with Vera and me, turning only to Pa to make some friendly remark that would require no response. The money he used to slip Pa, he began passing to Vera.

"Take care of your Pa and younger sister," he'd say to Vera, before disappearing down the dark corridor that smelled perpetually of mold and soup.

Vera proceeded to do just that, though I'm sure she hadn't needed Acek to tell her. She got a part-time job at a bakery. It sold Hong-Kong-style cakes and buns, and we gained weight from all the unsold items she would bring home. She took every after-school shift she could. I was nine and by then I could let myself back into the flat. That was one of the few rules my sister imposed: come straight home from school and wait for her and Pa to come back. Pa supposedly spent his days at the library using the internet and newspapers to hunt for jobs. I don't know if he actually did look through the job listings, but he began teaching himself Mandarin and getting obsessed with all things China.

What nine-year-old wouldn't get bored being cooped up in that flat every afternoon? I did my homework. I did my chores. I watched TV. Oh, those waste-era days, with cheap electricity and no household quotas! I could watch my fill back then if I wanted, but of course, there was often nothing good on. Then, one afternoon, the TV stopped working. I couldn't say I was surprised. We'd bought it used, and the picture quality was pretty bad. On a whim, I dismantled it to see if I could find out what was wrong.

That was how Acek found me—sitting on the lounge room floor, gripping a screwdriver, staring into the open back of the TV.

He'd gotten off work early and thought he might as well check in on me. I'd even pulled the main board out, though I hadn't dared disconnect any of the wires. I remember how, when Acek came in, I'd been admiring the structures on the board, their layout like the buildings of a city. I was worried Acek would be angry, but he didn't yell, just stood there, astonished.

"Vivi, what are you doing?"

When I told him, he laughed. "Do you want Acek to help you?"

I nodded. And he named all the buildings for me—capacitors and bridge rectifiers, resistors and transistors, the diodes, the towering transformer. Someday, I'd know what those names meant. Then he explained how electricity worked—little negatively charged particles, called electrons, flowing through routes built especially for them, like on that board. He pointed to the funnel-shaped thing attached to the screen—a cathode-ray tube. It shot electrons like a gun shot bullets, but faster, and more of them. It shot them at the inside of the TV screen, which was coated with a substance called phosphor. When pelted by electrons, the phosphor would light up. That was what made the images we saw on the screen—getting the right colors and patterns to show was just a matter of calibrating the light.

Acek fixed it easily, though the diagnosis was too complicated for me to remember back then. Then, he sliced one of the apples he'd brought over, and we ate it together.

"Vivi," he said, munching, "did you really find it interesting? How the TV works?"

"Yes, Acek," I chirped. My child's mind was lit up. Like a bulb. Like a phosphor-coated screen.

He nodded thoughtfully. Afterwards, he helped me with homework and made fried rice for dinner (rice was to be had back then), as a surprise for Vera and Pa when they came back. Though Pa was indifferent, I could see how happy my sister was at not having to cook.

*

Emergency heart surgery. That's Nina's update. Lina's returned just in time to hear it. She's annoyed because Zoe did in fact remember to turn off the iron, and the trip was made for nothing, but she sets that aside for now. Acek's got major blockage in his aorta, and they need to put in stents, stat. We ask how long it'll take. Libby asks what his chances are, and Lina elbows her in the ribs—which is pretty rich, given that Lina's first impulse upon seeing Acek pass out on the shed floor was to yell out, "Shit! Arvin's dead!"

Nina's answer to our first question is that she has no idea. Nina's answer to Libby's question is that the doctor was optimistic. We all breathe a sigh of relief, and I'm surprised to find my eyes wet with tears. Nina's obviously been crying, though her eye makeup is budge-proof enough that the only signs are the redness of her eyes and the patches beneath, where she's wiped the foundation away.

She says there's no point in all of us hanging around the hospital until who knows when. She asks Lina if she minds driving everyone back. It goes without saying, but we all have the rest of the day off. No one tells her that Lina's already spent an extra round-trip's worth of petrol thinking she needed to save the shed from getting burned down—the information seems too insignificant and at the same time too unpleasant to deliver. Lina simply replies that she doesn't mind and leaves it at that.

But I ask if I can stay. The words are out of my mouth before

I have time to consider whether it's the best idea. Nina frowns, puzzled. Her impression of Acek's and my relationship is probably similar to what Zoe and Libby think. I've worked for Acek longer and have some distant family-friend connection, that's all. My mind is made up, though. I'd rather be worried sick here than worried sick at home, waiting for news over the phone.

Nina asks if I'm sure. Wouldn't it be better for me to take Cloud back? I lie, saying it's easier to entertain him here, that he'll just get bored in the house. But I do open my backpack and conduct a quick check for essentials: a fleet of toy cars, two of his favorite board books, a full container of crackers, and, most importantly, extra nappies.

What I don't realize at this point is that I'm setting myself up for disappointment. Genuine worry is only part of why I'm suddenly bent on staying. The other part is a desire to prove to Acek how much I care and somehow win him back. If he opens his eyes after his emergency operation and finds me there, next to Nina, he'll remember, won't he, how close he and I were, like he and his niece are close now?

I should have enough self-awareness to recognize what's happening and the foresight to know that this won't end well, but unfortunately, I don't. The other thing I fail to realize is the effect the hospital is starting to have on me. Until now, Cloud and I have stayed in and around the canteen. Now, as I follow Nina and Cloud—she's offered to carry him, and he carries Ion—to the designated waiting area, unpleasant memories begin to swell and cluster. Like grapes. Or boils.

Cloud and I have never been here before, but it's familiar all the same. All medical spaces bear resemblance to each other—bland colors, blank spaces, sterile smells. Cloud is far too little to remember how much time we spent in them during the first several months of his life.

We pass a young mother in a waiting area breastfeeding, and I recall sitting in a waiting area breastfeeding. At a week old, Cloud had begun fussing constantly, even after long and frequent nursing sessions, night and day. Even when they finally diagnosed the problem, they were in disbelief. Who had ever heard of a new mother not producing enough milk?

The patient lying on a trolley reminds me of me, lying motionless in a narrow tunnel, waiting for the scan to end. Gabe's theory was that, somehow, I'd skipped rebirth despite being wheeled back from the empty rebirth room covered in blood. He clung to it until the scan results came back, conclusive: despite my poor physical condition, the cellular tests showed that I had indeed been reborn.

The blue balloon in the gift shop window reminds me of the jar of balloons our GP used to keep on her desk. She blew one up for Cloud at the end of each visit, and I resented it because carrying him everywhere was hard enough without minding a balloon. Due to my mysterious condition, it was recommended that I bring him for checkups more frequently than usual. *Healthy mum, healthy bub*, goes the saying. So, conversely: unhealthy mum, risk to bub.

With each passing month, it became clearer that my ailment wasn't temporary. Like my milk, my new-mother energy wasn't ever going to "come in," nor my mighty mother muscles, nor my mighty mother brain. No amount of supplements or rest or exercise or dietary changes was going to help. The best they could do was monitor Cloud, make sure he continued to develop and thrive despite my poor health. Yet, they couldn't comprehend just how poor my health was, nor the degree to which my functioning as a mother had been impaired. *Carrying a baby doesn't cause shoulder pain*, the early childhood nurse replied when I joked about inventing a cart specially for wheeling babies around. *I see*, said the GP coldly when I called requesting an urgent prescription renewal for Cloud's formula—it had kept slipping my mind, and I'd seen only that morning we were almost out. *Please calm him*, snapped the technician performing Cloud's ultrasound for possible hip dysplasia. All sorts of tests were ordered for Cloud. Something had gone wrong with me; therefore, it was possible that something might be wrong with him. We had both incubated in the same womb after all. Defects might be infectious. *Take your son's health seriously*, scolded the pediatric heart specialist, or was it the pediatric lung specialist, or was it the pediatric gastroenterologist—whoever it was when I showed up forty-five minutes late, panting, apologetic for oversleeping. The baby had been up all night, I'd tried to explain. I thought I'd catch a ten-minute nap during his nap, but I'd forgotten to set my alarm. *Do you really need me to*, huffed a nurse at the child and family health center when I asked her to write down the eight exercises she recommended for increasing his strength and motor development. And when I said meekly, *Yes, please*, she obliged with a loud sigh.

"Are you all right?" asks Nina, stopping beneath a sign showing the way to endoscopy, endocrinology, and nuclear medicine.

"Yeah," I lie.

She looks concerned, nonetheless.

Soon, we arrive at our destination: an area with rows of chairs, like the other areas with rows of chairs we passed on the way here, broken occasionally by low tables scattered with pamphlets and severely out-of-date magazines.

"They'll call us once the operation is over." Nina points to the double doors.

"Have they already started?" I ask.

"I think so, but I don't know."

There's nothing in this space to keep a small child entertained. No pictures on the walls, or windows to look out, or interesting structures to crawl under or climb. And not a communal toy in sight, not even the usual crappy ones you find in waiting rooms. But Nina is inventive. She hides Cloud's toy cars in various spots, then challenges him to find them. This buys a surprising amount of time. Then, Cloud comes up with the idea of having Ion find the cars, followed by him playing with the cars by himself for a spell.

What I appreciate about Nina is what I appreciate about Zoe: she genuinely seems to enjoy Cloud's company, and she doesn't get disoriented by the interruptions that inevitably happen when he's around. I don't have the gift that normal mothers do of being able to carry on seamless adult conversation while responding and tending to their child. I've noticed most non-child-havers get confused by the breaks—*Yes, that's a spoon. No, don't put that in your mouth. Wait, let me get that for you*—and either try to plough on through, or stop trying to converse at all.

As the eldest of five, Zoe is accustomed to kids, but Nina is an only child and has none of her own. So when you think about it, in her, these qualities are rather extraordinary. I feel suddenly sad remembering that she can't have children—and extremely guilty about my previous resentment. I can have Cloud, and she can have Acek to make up for our respective losses. Isn't that more than fair? My awareness of my pettiness cascades. Today, she came awfully close to not even having Acek anymore. Even now, after knowing it will probably be all right, there's still the small chance that it won't. And if I feel it, she must feel it more because she's his flesh-and-blood niece, and I'm not. Plus, there are the worrying long-term implications for her uncle's health. If I'm thinking about them, then she must be too.

"Are you sure you're okay?"

I wonder what I must look like for her to ask the question a second time.

She persists. "What are you thinking about?"

I can hardly tell her my latest thoughts about resenting her, so I backtrack a bit.

"Just remembering when Cloud was born. They were worried about him because of my condition, so we had to do a lot of checks and tests. Spent a lot of time at hospitals and clinics." I gesture around us and automatically scan for Cloud. He's at the far end of the waiting room, racing cars off padded-chair cliffs.

"They did some tests on me too," I add, "but they could never figure out what happened exactly."

"Not at all?"

I shook my head.

"My husband thought maybe rebirth didn't happen, but they ruled that out. The eventual diagnosis was malabsorption."

"What does that mean?"

"They think I didn't properly absorb the nutrients I was supposed to get from eating my old self," I explain.

"Do they know why?"

"The doctors had a few theories. Maybe I didn't finish the consumption process." As the words leave my mouth, I imagine my roasted carcass on a platter, partially eaten, a woman in a white coat clicking her tongue, "Don't waste food!"

"But they ruled that out as well," I continue. "The hospital records would have said something. Plus, the midwives check."

"Check what?" asks Nina uneasily.

"The room. Once mothers finish being reborn, they check to see if there's anything left."

Cloud runs up. He's hungry. I open the box of crackers, and he takes one and runs away.

"The most likely explanation is that my new digestive system wasn't fully operational yet. Basically, nutritionally speaking, I didn't get what I was supposed to get out of me."

I give a bitter chuckle. Nina continues to look queasy and troubled. She shifts the subject slightly.

"If you don't mind me asking, what happened with your husband?"

Cloud takes another cracker as I consider how much I should say. It's been a year, but I haven't really told anyone all the details, not even Acek, who's never asked. The one person I did tell was my sister, and she told me I was unreasonable and self-centered, so I haven't felt the inclination to share my story with anyone else.

But Nina isn't Vera. I recall the other day when Nina rescued me from the mother at the playground. I recall us eating ice cream on a bench in silence and her letting me be.

"Have you heard of rejuvenation therapy?"

Nina shakes her head.

"It's a relatively new thing. Very expensive. Most clients are wealthy or celebrities. It's basically rebirth, but without the pregnancy. They trick your body into thinking it's pregnant. Then they trick it into going into labor, and boom: brand new body, new-mother functioning. It doesn't even take as long as real pregnancy—only four months."

Cloud comes to take another cracker, but instead of leaving again, climbs into my lap. He's grown bored with the cars, and I'll have to find another way to entertain him soon. In short, if I want to finish the story, I don't have much time.

"Anyway," I resume in a rush, "one of the specialists suggested I do it, and Gabe thought it was a great idea. And I refused. And he said he'd leave if I didn't."

Until now, I've been avoiding eye contact with Nina, but I summon the courage to find her face. Her forehead is creased. The compassion of her gaze strips me bare. Her lips part to speak, but the words don't come.

"Oh, Vivi," she murmurs at last. "I'm so sorry."

Again, like that day, the tears spill over. It's embarrassing. Usually, I never cry, but Nina must think of me as a human fountain by now.

This time, tissues are necessary. She takes a pack from her bag and hands it to me.

"Silly of me, huh," I sniffle. "I've already been through rebirth, right? So what's the big deal?"

"No," says Nina, touching my shoulder. "It's not silly. Not silly at all."

The weight of her hand is reassuring, its warmth radiating through my shirt, into my skin. How long has it been since I've felt anyone's touch besides my son's? From my lap, Cloud cranes his neck to look up at me. He offers me a cracker. As I nuzzle his cheek, I think about how my emotional instability will scar him for life. My sister's words come back to me, a sharp contrast to Nina's. *Vi, you're a mother now. You can't be selfish anymore.*

I've been waiting so long for someone to tell me what Nina has: that I'm not silly. For a whole year now, I've been holding my breath. I picture myself submerged in a bathtub, coming up only now for air. At last, I can breathe.

What happens next is completely unexpected. As I predicted, Cloud is growing irritable. Nina suggests I take him outdoors. Her assessment is that it'll be at least a couple hours more, if not longer, so no point in cooping Cloud up right now.

I follow her advice. I take him all the way back to the green space outside the canteen. He, of course, hunts for more ants, and we discover some pill bugs too. He does a poo and I change him. We sit on a ledge under a tree, and I read him a book—*Woolly Bear, Beware!*—five times. I suggest he make a bouquet of dried gum leaves to bring back to Aie Nina—an indirect token of my own gratitude. We buy a chocolate-chip cookie, too, for us three to share.

But when we get back, something's changed, and I don't know why. At first, I don't even notice, but as the minutes pass, it dawns on me. Nina's quieter. When I ask her something or make a remark, her responses are brief, almost curt. She still talks and plays with Cloud, perhaps even more than before. But it's almost as if she's seeking an excuse not to engage with me. She eats a small chunk of the cookie we've brought back, but it's obviously a token gesture. I ask her if everything's all right. She says she's just tired and worried, and I feel stupid for asking. Her uncle is having emergency heart surgery, after all. But still, I don't understand why she's acting so differently from before.

Gradually, she and I lapse into complete silence and, when we're not entertaining Cloud, resort to leafing through the outdated magazines to pass the time. I feel myself shriveling inwardly, ashamed of confiding so much, exposing myself, depending so excessively on her for affirmation. I replay her reaction to what I told her about refusing rejuvenation therapy and wonder if I misinterpreted. I mistook politeness for sympathy. I misread discomfort as compassion. As I read Cloud his other book—*Farm Animal Fun*—my lips describe barnyard life as my thoughts spiral around the matter of Nina's sudden coldness like dry leaves caught in a looping wind.

Eventually, someone comes to put me out of my misery: the surgeon in charge of operating on Acek. "The family of Arvin Japutra," he calls out, pronouncing Acek's family name "Jap Putt Ra." Nina and I both stand.

He tells us the procedure went smoothly, and that it may be a couple hours more before Acek regains consciousness.

My original plan to stay and greet Acek when he wakes up suddenly seems unbearably unpleasant. How long can I endure the humiliation and shame of remaining in Nina's company? My backpack seems overwhelmingly depleted. We've burned through the cars, the crackers, the books. Nina is obviously thinking about how disagreeable this situation is as well—How long can she stand the company of my self-pitying, selfish self?—because she turns to me and says, "There's no point in you and Cloud staying any longer. Who knows when he'll wake up. I'll take you home."

Wordlessly, I nod. It's for the best. We gather the cars, the lion, the snack box, the books, but do a final sweep of the waiting room all the same. In the car, Cloud falls asleep. Nina maintains her silence. I stare ahead and remember how, early this morning, I forgot to put the nappies I washed last night out to dry. Again.

As we hurtle along, I think again about the road that is my life, and the body that is my vehicle, and how, though my vehicle continues moving ahead, the passenger in the vehicle—my self—keeps on shuttling between present and past. As if to illustrate my point, my mind shoots back to a distant memory of when the government announced the grid shift, and Acek explained to me what we were shifting from and to.

Not too long after the TV dismantling incident, Acek asked my father if I could help him a little on the weekends, just with some light repair work he'd started doing on the side (in addition to his apprenticeship day job and the nighttime waterworks gigs). I noticed Acek made the request as casual and vague as possible and timed it for when Pa was retreating to his room. He said he could really use the help and noticed I had a knack. He said there would be money.

"No need to pay her," mumbled Pa as he walked away.

Anyway, I'd begun spending Saturdays and Sundays at Acek's place (for which he did pay me, despite what Pa said). The repair work he was doing came mostly from people he knew, or friends of people he knew, who wanted something fixed but couldn't afford much. They were the kind of items we'd later receive at the shop when Acek went into business for himself: toasters, rice cookers, electric fans, sewing machines, clothes irons, humidifiers. And usually, the required fix was small: frayed cords, burnt-out plugs, broken thermostats, faulty capacitors, blown-out fuses, and the like. They were ideal projects for a rookie like me to cut her teeth on. But then came the day when I walked in and Acek handed me a letter. The official-looking kind, typewritten with a logo in the corner, that began *Dear Resident*.

"Your Pa and Ci tell you about this yet?" he asked.

I shook my head.

"Read it. See if you understand."

I tried my best.

"They're changing the electricity?" I asked.

He nodded. "That's right. From AC to DC. *R*-DC."

He began to explain. AC stood for alternating current. DC stood for direct current. With AC, the electric current periodically reversed direction—hence "alternating." With DC, the current moved consistently in one direction—hence "direct." Until now, electricity had always been distributed using AC. It was more energy-efficient over long distances and was easier than DC to convert to higher and lower voltages. But recent breakthroughs in DC technology had reached a point where AC no longer had these advantages. With RDC tech, as they were calling it—*revolutionary* direct current—DC had become better in all respects. And machines that ran on DC rather than AC tended to be inherently more efficient anyway. *Plus*, DC was more easily stored, making it ideal for use with renewable energy sources. In short, the advent of RDC meant energy sustainability on a scale unimaginable, which was why, at the last L20 Summit, consensus had been reached regarding a global phasing out of AC in favor of RDC grids.

A question occurred to me. "Will the old machines work? The ones we use now?"

He shook his head. "Not the way they are. They'll have to be modified."

"How?"

"Us."

"Us?"

"Yes. We'll do the modifying. It's a good business opportunity. The grid shift will be gradual, over several years. So we have time to get good at it."

We weren't the only ones who had this bright idea, obviously.

Here and there around the city, the state, the country, the world, people were having the same idea we were—little brains lighting up across the globe. In the end, it was called *hobbling* not *modifying*, a reference to the radically lower voltages that AC appliances had to operate on in order to run on the RDC grid.

To cement my comprehension of AC versus DC, Acek folded the grid-shift letter partly along one of its creases. He had me hold it while he dropped a few roasted peanuts in the paper trough. They formed a single line. With one finger, he slid the peanuts back, then forward, then back again.

"If the peanuts are electrons," he asked, "then is this AC or DC?"

"AC, Acek."

He shifted the peanuts all the way from one end to the other and stopped. "And this?"

"DC," I replied, model student that I was.

I'm thinking of that now: AC and DC. How I'm forward and backward—AC in a DC world. How my brain keeps sliding back to the past while my body's in the present. How my body has somehow managed to be brand-new and worn-out all at once. How Gabe offered me the chance to move on, and I insisted on remaining in my backward state. How I started anew just to stay where I was. How apparently fearful I am of being better than I am now. How Cloud deserves a future, and I want him to have one, except I persist in driving in reverse.

vii.

Looking back at my marriage is like looking at the handful of childhood photos I still have. They're evidence of reality. But at the same time, they're surreal. Take the photo of my third birthday. I can see Ma lighting birthday candles in our home in Medan. I can see Pa is capable of smiling. I can see Vera's taller than me. But it's a world that doesn't exist anymore.

Gabe loved me. Call me a fool, but I do believe that, even though it turned out to be a conditional sort of love. And I do believe I loved him in return. But now I don't miss him. How can I miss the person who loved me if he's no longer a person who loves me? I'd have to be the person he once loved, which I'm not. I'm not lovable in my present state. He told me so himself. My love for Gabe turned out to be conditional, too, a mirror image of his love for me. When the mirrored object moves out of view, the image vanishes as well. It doesn't mean my love for him wasn't real. A plant is real, but it's also an outgrowth of the soil. In the absence of the soil, the plant can't grow, that's all.

I would never have taken the initiative to fall in love with someone so well-adjusted, so good-natured, so likable as Gabe. I would have been too worried that he would realize, one day, that I could never be like him. My worries proved correct.

While I was pregnant, I had a strong sense that Gabe regarded the conclusion of my pregnancy as the solution to my problem—my problem being, of course, my fear of being killed, eaten, and replaced. Once I had gone through rebirth, I would stop worrying about it. You can't dread something that will happen if it's already occurred. And I felt strongly that this was the reservoir from which he drew his sympathy, good humor, and willingness to comfort me.

I get this. Nowadays, I try to adopt a similar mindset when I comfort Cloud. I reason that he can't cry forever about having to put on shoes; being offered a broccoli floret; having to get off the bus; me finishing his leftover toast because he still wanted it, even though I asked him multiple times and he shook his head no. You can endure something much better if you know it will end.

No one suspected anything at first. I felt great, exactly like everyone said I would. Full of energy, clear-minded, happier than ever. It was as if some defect had been removed, some faulty component replaced. I remember holding Cloud as he suckled and dozed, sensing his every mood and desire and need as if his consciousness were an extension of mine, my brain automatically processing and organizing what had to be done in order to create the best conditions for our son, for our family to thrive. *So this is my life's purpose*, I thought. *So this is how I was meant to be.* I didn't know it was humanly possible to feel so luminous, whole, and strong.

Then, over the next few days, it vanished. All of it. The energy, the clarity of mind, the deep sense of satisfaction and purpose and connection and calm. It receded slowly. I remember noticing for the first time, wondering why I felt so reluctant to get up from the sofa. Almost as if I were tired. Later that afternoon, Cloud woke up from napping in his cot, and I only realized it when I heard him cry. At midnight, while reorganizing the kitchen—one of the many projects I'd been saving for when I had new-mother enthusiasm—I found myself struggling to lift the turbo mixer. Two hours later, while ironing, I felt my eyelids go suddenly heavy, as if I were sleepy. Absurd.

Things only worsened from there. I've heard that when babies are first born, they are capable of surviving some days without being fed (God forbid). Their little bodies contain enough emergency reserves of fluid and glucose to keep them, for a period, alive. Maybe I was like a newborn baby—subsisting on stockpiles of whatever nutrients newborn mothers carry within them, independent of what they acquire through thc succcssful digestion of their old selves. Once I'd burned through it, I must have had nothing left. When I woke up to feed Cloud in the dead of night, I could barely drag myself out of bed. I was a zombie during the day too. I lost all sense of what Cloud was feeling or needing and couldn't soothe him effortlessly, like before. My breasts stopped producing milk. My muscles atrophied. My back and shoulders began aching all the time. My brain stopped telling me what needed cleaning, washing, drying, storing, reorganizing, buying, folding, cooking, changing, sterilizing, preparing, packing. Our apartment was always a mess.

Everything seemed to slip my mind. I made to-do lists, but missed items anyway. I kept a planner, but would sometimes forget to write an appointment in, or would write down the wrong time. I was perpetually running late. I'd get tired from carrying

Cloud and the diaper bag, and I would have to slow down or rest; or I'd start out with plenty of time but have to circle back to get something vital I'd forgotten: nappies, inserts, the thermos of boiled water for preparing formula, my wallet, my house key—twice. The first time I forgot my key, it was late afternoon, so I waited for Gabe to come home. The second time, it was morning, and I had to call Gabe's office from our neighbor's phone so he could come back on his lunch break and let me in. My neck and back continued to bother me, and my left shoulder began hurting especially, so I began wearing one of those fiddly ergonomic baby carriers for eager fathers, despite the fact that it attracted a lot of stares. At the supermarket, I'd watch with envy as other mothers strode out, baby in one hand, diaper bag and six full bags of groceries dangling easily off their other shoulder and arm.

Gabe was a huge help during this time—he had to be. My condition left him no choice. His mood remained buoyant during the early months, but then it began to sink. Gabe enjoyed cleanliness and order, which I'd always known and appreciated. His expectations had once been simple to meet. Putting things back where they belonged, making the bed, taking out the trash and recycling, folding clothes while watching TV, leaving the kitchen clean after every meal: too easy. Now the most basic tasks became daunting. Unless he was sleeping, Cloud had to be held or spoken to or in motion, or else he would cry. The playmat, the activity center, the bouncer—Cloud would stay in any one of them ten minutes tops before screaming to get out. So, beds were half-made, dishes were half-washed, clothes were half-stored, items remained out of drawers and cupboards. All was abandoned when Cloud needed my attention, impossible to do in my condition while carrying or tending to Cloud. But instead of taking full advantage of Cloud's daytime naps, I would often sit slumped on the sofa for far too long, staring into space, half-dozing, before hauling myself back onto my feet to do what still needed to be done. And nighttime productivity was out of the question in my state. When functioning new mothers were at their busiest—cleaning, cooking extra meals to freeze, reorganizing toy storage areas, sewing quilts, reading parenting books, doing extra loads of washing—I lay snoring between Gabe and Cloud, waking up only to give Cloud bottles and pat him back to sleep before crashing into deep slumber once more.

All this meant that Gabe would have to come home from a full day at the office, roll up his sleeves, and set about tidying. It was worse because he'd recently been promoted and had been counting on my post-rebirth energy to turn me into the domestic goddess I'd never been. I felt awful. I'd tell him he didn't have to, but he'd insist. He *wanted* to, he said. That was worse, to be honest, to know that I'd allowed our home to descend into a state so unacceptable that he couldn't bear to leave it be. Over time, he began to not just look tired, but act tired as well. And, occasionally, curt. He began to make pointed remarks, like how the lid not being able to shut was probably a sign that the bin should be emptied. How I should learn a few more recipes. How it took only a few additional seconds to put an item away after use. I always apologized because he was always right. Why hadn't I done X? I asked myself. Why hadn't I seen to Y? I wasn't so busy, was I? Except for the odd errand, or Cloud's extra health checks—all of which were, thankfully, turning out clear—I hardly ever left the house. Even my sister had to come to me, since I'd stopped going to her place for dinner. Once a week, during school hours, Vera would arrive, baby in tow, bearing freezer meals and boundless energy. Gabe could always tell when my sister and niece had visited: Vera left the place spotless. It always put him in a better mood too. He'd make an effort to smile and chat to me, not just to Cloud. He would look like himself again—lighthearted and happy, like he was meant to be.

Maybe I should have made even more of an effort. But I genuinely felt exhausted through and through. Especially at first, when I could barely see each week's schedule through the thick forest of medical consultations and checkups and follow-ups, through eyes bleary with lack of sleep and the thick fog clouding my brain. I didn't even make an effort to see Acek in person until Cloud was ten weeks old. Acek, who had called faithfully every other day to check in on me after I'd stopped coming in to work, a month before Cloud was due. He was never one to chat. Whenever I'd been able to pick up, our exchanges had lasted less than a minute, and when I hadn't been home, he left short messages with more or less the same content as our brief calls: he hoped I was doing well. I mustn't forget to remind Gabriel to call him when I went into labor, no matter what the time. I should take care to eat enough and get plenty of rest.

After Cloud's birth, he'd called only once, to leave a voice message: he had received the birth announcement in the post and congratulations to me and Gabriel. Acek probably didn't want to bother me, and I'd been meaning to call him back, but it felt like there was so much going on.

I did ring him, finally. We arranged to meet in a park just a short walk away from where Gabe and I lived. It was the time of year when it wasn't exactly cold yet, but if the wind blew, you remembered winter was on the way. A healthy new mother wouldn't have needed one, but I wore a heavy cardigan and dressed Cloud in layers that I could peel off as needed: a knit vest and jacket over his bodysuit. With no sensory bond with Cloud, I had difficulty gauging whether he was wearing too little or too much.

That was before I bought the baby carrier, while I was still conveying Cloud the way a new mother should—naturally. I'd misjudged the time it would take to reach the park, and I was twenty minutes late. I'd left the entire diaper bag next to the shoe cupboard and had to circle back. In addition to that, my shoulder had begun to ache, and I was slow. I worried Acek might leave, thinking I'd forgotten, but to my relief, he was still there.

He was sitting on a park bench feeding bread scraps to pigeons—a habit of his since my childhood, back when he and Pa were still friends, and he would take Vera and me to the park to feed the birds. When I got older, I would inform him that bread wasn't good for pigeons, and he would tell me pigeons had a rough life and deserved to eat what they wanted, and he would keep feeding them. Like he was doing now. I felt comforted by this steadiness. Acek would never change.

I greeted him. And though he tried to hide it, his shock was visible.

"I'm fine," I assured him despite my sudden shame. "It's nothing. Just some rebirth complications. I'm seeing a specialist soon. Gabe's sure they'll find out what's wrong."

By way of deflection, I introduced him to Cloud.

"Say hi to Akong," I said in my best mother voice (melodic, happy, et cetera), propping Cloud up and waving his little hand.

When Cloud gripped his finger, Acek smiled. But even so, I sensed a certain unease in his expression.

Our conversation was awkward, and even now, thinking back on it, I'm torn as to the reason. Was it because of my condition? Was it because his niece had already begun to take my place in his affections? Was it because of what he was going to say next?

"Vivi," he said, passing Cloud back to me after he had held him for a while. "I have something to tell you. I'm moving to the country. Up near Port Macquarie."

I stared in surprise, but he didn't want to look me in the eye.

"What do you mean, Acek? What about the shop?"

"I'm moving it too. It's my niece," he explained. "She's been alone since my older brother and his wife died. She just started living in their old house, and I thought I'd keep her company there."

I hadn't even known that Acek had a brother, let alone a niece, in Australia. I'd always thought of him—assumed he was—alone.

"My brother and I weren't close," he added, as if reading my thoughts.

I was too shocked to speak.

"You said it yourself once, remember? 'Better move to the country'?"

He tried to laugh, but let silence overtake us again.

"I did say that," I acknowledged.

"You'll be fine, Vivi. You have this little one to look after. And you and Gabriel probably want more children after him."

I supposed he was right. There had been a plan to have more.

The conversation ended not long after.

"Take care of yourself, Vivi," he said, giving Cloud's little hand a squeeze.

What choice did I have, I remember thinking. And as I sat on that bench, watching Acek trudge away, I tried to place what it felt like, because it did feel like something familiar. I couldn't put my finger on it then, but later I would.

It would be a week later, when Gabe took me to the specialist that he'd booked, and the same feeling came creeping like a cold shadow. When I learned the specialist's exact area of expertise only after we arrived and read the clinic's sign. When Gabe said, reasonably, that we might as well explore all our options, and I reminded myself he was trying to help. When the specialist began going into the details of her recommended treatment, and I thought instantly, *not again*. When I wondered, like I did on the maternity-ward tour, if it was all one colossal joke.

Yes, that was the feeling, spreading inside me as the specialist explained the rejuvenation procedure, and I saw Gabe's face lighting up the same way it lit up when I told him I was pregnant that night. It was after I'd thanked her and said I would think about it, and Gabe's face fell because if it were up to him, I would have said yes right then and there. When Gabe was paying the bill for the consultation and I was giving Cloud a bottle before we went out to catch the train—that was when I finally pinpointed what the feeling was. It was like all those nights when I was a kid and Acek would say goodbye after dinner. When he'd disappear down the corridor and it felt like someone had shut off all the lights.

*

Gabe and I didn't start arguing immediately. On the contrary, our discussion after the specialist consultation was quiet and loving, creating the illusion that the matter had been resolved. Gabe had taken the whole day off to accompany me to the specialist, so we stopped afterwards at the gourmet grocer's for a leisurely shop. Back in the apartment, we took turns minding Cloud and doing chores before Gabe made dinner: mushroom risotto and something that he called an autumnal salad, which was delicious and full of ingredients I couldn't identify. In short, it certainly wasn't a usual weekday evening. The apartment wasn't cluttered and chaotic after a day of Gabe being absent, with me too overwhelmed and exhausted to do anything about it. We weren't eating my mediocre cooking or one of our Vera-given defrosted meals. So maybe Gabe was in a better frame of mind when it came to hearing out my misgivings, and maybe my condition didn't seem as dire or insurmountable as it usually did.

When Gabe asked me what I thought about the specialist's recommendation, I admitted I was hesitant. As he knew, I had been terrified of rebirth before. Even now, having already gone through it, I didn't especially want to go through it again. As I spoke, I was aware of the need to express myself calmly and coherently, to talk about my fear without appearing dominated by it, to present myself as optimistic about managing my condition and improving my maternal and domestic performance over time. This faint pressure steadied me, like a weight.

To my relief, Gabe said he understood where I was coming from. He did remember how anxious the prospect of rebirth had made me. He acknowledged this was a big decision and that I would be the one who'd have to go through it, so it was ultimately up to me.

That night, we even had sex—an infrequent occurrence since Cloud had come along. We were usually too tired, too grumpy. Afterwards, as I lay in Gabe's arms, I felt hopeful. I believed what I'd said. Things would improve. I believe he believed it too.

But the situation continued to sour. As Cloud grew, so did his needs and my fatigue. He started eating solid foods, which meant more planning and preparation and freezing and thawing and gentle reheating, and a lot to clean up. He still disliked being left on his own for too long, and when held, he wanted to be constantly walked around or spoken to. He refused to sit still in my lap, preferring to stand and jump while being supported under his armpits. It was admittedly very cute, but my left shoulder burned with hate for me and how I let my child cause it so much pain.

In order to get me out of the house more and boost Cloud's social and sensory stimulation, Gabe enrolled us in various courses and activities. Not only the Mothering Made Simple class, but also a music playgroup, a motor-skills playgroup, baby swim lessons, and a biweekly Messy Play experience. At least Cloud had fewer medical appointments—the doctors and nurses were becoming increasingly confident that his development was on track (not optimal, but for a non-breastfed baby, he was doing surprisingly okay). With all the new activities, however, the schedule filled up once more, like stones filling a sack.

That was the next time rejuvenation therapy came up. I'd asked Gabe to stop scheduling new activities for Cloud and me. I knew he meant well, but I was starting to feel overwhelmed and exhausted. (I was careful to use the word "starting," as if I were neither of these things already.) Admittedly, my timing wasn't great. I brought it up just as he was leaving for work.

"But they're fun activities," said Gabe, lacing up his dress shoes. "It's good for Cloud to interact with other babies and have new experiences. And I thought you could meet other mothers. You know, make friends."

"But I've never had friends," I protested, holding Cloud.

Gabe laughed in that easy way I used to find disarming but was beginning to perceive as dismissive.

"You should try it, Viv. It's really not so bad."

"I'm just starting to feel like it's too much, that's all. You know it's hard for me."

He pulled on his suit jacket. "Well, it doesn't have to be," he mumbled.

"What do you mean?"

He kissed Cloud goodbye.

"Hey, what do you mean?"

His eyes met mine. "It doesn't have to be hard, Viv. You just want it that way."

I could only stare dumbly after him. The door shut, and he was gone.

Later that day, as I sat among the other mothers at Messy Play, watching Cloud sit among other babies in an inflatable pool filled with overripe tomatoes, I thought about how naïve I had been—how I'd thought, once we'd closed the door on rejuvenation therapy, that the room where it led would disappear. But the door had reopened. And would reopen again. And wasn't even a door to a room, but a portal to a parallel world in which I was the mother I was meant to be. And how every time Gabe looked at me, he was staring wistfully through that portal at the new me—the *newer* me—who could get rid of me properly, and not repeat the botched job I had done.

Sure enough, every mistake, every shortcoming became an opportunity for Gabe to raise the subject: missing the first baby swim lesson of the term; failing to install the car seat properly when Gabe and I were using the car share and having Cloud's seat fall forward while driving on the motorway (thankfully, Cloud was unharmed); running out of laundry detergent; being insufficiently enthused about buying and preparing an assortment of brightly colored fruits and vegetables so that Cloud could "eat the rainbow," as advised by the Mothering Made Simple instructor. Gabe alternated between casual hints and sarcasm, guilt trips and logic. When longer discussions broke out, like when I forgot to set a timer and melted the bottles I was sterilizing on the stove, I tried to summon whatever magic I'd been able to deploy that very first argument, when I'd actually convinced him for a time to leave me alone. But it was useless. It gradually dawned on me: Gabe had stopped taking my concerns seriously. Not unlike how, that day outside the baby shop, his words had lost their ability to calm me down.

I began to feel disconnected not only from Gabe, but from life in general. As if my body wasn't part of me, but a machine I inhabited—a big human-looking machine through which I interfaced with the world. Whatever I desired to say with my own mouth wasn't audible from the outside. To be heard by Gabe or anyone else, I had to get the machine to speak. On the plus side, though, Gabe's words couldn't hurt me. No one's could. I heard them, but only through the machine's mechanical ears. When they reached me, they were muted, softened. I could react to them dispassionately, or choose not to react at all. The same went for events. As the weeks passed, along with Cloud's milestones—teething, babbling, sitting, crawling, cruising—I found myself slipping into this mode more frequently. Not that I had any control over it, but I found it a relief. Inside the machine, motherhood was no longer too much.

That day—that fateful day, which pretty much spelled the end for me and Gabe—was a day spent mostly in the machine. I was supposed to have taken Cloud to music playgroup at eleven, but I decided not to. Or rather, I let the window for doing so pass. I had fully intended for us to go. I'd checked the bus schedule and packed our bag and everything. I had even successfully prepared my assigned snack contribution—seedless grapes, clearly labeled, sliced lengthwise into quarters to prevent choking (people used to think halves were sufficient, but they weren't anymore). But I realized I was still in pajamas. Then Cloud woke from his morning nap. And then it just seemed too much to get dressed in time for the 10:46 bus. And then I thought we could just head to the bus stop as soon as possible and catch the next bus, whenever it came. Better late than never, right? Then Cloud did a poo and needed changing. Then I noticed his nails needed clipping as well. Then it just seemed impossible to leave the apartment. The world wouldn't end if we missed one music playgroup—what a liberating revelation that was.

I made Cloud a bottle. We got to eat the grapes ourselves. Then we ate toast on the sofa and crumbed up the cushions. I put on a Wiggles DVD, and whenever it got to the end and Cloud fussed, I pressed play again. At some point I realized, vaguely, that I'd been meaning to mop the bathroom floors that day, so I made a start. Then I heard Cloud break into a sudden wail and came out and saw he'd pulled himself up to standing at the bookcase and dropped a heavy hardcover on his foot. Normally, Cloud's distress would have caused me distress. Instead, I was able to tend to him without feeling overly upset. I applied an ice pack and inspected his injury, and held him in a cuddle until the tears stopped. I said yes to another season of Wiggles. While I was doing that, Cloud wandered off, found the laundry basket of clean, folded clothes yet to be put away, and scattered them all over the living area floor. On another day, I might have been frustrated. Instead, I saw I could re-fold them all some other time, and I lay down on the sofa, watching the Wiggles along with Cloud. I made another round of toast.

Every time we were done with a plate or cup, every time Cloud was done with a bottle, I simply left it in the sink for later. Cloud fell asleep watching TV on one end of the sofa, and I took the opportunity to crawl away to sleep in the actual bed. I was still in my pajamas, so it was perfect. I slept for maybe an hour or more and woke up before Cloud did, so I gazed out the window and wondered at how fast the day was slipping by. Cloud eventually did wake up, and I changed his nappy and put on yet another show, *Play School* this time. I thought about how dark it was getting in the apartment and how I should turn on the lights and start getting dinner made.

But it was too late. The key was turning in the lock. I sat up to see the foyer light turn on.

"Hey," I heard Gabe call.

"Hey," I echoed, thinking how I should stand up and busy myself somehow.

Gabe rounded the corner. At the sight of the state of things, the smile on his face froze.

"Watching TV in the dark?" he asked, glancing around. The laundry Cloud had scattered was everywhere.

"Yeah." I sounded so far away.

My hands reached for the remote control, but I stopped them. To switch the TV off would be to call attention to the fact that I'd been doing something wrong.

"How was music playgroup?"

"Oh. We thought we'd skip it for today."

"Did something happen?"

"No. Things just got busy, that's all."

Gabe was quiet for a few seconds. "Still in your pajamas?"

I shrugged.

"Where's Cloud? He's not napping this late, is he?"

"No, he's—"

I glanced around. Cloud was gone.

"He was right here . . ." I began to explain. But Gabe was already bolting in the direction of the bedrooms, his voice panicked but attempting to sound calm.

"Cloud? Cloudy? Where are you? Daddy's home!"

How strange to be worried, I wondered as I followed after him. Cloud was obviously in the apartment somewhere, and here Gabe was, acting as if he were lost.

Sure enough, he was in the bathroom, happily playing with the bucket of water I was using earlier to mop the floor, his onesie soaked in gray, soapy water. Gabe scooped him up and quickly washed his hands off under the tap.

"I'm sorry. I'll bathe him," I heard my voice say, modulating itself to sound repentant.

"It's fine, I'll do it," said Gabe, sounding artificially upbeat. I could tell he was trying hard to shrug the incident off. He changed the subject. "What's for dinner?"

I had no idea. I tried to remember what meals we had left in the freezer.

"Tofu curry."

He frowned. "The one your sister gave us? Didn't we have that yesterday?"

"Oh, yeah. I guess we did."

"What will Cloud eat?"

"Ryce. I'll make some."

I waited for the questions that would come next. Shouldn't

Cloud be eating vegetables and protein? Did I really just "plan" the adult portion of the meal without thinking of our nine-month-old child? Was I really starting dinner only now? Shouldn't I at least have set the ryce going already? What exactly had I been doing all day long?

But Gabe whisked Cloud off to the bathroom without a sound. A few minutes later, I heard the baby tub being filled. I set to work in the kitchen, but dinner still took half an hour to prepare—ryce only cooks so fast. I began to regain feeling again—those horrible feelings: guilt, loneliness, inadequacy, anxiety, remorse. I took the opportunity to add frozen green beans to the curry, and to cube and steam half a sweet potato, one of the foods we were trying to convince Cloud to enjoy. *Persistence is key. Your child's nutritional well-being is at stake.*

In addition to being late, dinner was dismal and messy as usual. Gabe airplaned some sweet potato into Cloud's mouth, which Cloud promptly spat out. Cloud ate around half his ryce before he began smashing the rest of it into the high-chair tray with his elbows and between his fingers, reminding me why we usually waited till after dinner to give him a bath.

"No, no," I chided, reaching for the wet washcloth.

Gabe stopped me from stopping him. "It's fine. He's exploring texture. I'll clean it up."

The rest of dinner passed in relative silence, as did afterwards, with me doing the bedtime routine while Gabe stayed in the kitchen and cleaned up. He made no comment about the sink full of dirty dishes and bottles, and this made me feel a certain dread. A capacitor came to mind, its electrical potential gradually mounting, waiting to discharge. I noticed my senses sharpening and everything turning more vivid, as if my body knew that some sort of end was coming, and therefore these peaceful moments were to be savored to the full. Cloud's cheeks flushed pink as he drained his warm bedtime bottle. I changed him into a night nappy and fresh onesie, kissing his baby belly and squeezing his baby thighs. I observed how white and perfect his four teeth were as I brushed them. I zipped him into his winter sleep sack and placed him in the bedside cot. Lying beside him, I watched his eyelids lower and his breath slow as I patted him to sleep. I remained there, inhaling his sweet milk fragrance, the sound of gentle snoring in my ears, and I counted the seconds, marveling at each one as it sailed by.

"Viv, can we talk?"

Gabe's tone was gentle.

We went out into the lounge area. He poured us chamomile tea from a pot he had brewed while washing the dishes. I noticed he'd vacuumed up all the toast crumbs.

"We can't go on like this," he said.

I didn't necessarily disagree, but to assent would be to surrender.

"I'm sorry," I said. "I know today was a bad day, but I think I'm improving—"

He cut me off, firmly and loudly. "No, Viv." Then more quietly, "No. You're not."

He took my hand, but I saw how he did it, as if overcoming revulsion. Then muscle memory seemed to kicked in, of a time when he loved me, and his grip softened and warmed. His gaze locked onto mine.

"We've tried, Viv. We really have. But we have to face facts: it's not getting better. And it's not just about you. Your condition affects my life, and it affects how well you take care of our son."

I thought of Greta Wilde's carcass, limp and bloody and torn open, the new Greta plunging her hands into organs, like Cloud eating spaghetti from a bowl. Peering at Gabe through the windshield of my eyes, I thought, no, I didn't want that.

Gabe continued. "Believe me, Viv. I was hoping as much as you that we could avoid it. I know it's not an easy decision to make and that you've always been anxious about rebirth. I hear you. I really do. But I can't do this anymore. I just can't."

I noticed my hand was still in his. I pulled it away. To my surprise, it was trembling. I gazed at it and, with some effort, willed it to stop.

"If you don't take the rejuvenation option, it's over."

"What's over?"

"This marriage. Us."

To my great surprise, his voice broke and he began to sob. Like a baby. "I didn't sign up for this, Viv."

Inside my head, I tilted my head. "But you think *I* did?"

At this, his self-pity turned into anger. "Yes, Viv. I think you're signing up for it every day."

He stabbed his finger in the air. And kept stabbing—a gesture comic in its repetition.

"*Every. Day.* You have a way out, and we have the money, but you still won't take it. It doesn't make any sense!"

He kept going, and the comic element disappeared.

"Maybe I could understand the first time. But now that you've been through rebirth, what's the big deal? Was it painful?"

He waited for an answer, which I gave.

"No."

"Do you remember any of it? At all?"

He waited again.

"No."

He kept going like that, though at some point I stopped replying. The whole situation was bizarre. I hadn't wanted to be killed and eaten before, so was it surprising that I still wasn't keen? Did going through it once mean I should be all right with subjecting myself to it again—so life could be easier and more convenient for him? I didn't enjoy my condition, but I could certainly live with it in order to avoid a grisly death. I recalled my last lucid moments before the rebirth—the fear, the attempt to struggle, Cloud being pulled from my arms. *Poor woman*, I thought, because when I thought harder about it, facts were facts: that wasn't me—though I felt as if it were. I was merely her replacement. And now my loving husband wanted another, better replacement to take her replacement's place.

I raised my head. Gabe was still crying, still pleading, still ranting, for me to be reasonable and practical—for the sake of our future as a family, for the sake of him and our son. And I felt I'd had enough. I shot out my hand. It picked up my cup of chamomile and smashed it against the coffee table.

"What are you doing?" he yelled.

I listened for the sound of crying from where Cloud slept. Nothing. Good.

The same hand picked up the teapot and hurled it against the opposite wall.

"Stop talking," my lips ordered—reasonably, because Gabe had requested I be reasonable, and I felt it was all right to grant that particular request.

"You're crazy," he said.

The hand reached for a book—the one Cloud had dropped on his foot—and I made to throw it at the TV.

"Don't!" he shouted.

How funny, I thought. He didn't want to replace his TV, but he couldn't wait to replace me.

"I'm not doing rejuvenation therapy, Gabe. I'm fine with getting a divorce, but I don't want to talk about it anymore."

"Okay, okay. I'm sorry."

He seemed like he actually meant it. As I lowered the book, the machine receded a little. Remorse trickled in, as did anxiety.

I used what was left of the machine to make my final demand. "I want to keep Cloud."

He stared at me, hurt, as if he'd ever try such a thing. "Of course. You're his mother."

I straightened. Yes, of course. Children belonged with their mothers, even mothers like me. It was nature's way.

Gabe rubbed his face. How tired he looked. And sad.

"I'm sorry, Viv," he said at last. "I love you, but I can't love you like this."

Unexpectedly, I sniggered. He looked indignant.

"What's so funny?"

"Nothing," I replied.

But what he'd just said reminded me of a question I'd asked a long time ago. Back when I was still pregnant and turning to Gabe for comfort, although his words had ceased to reassure. I was showing him the album I'd brought back from the holosonogram. We were admiring the images of our soon-to-be-born and not-yet-named son. Gabe spotted my embryonic self in the corner of one photo and pointed.

"Viv, is that you?"

I tried to turn the page, but he stopped me.

"Don't. You're beautiful," he cooed, stroking the blob lovingly. "Hello, baby Viv."

I laughed so hard that I cried. Or was it the reverse?

"But won't I miss me?" I asked once I was able to speak again.

Then it had been his turn to laugh, but without the tears.

I cleaned up the fragments of cup and teapot while Gabe dealt with the spilled chamomile. An anti-climactic conclusion to our dramatic fight. We slept with our backs toward each other, me facing Cloud, Gabe facing the wall. Cloud woke up once for his middle-of-the-night bottle, but I barely recalled waking up to prepare it, I was so tired. Apart from that, I slept deeply, without dreams, as if the fight with Gabe had been all the nightmare my body could take.

The sound of Cloud waking was what made my eyes flicker open. It was almost half past seven. He had slept in. Gabe had already left—for the office, but after last night's confrontation, the apartment's emptiness felt eerie, as if he were already gone for good. He'd even tidied up. The mop and bucket were drying in the sunniest corner of the balcony. The clothes Cloud scattered yesterday were back in the laundry basket, folded and stacked. The only signs that Gabe had recently been there were the bowl, spoon, and cup in the dish-drying rack, washed but still wet. I thought to myself how I should enjoy it for now—waking up to a clean home. It wouldn't be the case after the divorce. Cloud and I would probably be the ones leaving, given that the apartment was in Gabe's name. Where would we go? My sister's? It occurred to me I should tell her the news. I fed Cloud a bottle and gave her a call.

Vera came over right away, with all three kids in tow because it was school holidays, plus the meal she'd been cooking when she picked up the phone. She swept in like a hurricane, handed Cloud to Terry, and ushered all the kids into Cloud's room to play until lunch was served.

"Terry's responsible," she assured me. "And Haze just *loves* babies. It's a phase girls go through—they love pretending they're mothers."

My immediate reaction was to feel sad for girls. But I set it aside to ask how Pa was doing. I'd seen him maybe . . . two or three times since Cloud's birth? Pa hated leaving the house, and the first time I'd gathered enough energy to take the train and show him Cloud, he'd seemed so uninterested, I wondered why I had bothered at all.

"Pa's fine," replied my sister. She finished setting the table and moved on to briskly laying out lunch: brown ryce, tofu mince and broccoli, bakwan jagung, mixed bean salad. She apologized for the bean salad being left over from last night, not freshly made.

Meanwhile, I was still wearing the same pajamas.

"I'll start feeding the kids," she offered. "Why don't you get changed?"

I returned to a merry table of eating and chatter. Cloud's plate had some of everything on it, and though he was sticking exclusively to the brown ryce, he wasn't throwing the rest of the food onto the floor.

I knew we would have to wait until after lunch to discuss the matter. My sister didn't think children should listen to such things. She was right, of course. Once they were finished, she directed them back into Cloud's room.

"Vi," she said gravely, scraping the uneaten food from the kids' plates onto her own—waste not, want not. "You need to reconsider. You're making a mistake."

The surprise I felt: was it because I didn't expect her to say what she did? Or was I surprised at myself for not seeing it coming? I didn't know, but I felt the blow, like a sudden gust, hollowing me out as I sat stupidly in my chair.

My sister went on. And as she did, she seemed to get angrier. "Vi, do you hear me? You're being ridiculous. Gabe's basically a perfect husband, and you're leaving him because he wants to pay for an expensive treatment to cure you. You're insane."

She stood up and began clearing the table loudly, banging the plates one on top of the other, clattering the cutlery.

"And how are you going to take care of Cloud alone in your condition? You're a mother now, Vi. You can't be selfish anymore."

"Selfish?" I repeated. "Just because I don't want to be—"

"Murdered and replaced? Yes, I know. In case you forgot, you spent your entire pregnancy worrying about it. As if every other mother in the world doesn't go through it. What do you think Ma did twice to have us? What do you think I've been through three times? Just get over yourself, Vi."

Terry came out of Cloud's room. "Mum, why are you yelling? Is something wrong?"

"Not at all," said Vera, the faintest trace of guilt in her bright voice. She looked at her watch. "Tell your brother: we're leaving in fifteen to catch the train to BJJ."

"What's BJJ?" I asked.

"Brazilian jiujitsu. It's like kung fu, but more practical," my sister explained.

Terry went back inside, and my sister began washing up.

"You can use the dishwasher," I offered.

Vera merely laughed. In a few minutes, the dishes were done.

She hadn't resumed scolding me, and at first I was relieved, but then it occurred to me: "What do you mean by 'selfish *anymore*'?"

She busied herself by putting the leftovers in the fridge.

I persisted. "Ci, what do you mean?"

She turned and contemplated me. As if she were sizing up the situation: was now the right time? Then she took a breath and let out what she had to say. Something she must have been yearning to say for a good long while.

"Vivi. Believe me, I understand why you're the way you are. You've never really had to grow up. You've always had other people take care of you—me, then Acek, then Gabe. But like I said, you have a child now. You have to take responsibility for his sake. You can't just abandon Gabe like you abandoned me and Pa."

"What are you talking about? I never abandoned you and Pa."

She shook her head, lips pursed in a bitter smile. "Yes, you did, Vi. You're just so self-absorbed you don't even know you did. After Pa and Acek fought, you left me to take care of Pa by myself."

"No," I protested. "No, it's not like that. I've always helped out. But most of the time you won't let me. You always try to take care of Pa yourself."

She laughed, then. A laugh of disbelief. And when she did, I saw how strong she was—vibrant and full of energy, like all new mothers—but also, how thin. Like a greyhound. The ones they rescue from racing. She'd been thin for so long, I'd stopped noticing, I suppose. Her eyes glittered when she opened her mouth again to speak.

"There's always some excuse, isn't there? But not this time, Vi. Do you hear me? You have a great life, and if you blow it up, you're a fool. You have a husband who knows how to cook and clean, and who's super hands-on. And thanks to his high-paying job, you live in the lap of luxury with an expensive kitchen and TV and *internet*—who can afford to pay for internet, Vi? James and I can't even afford to heat our house. Yet you still have the nerve to sit here and whinge to me whenever I come over and expect me to listen and agree as I tidy up and stock your freezer with meals."

She checked her watch and grabbed her bags. "Terry! Matt! Haze! We're going! Put on your shoes!"

As they trotted past us to the foyer, my sister kept speaking, though she kept her voice low.

"One more thing, Vi. Maybe you have the luxury of whimpering and crying about how scary rebirth is, but some mothers are grateful for it. Not some—most. For *most* mothers, it's something we want and need. Five years of being superhuman! Do you have any idea how tired I was before kids? If James's salary could take it, I'd have another one in a heartbeat. So just take Gabe's offer, okay? For once in your life, start pulling your weight."

She ushered the kids out and closed the door. Meanwhile, Cloud rounded the corner, bawling. He was crawling after his cousins. He wanted them to come back. It was too hard for me to pick him up from the floor, so I sat down in the hallway and pulled him into my lap to console him. Once his tears had dried, I decided we should go to the park.

I called it the park, though it wasn't. Just a corner patch of green at the end of the block with a pink camelia tree. It was close enough that I could carry Cloud there easily, without even using the baby carrier. And whoever maintained it kept the grass lush. The tree was in bloom, and the ground was dry. We sat among the mess of browning pink blossoms. Cloud loved to squeeze them in his fists until the petals separated and the flowers fell apart.

I mulled on what my sister had said about me being selfish for not wanting to go through with rejuvenation, and about how I'd left her to take care of Pa. I thought of the night Pa and Acek fought—the last time Acek ever came to our place, the last time he and Acek ever spoke. The fight took place over dinner, so Vera and I witnessed the whole thing.

It had started when Pa informed Acek that he was thinking of migrating to China. Not to Fujian, our ancestral province, but to Shanghai. That's where things were really at.

By that point, Pa rarely spoke to either of us daughters, much less Acek, anymore. So the mere fact of him speaking, combined with this unexpected piece of information, added to my surprise. Acek had merely nodded and continued eating. Until Pa got up and brought back a folder. He'd gone to the Chinese consulate, he said, and obtained the information and requisite forms.

Acek didn't open the folder. "What about the girls?" he asked.

"They'll come with me, of course."

Acek turned his gaze on Vera and me. I felt its heaviness.

Soon, Pa's reason for bringing it up became clear: he needed money for the migration process. He'd pay Acek back.

Acek, politely, tried to change the subject, but things only escalated from there.

"You tricked me into moving to this country," Pa spat. "This place is nothing but a dead end."

"You're the one who wanted to leave Indonesia," protested Acek. "Remember? After Ahun died?"

Pa raged on. "We wouldn't be here if it weren't for you. I know better now: we need to be in China, where we belong. The motherland. *Wo men qin ai de zu guo*." I didn't know Mandarin, but even I could tell how lousy his accent was.

Acek went quiet. "Well, you didn't know then. And you're here now. Might as well make the best of it."

"You cheapskate. You just don't want to lend me the money, even though I'll pay you back."

"I've given you plenty of money already," Acek said at last. He didn't sound angry or resentful, just sad. "Anyway, you don't know anyone in China. At least here, I can help raise the girls."

Pa's stare was cold. "I don't need your help raising my children, you homo. Get out of my house."

Acek's face turned gray.

Pa didn't stop. "Maybe Australia's a great place for perverts like you, but you didn't need to drag us here as well."

I held my breath. Slowly, without a word, Acek pushed back his chair and stood up to leave. I got up too, to see him off as usual, but Vera didn't move. When he saw I'd followed him, it seemed to cheer him up a little. I could tell he was trying hard to shake off what had happened.

"See you Saturday, Vivi?" he asked as I opened the door for him.

Something inside me lit up.

"Can I still come?" I whispered.

His mouth smiled, but his eyes didn't—as if they were looking far away at something else.

"It's up to you, Vivi. Remember that. For everything. Even when people say it isn't, it is."

He ruffled my hair.

"Goodnight. And tell your sister goodnight for me too," he said before vanishing into the damp, black hall.

I helped Vera wash the dishes. We worked in silence, even

though Pa had already retreated to his room. Only later, in the sanctuary of our bedroom, did we dare to talk.

"Do you think Pa's really going to make us move to China, Ci?"

Vera turned to me. We shared a double bed. "I don't think so. Pa's not well enough to pull it off. Just don't bring it up."

Her remark startled me. I'm pretty sure we'd both known for years that something wasn't right with Pa. But it was the first time one of us had said it out loud.

"Pa was so mean to Acek," I remarked.

Vera was quiet, not agreeing or disagreeing. All she said, after some time, was "We have to take care of Pa."

"Why? He doesn't take care of us. Not anymore."

"I know," she conceded. Then sighed. "But he's our Pa."

Then she fell asleep, or pretended to fall asleep. And I tried, but my brain whirred inside my skull. I was eleven, so I already knew what "homo" meant and that it wasn't a nice thing to call people who were gay. Whether Acek was really gay or whether Pa had called him that just to be mean, I had no idea. But I knew that Acek was kind to me and liked having me around, and I liked him infinitely better than Pa—even if Pa was our Pa, as Vera had pointed out.

I did go over to Acek's that Saturday. And Sunday. And I kept going over. And even though Vera never stopped me, I was aware that she didn't entirely approve. Acek still tried to slip her money—through me. He'd give me extra with my wages. But Vera would always make me give it back.

One day, she gave me a note for him, which I unfolded and read secretly before passing it along. It was short. *Thank you for taking care of us in the past, Acek Arvin. I got a good job. Don't give us any more money. We will be all right. Vera.*

She had indeed gotten a good job. She'd found another part-time position at a supermarket, and they'd promoted her to assistant manager. It was more than even the paper salary Pa had received once upon a time. Meanwhile, Acek had started paying for my TAFE courses. After that, I started working as his apprentice, and then his employee.

At the time, I'd thought I was lightening my sister's load, even chipping in with what I could until she married James, and Pa moved in with them.

But was that what Vera had felt all that time—that I'd left? That I'd deserted her and Pa for Acek and then never returned? That our family life was a prison I'd escaped, while she had chosen to remain behind? Had it been my duty to remain behind as well?

Was that my duty now?

A smooshed camelia fell into my lap. Cloud had crawled over to show it to me.

"For me? Why, thank you," I gushed, and he broke into a grin.

Taking advantage of gravity, I swept him into my arms and num-nummed his cheeks and neck, which always made him laugh. I reached to my right and picked up a blossom myself, pulling apart the petals and throwing them like confetti.

"Whoosh! It's a parade!" I exclaimed.

I gave him more petals so he could try for himself. See, I could make Cloud happy. I didn't need to be replaced. More importantly, I didn't want to be. Then it wouldn't be me nuzzling his little neck, holding his little hands, rubbing his little belly. She'd think she was me, like I thought I was me, but technically speaking, it would be someone else. *It's up to you, Vivi. Even when people say it isn't, it is.*

I threw us another hot-pink parade, and we giggled some more.

I thought about what I was going to do when it was time to head back home. I would call Acek at the new number he'd given me, for his niece's house in the country. I'd explain the situation and ask if Cloud and I could move out there, if I could work for him again. Then there'd be a startled silence, followed by a "Yes, of course, Vivi. You and the baby. Of course you can come." We'd leave this life with Gabe like I'd left that life with Pa and my sister, but I'd know that I'd chosen it this time. It would be difficult, but worth it because I would get to stay alive, and Cloud and I would have each other. We'd be fine.

viii.

It's been a few days since Acek's surgery. We've been back at work since the day after he was discharged. Lina was the one who called to tell me, and I felt irrationally hurt that Nina hadn't been the one to phone. After hanging up, I thought about how I shouldn't be upset. Nina had enough on her plate, I shouldn't add to her burden. I should just be happy that the procedure went smoothly and that Acek was recovering. I should try to be less selfish—because it was precisely my selfishness that caused me to blow up Cloud's and my former life.

I don't usually feel our current life is this bad, do I? This utterly exploded? This wrecked and charred? But ever since what happened with Nina at the hospital, something's begun to change. A thick fog has rolled in, and I can't tell if anything beautiful is left or, for that matter, if what's left is beautiful anymore. As I perform the usual household tasks, work tasks, mothering tasks in their endless cycles, I find myself wondering more frequently, *what's the point?* "Wondering" is, in fact, the perfect word. Isn't it a wonder that the chore of living is made up of so many smaller sub-chores despite being, itself, futile. This is the true miracle of life.

There are parts of me that recognize what harmful thinking

this is. They attempt to intervene. One part observes that my nights have been restless, coloring my outlook on life. Of course I'm not sleeping well, I respond. What future do Cloud and I have out here? How can we go on like this? These are matters that should rightfully cause me to lose sleep. I am merely comprehending fully the reality of our situation.

Another part notes that Cloud's been acting up a lot. He threw a tantrum this morning because I told him the T-shirt he wanted to wear was in the dirty clothes pile. Yesterday he lost it when his banana slices were touching the pasta on his plate. He also lost it at the bus stop because we were boarding the "wrong bus" ("NO DIS BAAS!") and the driver wouldn't wait, so we had to take the next one. It came forty minutes later and was also the number 38, because only the number 38 stops at our stop, so there are, in fact, no wrong buses, my dear Cloud. And these three incidents were just the major ones. There have been other, more minor incidents of upset. So, no wonder I'm feeling a bit low and doubting my mothering abilities. But this is how toddlers are. Be kind to yourself. This too will pass, this part of me says in a soothing voice.

You're wrong, I tell this part. It won't pass for another several years. Cloud's just turning two and tantrums last until, when, four? Five? Six? And how should I have responded to this latest slew of awful behavior? Always with calm explanation, gentleness, and cuddles, which I have failed to do. This has been my response only sixty percent of the time, more or less. The other forty percent of the time, I have responded with frustration, stern words, yelling, or a smack on the back of his hand. Forty percent of the time is basically fifty percent of the time—so, half the time, I am responding to my child's normal age-appropriate behaviors with abuse. This is because I'm literally medically unfit to be a mother, with none of the boundless reserves of patience, energy, and emotional intuition that a healthy mother would have. So you see, Vivi, this isn't just a brief bad phase—it's a very long bad phase caused by me being me, and by the time it's over, I will have ruined my own child's mental health for life. That is, if we make it through the phase at all.

Everyone dies at some point, so if I can just postpone our deaths, it will be okay. I have been trying to repeat my usual mantra, but I find myself trailing off when I'm barely getting started. *Everyone dies.*

These are the thoughts running through my head like current as I rewire this air-conditioning unit. It's the same one I've been working on since Acek's collapse. I can't seem to get ahead with it. Cloud keeps interrupting me. I keep making mistakes that need fixing. The quieter atmosphere in the shed only adds to my feeling of abandonment. The sense that no one cares. Classes have started, and Zoe and Libby aren't in today—it's just Lina, Nina, and me. Nina's still acting strange and avoiding me, although she plays with Cloud. Acek's been recuperating in the house, keeping to his room.

I've seen him exactly once since I failed at waiting till he came out of surgery. It was when Nina brought him back from the hospital and helped him into the shed to say a group hello. We presented him with a fruit basket and a get-well-soon card from all of us. He thanked us in his usual gruff manner, followed by "Well, you should get back to work."

Everyone laughed, including me, but only for show. I wondered if Nina had told him how worried I'd been, and how I'd tried to wait. I wondered if somewhere, behind that sweeping gaze of general appreciation directed at the whole lot of his employees, there was any memory at all of how I once was a child he was fond of, someone he saw almost every day, someone he took under his wing. Someone who spent over a decade working at his side, who eventually grew up and got pregnant. Someone he consoled as she sat on his floor, fearful of death. I wondered if he remembered dimly somewhere. Perhaps the memory was like a small screw, in a box of screws, on a shelf stacked with other boxes, in a storeroom filled with such shelves. In which case, the memory might be small, but it would still be there.

Today, while tightening a tiny real-life screw, I wonder what it will take to dig the memory out of its box. I don't even want to use it, necessarily. I just want to know if it exists. And I have an idea. It's midday. I set down my tools, grab Cloud's lunch box, and go in search of him and Nina. She offered to take him to watch a DVD half an hour ago so I could focus. Or more specifically, she ignored me and asked Cloud, "Do you want to watch TV with Aie Nina while she prepares lunch for Akong?"

I slip out of the shed and through the back door of the house. Sure enough, Cloud is watching an old *Play School* DVD with Nina while sitting in her lap. My heart quickens in my chest. You'd think I was on a top-secret mission or something. I spy the tray with Acek's lunch on it, sitting on the kitchen bench. Ryce and sides. Pa's the same way: it's not a real meal if there's no ryce. I take a deep breath and come around the corner, all smiles.

"Oh, you're still watching. I have Cloud's lunch here . . ."

I open the box and show it to her. Inside are plain pasta spirals and a boiled egg.

I'm about to suggest that she feed Cloud while they watch TV when she does it for me: "I can give it to him. I don't mind. Then you can have more time to finish the air conditioner."

"Thanks!" I say, feigning pleasant surprise. I pass her the box. Cloud immediately grabs a spiral and begins munching, eyes glued to the screen.

I pretend to notice the tray for the first time.

"Is that Acek's lunch?" I continue before she can reply. "I'll take it to him for you."

She looks like she wants to get up, but she's pinned down by a munching toddler, lunch box in hand.

I'm already picking up the tray. "It'll only take a minute. I really don't mind."

I think I hear a faint "okay" behind me as I walk down the hall to Acek's bedroom. But I'm too upset to be happy that my plan is working. The look on her face—it was more than hesitation. It was panic. And I don't know why.

I knock on the door. "Acek?"

"Come in," I hear him say.

I open the door to find him sitting in bed, writing in a notepad, reading glasses on. When he sees who I am, his expression looks like his niece's—panicked. Like I've caught him out.

"Vivi," he mutters, taking off his glasses and putting away the notepad and pen. "I thought you were Nina."

"I know," I reply.

"Just put it there," he says, motioning to the top of the dresser.

I follow his instructions. It's now or never. I wheel around.

"Acek, what did I do wrong?"

He stares, bewildered. I press on, voice shaking. "Did I do something? Is that why you're mad?"

Now the words have started coming, they won't stop, like I've opened a tap.

"You shouldn't have told me we could come, Acek. If you were going to treat me this way, you shouldn't have said yes."

I wipe my eyes. He still hasn't said a word, but his silence gives it away—I'm right and he feels guilty. But the questions remain.

"Why, Acek?" I ask again.

Then, for an instant, his face softens, and I see him—not the Acek of this past year, but the Acek I've known since I was a little girl. He opens his mouth.

"I'm sorry, Vivi."

I wait, expecting more. But that's all he says.

We stay like that for some time—me standing, hoping he'll say something else, hoping at least that he'll explain; him sitting in his bed, eyes downcast, waiting for me to leave, which I do, at last. Even as I look back through the door as I shut it, I see he hasn't moved. As if he's turned into a statue.

I walk straight through the house and through the back door without stopping to look at or talk to Nina and Cloud. I head to my workbench and pour all my concentration into fixing the air conditioner. It's easy to focus, now that I've received my explanation, which is that I don't deserve one.

Cloud is returned to me while I'm testing the unit. He's full and happy. I change his diaper and take him out for a walk. It's a perfect afternoon. The sun is shining, and it's not too hot. I stoop a bit so I can take Cloud's hand in mine. We toddle to the shady side of the shed and, like that Chinese New Year's Eve day, I bounce him on my knees and hum. Today is different, though, and I'm sure the difference would unsettle me if I could feel anything right now. I remember being happy that day. Positive and optimistic. I remember it with some disbelief. I turn my gaze on my son, his child's face giggling, and I feel like the operator of an amusement park ride, watching, bored, from a windowed booth at the base of the machine. It occurs to me that, though I've been in machine mode before, I've never experienced it quite like this. I've always been able to feel *something* for Cloud. Even that day when we didn't leave the apartment at all and he dropped that book on his foot: I didn't feel distressed, but I still felt the need to comfort him, to make him happy again. Now, I feel no such need. I am entirely free of the burden of emotion—his and mine.

But I'm still aware of what is expected of me, the tasks I must perform in the meaningless sequence of events that is life. In between tending to Cloud and keeping him busy, I put the finishing touches on the air-conditioner, tally up the repair costs, and spend the rest of the workday doing general chores: sweeping, tidying, unpacking new supplies. Weirdly, no one seems to suspect that the Vivi they're interacting with isn't me at all, but a shell, with the true me small and safely tucked away inside. The minutes pass, accumulating into evening. As usual, Nina drops us home—just three of us today, Cloud and me, followed by Lina.

Cloud and I wave Lina and Nina off. I let us into the house.

"Mama needs to make dinner," I hear my tired voice mumble as my body kneels and slips off Cloud's shoes. "Play by yourself for a while, okay?"

He doesn't, of course. But it's all right. I don't feel particularly annoyed, or anything else, even when he toddles into the kitchen every few seconds to show me something or tug at my leg. Dinner's not complicated: boil up the last of the pasta spirals; chop up a cucumber; microwave some canned mushroom soup. I stare through my eyes out the kitchen window at the graying sky. It's started to rain. I leave the house to retrieve Cloud's drying diapers from the rack outdoors. When I return, Cloud is standing at the screen door, screaming in rage. I was only gone for a few minutes, but he didn't want to be left behind.

As I calm him, I'm faintly bemused at how strongly he feels. He's hyperventilating, he's so upset. Tears and snot pour from his face. It's not a big deal, I want to tell him. Nothing's a big deal. Not me leaving him in the house for two minutes, not the mistake I've made by moving us out here, not the tedious pointlessness that is living. It's all about perspective.

Dinner is ready: cucumber and pasta for Cloud, the same for me, plus soup. I hoist Cloud into his high chair too carelessly and my shoulder feels like it's been stabbed. But even that doesn't matter. I experience the pain as a dull, faraway throb, light and sound on the periphery of the vast dark field in which I stand. I pour Cloud soy milk and set it in front of him. He bursts into flame.

"No dis!" he screams. I stare at him before registering what he's upset over. He wants his favorite cup.

"The red cup is dirty," I say dully, not wanting to wash it. It's in the sink.

He keeps repeating his protest. "No dis cup! No dis!"

I put the milk away. Behind me, the screams continue. Then something clatters to the floor.

My body turns and clanks over to the high chair. The cup is underneath the table, milk pooling and spattered all around. Cloud's fury hasn't abated; it's worse. The force of his kicking and pounding shakes the high chair. Next to go is his plastic plate, face down, spirals and cucumber sticks rolling and skittering across the wet tile. Cloud is still screaming when my hand reaches for his, stopping it in mid-pound. And he screams even louder when the hand refuses to let go. He struggles to free himself by beating my forearm with his left fist, which my other hand closes around as well.

I hear a single word rise from my throat: "Stop." It sounds calm and eminently sensible.

Cloud doesn't obey. The hands—my hands—tighten their grip. Cloud yelps and struggles even more.

"Sshhh," my voice is saying now. A neutral hiss, like air escaping. "Sshhhh."

Abruptly, another emotion enters Cloud's expression. Fear. His shrieking turns to wild sobbing. Sobs to pierce the heart, but my body's walls are steel and thick, and the sound doesn't penetrate. My heart and I watch, but we cannot be reached.

The hands keep pressing. They will stop when Cloud does. All Cloud needs to do is obey the voice: *ssshhh*. But he won't, so the hands will keep going because, eventually, if they keep at it, the wailing will cease. Even now, it's turned into whimpering.

A sudden noise at the front door jolts me back from Cloud's high chair. I blink. My hands are my hands again, my body my body. I lift Cloud into my arms and clutch him close, peppering him with kisses. He clutches me back.

"It's okay," I whisper again and again. "It's okay. Mama's here. It's okay."

The noise comes again: a series of knocks. And a voice squeezes through the wood, muffled.

"Hello? It's Nina!"

Nina?

Shifting Cloud's weight to my right to accommodate my shoulder, I head to the door, still horrified. Did that really happen? Did I do that to Cloud?

I swing the door open to find Nina standing on the porch, holding a six-pack of Tooheys. She looks bewildered, as if she's surprised that I've answered at all.

"So," she begins awkwardly, "after dropping Lina off, I thought . . . well . . . it seemed like you had a bad day."

She holds up the Tooheys. "Can I come in?"

Someone noticed. I'm touched. But I catch myself, remembering Nina's about-face at the hospital. I can't have that happening again.

It's as if she knows what I'm thinking. "About the other day at the hospital. I'm sorry for acting so weird."

Her apology disarms me, and though I'm still wary, I let her inside.

"What happened here?" she asks when she sees the mess. I grab a rag.

"Nothing. Just an accident," I say, grateful that Cloud can't really speak yet, can't explain who's to blame for his red face and teary eyes. I feel guilty for feeling so.

I'm still carrying Cloud. After what happened, I don't want to let him go. But my shoulder hurts too much when I try to bend down to wipe up the mess. Nina takes the cloth from me.

"I'll do it. Don't worry. You can feed Cloud dinner."

The incident has made me docile. I keep him on my lap and feed him from my plate while I feed myself the mushroom soup. He eats only the pasta, but I don't care. I'm so grateful he's alive. I get his favorite red cup—Nina's already washed it—and fill it with soy milk, which he gulps down.

"I might put Cloud to bed," I say.

"Go ahead. Just pretend I'm not here."

"It won't take long."

It doesn't. I brush his teeth and change him into a nighttime nappy and pajamas. We can skip bath time tonight—he hates washing his hair, and I don't know if he will survive if he throws another tantrum. What if the same thing happens?

That's the one thing I think as I lie next to him, stroking him to sleep. What if it happens again? What if Nina hadn't randomly decided to come by? If she hadn't knocked, would I have been able to stop myself? Would Cloud be hurt? Would Cloud be dead?

Cloud must be exhausted—by the tantrums, by the terror, by his own mother almost murdering him. He's asleep in no time flat.

I come out of the room to find the dining table cleared and clean, all the dishes washed and in the drying rack, the toys being herded into a pile in the corner by Nina, who looks up at my approach.

"Is he asleep?"

I nod.

"I'll get the beer. It's in the fridge."

I sit on the sofa, not attempting to help. She hands me a bottle and I take a swig.

I'm still dazed, so I leave her in charge of the conversation. This means we sit in silence. I'm fine with that.

I don't know how long we stay there, incubating. It feels like forever and no time at all. Eventually, Nina clears her throat.

"Hey. I've been wanting to say this for a while. I really am sorry. Not just about that day at the hospital. I know how Acek's been acting towards you. It can't be easy. Since you were so close to him."

I'm startled. So, she's aware.

"It's not your fault," I concede, the words coming out a bit fuzzy. I suppose I should have eaten more besides soup before starting on my beer.

"I'm going to make toast," I say. "Do you want some?"

She smiles that sad smile of hers. "Sure."

I get up and sink back down. I'm no heavyweight, but I've only had one bottle. Less. That's when I realize something is wrong.

My gaze meets Nina's. Suddenly, past the heavy makeup, past Acek's square jaw, I see.

Her voice is the last thing I hear before the world goes dark. "I'll take good care of Cloud. I promise. I'll take good care of our son."

II.

NINA

i.

I like mornings the best. They leave me no room to fall down into my thoughts. Before I'm properly awake, sounds lift me to life's surface—the call to prayer over mosque loudspeakers, roosters crowing, birds chirping in the trees. The traffic comes next: the tinkle of bicycle bells, the growls of trucks, the hum of angkot, and the very occasional motorbike and car. My head's already outside on the street with all of them by the time the sun has risen, and I swing my legs out of bed. Then there's a set sequence to follow; I bathe and dress, make breakfast, see Iwan out the door, head downstairs to open the shop. I don't have time to reflect or regret; my focus is on organizing the jumble of tasks that need doing that day: which jobs to finish, which jobs to start, parts to order, deliveries to unpack.

Only when I've reached mid-morning does my mind begin to sink below the surface of the here and now. Not when I'm working on anything complicated, but during easier tasks: simple rewiring, oiling motor parts, testing fuses, taking inventory. It comes like background music, wafting in like the radio that plays all day in Shirly's cooking-supplies shop next door: I don't notice it until I do. And then I'm bobbing in and out of it all day long. Even after

I close the shop, even after Iwan comes home, even as I lie in bed falling asleep, I can't escape it, thinking of you.

Is that any consolation? That not one day passes without you in my head?

Today, as I sit soldering, the rosin core giving off its faint pine fumes, it's the morning of our excursion that I remember—that first day of the Lunar New Year, when I invited you and Cloud to the beach for our day off.

Did you hear my voice tremble over the phone when I called you that morning, Acek standing at my side to steel my nerves? Did it matter if you did? It didn't stop you from saying yes. I still remember the drive over, my breath soundless and shallow, my heartbeat soundless and shallow, my mind rehearsing what to say and what to avoid, reminding me to maintain my Nina voice—low and monotone, like Acek's. You don't need to be chatty, I told myself, you just need to make her comfortable. That could be done in silence. In fact, if I knew myself, which I did, then silence was probably best.

Pulling up the dirt driveway of your house, I saw you were waiting already, sitting on the sagging front steps, our son toddling around barefoot, a slice of white bread clutched in his hand. I still remember the stabbing sensation that came then, the rush of cold through my chest that pinned me to my seat so that I could only watch from the car as you led Cloud over instead of getting out to help or say a proper hello.

Now, nearly twenty years later, as I watch my younger self sitting in the car, gazing at you and Cloud and the house, I feel a different sensation. Gentler. Like nostalgia but not. I'm not yearning for what happened but for what never could. A longing for something still formless, that never was and therefore can't be articulated. It's like squinting at a blurry photo, waiting eternally for the features to sharpen and resolve. What if you and Cloud hadn't had to end for me and Iwan to begin?

At noon, I take my usual half-hour lunch break. Today, I cycle to the place that serves bihun bebek, ten minutes away. It's one of Medan's trademark dishes. The herbal broth here could be better, but they make up for it by mixing genuine duck in with the shredded mock duck and tofu. Another thing Medan is famous for: widespread flouting of the federal ban on meat, in line with its general reputation for lawlessness. As the locals say, "*Ini Medan, Bung!*" This is Medan. Anything goes.

I don't claim to be a local myself, even after all this time. Though my Hokkien and Indonesian have improved considerably, I've never been able to get rid of the trace Aussie accent that makes someone hearing it for the first time furrow their brow. Right now, for instance. The woman who usually takes my order knows me, but today, there's a new employee who does a brief double-take before jotting down what I want. I'm more relaxed about it these days, but you can imagine how it was when Iwan and I first arrived, and my accent and language skills were worse.

It's more crowded than usual, and my meal takes a little while to come. I slurp it up quickly and head back to the shop, but no one's waiting when I come back. Only two people come in the afternoon: at one-thirty, a relatively new client, to pick up his TV set; and at four-fifteen, my neighbor Shirly, who ambles over for a chat. Shirly's six years my senior and a widow. Her husband died of liver failure. She had kids much younger than I did—her two daughters are already married and have children of their own. Every now and then, she goes to see them in Jakarta. I notice they hardly come back to visit her.

She's probably the closest friend I have here, or perhaps have ever had. As you know, you and I were never the social sort. I invite Shirly up for tea. She tells her employee to mind the shop. I lock up and put out the sign instructing customers to ring the bell.

We climb the narrow stairs to the living quarters, which consist of two dark, cramped floors: kitchen, living area, and bathroom on the first level, and Iwan's and my bedrooms above. I don't invite Shirly over often, but when she visits, she feels right at home. As do I when I go over to hers. The layout is the same for all the shophouses in the row.

"When does Iwan get back from school?" she asks as we wait for the tea to steep.

"It depends. Recently, he's been staying back to rehearse for graduation. The whole class is singing a song for the ceremony."

"They grow up fast, don't they?" Shirly sighs.

A memory surfaces: Iwan at two, locked with me in the soundproof room, pushing me away, crying not for me but you.

I lift the teapot lid to check on the leaves. "Yes, they really do."

The conversation drifts—to her daughter's new job and her latest grandchild, to advising me for the nth time to hire an employee to help in the shop.

"I was stubborn like you," she tells me. "When Abing died, the girls kept nagging me: 'You can't run things alone. You have to take care of your own health.' I ignored them for months, but when I finally gave in, whew, what a relief!"

She yammers on about how it's important to find the "right" one. How the first employee was great but stopped showing up after six months. How the next one was lazy and had to be let go, but how this current one is an excellent fit.

It's the price I pay for Shirly's company: the nattering. Her good-natured self-absorption is something I'm grateful for. She's not nosy at all and doesn't seem to realize how little she knows about my past.

Shortly after Shirly leaves, Iwan returns. The key turns in the door downstairs. Years of being on the alert have made my ears sharp. I hear his long legs bolting up the stairs two at a time. The first thing he does after greeting me is seize a banana from the counter. In a few seconds, he's done and lunges for another.

"Hungry?" I ask, amused. We speak English at home. English is easier for me, even after all these years.

"I had a bun, but it wasn't enough," he mumbles, mouth stuffed.

"How was rehearsal?"

"Good. How was your day?"

I reach up and muss his hair. "Good."

I think how, if I can hardly believe it, you'd never be able to either: how tall he's grown, how deep his voice is, how huge his feet are, how much he reeks when he doesn't wear deodorant. And, if it's possible, he looks even more like Gabe than he did when he was little. "His father must have been handsome," Shirly once remarked. She thinks I'm a widow, like her. So does Iwan. I told him his dad died just after he was born. I think about Gabe sometimes—not the same way I think of you, of course. But he crosses my mind every now and then: how he's doing these days; how his new wife and kids are doing; how much thought he spares, if any, for his missing ex-wife and first child.

Iwan may look like Gabe, but his personality is mostly yours and mine. We sit happily in silence before he withdraws to his room upstairs. I contemplate where to buy dinner. I'm still not a great cook. That's something I don't miss about Australia. Here, good food is reasonably priced and easy to find.

I'm just about to head out when the phone rings. It's probably one of Iwan's friends, but I pick up anyway. To my surprise, it's Acek.

"Nina?" he asks, cautious as always, making sure it's me.

"Acek? Is everything okay?"

Acek and I have a standing phone conversation on the last day of each month, but otherwise, we only call each other when something's wrong.

A long silence follows my question.

"Acek?" I repeat. "Are you all right?"

"I'm fine," he says finally. "But someone broke into the house."

"What? When?"

"Just now. While I was out. Smashed the window and climbed in."

The hairs on the back of my neck stand on end, and my breath catches in my throat. I lower myself onto the sofa. I've heard enough, but I know I should make sure.

"Was anything taken?"

"No. But she opened the drawer where I keep your address. The one I keep locked."

I shut my eyes and see you, unconscious, slumped back on your yellow sofa.

"Nothing is missing, but she left it open," continues Acek.

I understand all too clearly. You want me to know that you're coming for me.

"Nina, I'm sorry. I'm very sorry."

Acek's usually impassive voice sounds frantic. It also sounds tinny and far away. I realize the receiver is resting in my lap, where my hand has fallen. I raise it to my lips.

"It's not your fault, Acek. Don't worry."

"I'm sorry. I shouldn't have—"

"It's not your fault," I repeat calmly. "I'm sure everything will be fine."

After I hang up, Iwan pokes his head down the stairs and asks who it was. I tell him the truth: that it was Akong Arvin, that his house got broken into, but that he's all right. Iwan knows who Akong Arvin is—the closest thing to family we have, though Acek lives in Australia, though he doesn't have any memories of Acek firsthand. Iwan was too young when we left.

"That's awful. At least he's not hurt," says Iwan.

The fear hits surprisingly late, dissolving my insides. I don't want to go out. I ask Iwan if he can go out instead to buy dinner. "My head hurts," I lie.

Iwan obliges without complaint. He's a good kid, always happy to help.

Once I hear the downstairs door close and the key turn, my eyes dart this way and that, as if you're already here. As if you're hiding in the dark corner behind the cupboard, or crouched behind the rattan armchair across from me, or lurking in the bathroom, just beyond the half-open door. But then, out of nowhere, comes another sensation, tranquil and warm. I realize what your arrival will bring. No more suspense. No more wondering when you'll show up. The more I think about it, it's a relief.

I walk to the kitchen and turn on the light. I examine the free wall calendar I get from the life insurance company every Lunar New Year. I find today's date and mark it—a tiny black dash that Iwan won't notice. I calculate how quickly you might arrive. Though it's unlikely, let's say you board a ship from Sydney tonight. Sydney to Jakarta. Jakarta to Medan. On an old model like the one Iwan and I took when we left Australia—it'll take nineteen, twenty days. On one of the new liners that run on Eco-Quik tech, more like twelve. I score two more dashes, to indicate the earliest and latest dates you could possibly arrive. There's a slight overlap with Iwan's trip to Bangkok with two friends—to celebrate finishing high school and getting into university. You may miss him if you don't hurry. But if that's what happens, I'll let you know the situation so you can wait for his return—after you've dealt with me.

I re-hang the calendar. Because I've just made them, the three little dashes stand out. They remind me of notches on a prison cell wall. A way to count down to my execution and freedom, though maybe I shouldn't assume. There's a small chance I'm wrong. How well can I even claim to know you anymore, after seventeen years in a different country, nineteen in a different body? I know only what I'd want to do in your place, and I can't blame you one bit.

Our son returns. He's bought kwetiau goreng—the premium, charcoal-flame kind. Even after all these years, eating it reminds me of when Acek illegally cooked it that evening, on Sa Cap Meh. Like Australia, Indonesia's clamped down on charcoal and propane usage, now that induction technology's more affordable. But of course, people complain it doesn't taste the same and, if they can, go to places that charge higher prices to cover the cost of bribing the energy police.

I slice up some cucumber. Iwan gets the plates and chopsticks. We talk about his upcoming trip. He's more excited about Thailand than about graduating or continuing his studies. Of course, he is. I've never let him leave the country before. Now he's going all the way to Bangkok—the global hub of bioluminescent tech, where the streets glow all night.

I devote my full attention to him, basking in his boyish enthusiasm. Tonight's news has made our time together precious; he's no longer a baby, but he'll always be our baby to me. A full two heads taller than me and straddling adulthood. It occurs to me that maybe you've timed it this way on purpose, and I thank you for letting me finish raising him, letting me see out my time. What a long way we've come from my terror at first laying eyes on you, that floating blob of blue.

Only after dinner, after I've climbed the stairs to my room, do I allow myself to attend to practicalities. I slide your gift out from under my bed and open the lid to survey it in its near-finished state. I confess that I've been working on it at a leisurely pace, but please understand: I've been expecting you, but not knowing when to expect you has made keeping up momentum hard. To my credit, I've been steady. Now I have twelve to twenty days to finish it and tie up other loose ends. Perhaps longer, depending on when you start your journey, but I'll work as if it's twelve. There's really not much left to do. I've been putting it off, that's all.

As I put your gift away, I plan how, within the next few days, I'll have to visit Aie Ing Lan to put the final touches in place.

ii.

Was there another way? Of course there was. But once you chart a course, it's hard to stray. And as you're well aware, I became dead set on the route I planned. At some point, the costs incurred in following a plan also make it difficult to abort, though, in theory, one could. In theory, much is possible; in practice, the path of least resistance is the one we take.

And, believe it or not, what I did became the path of least resistance—over time, as all the components fell into place. Suppose I'd resisted the urge to see Cloud in the first place. Suppose I hadn't gone through with getting work done on my face. Suppose, even, that you hadn't asked Acek if you could come work for him—the equivalent of a bug flying smack into a web. Maybe I would have changed my mind. But once everything was in alignment, it felt as if there was no turning back.

There's an image that still pops into my head every now and then: the two lines, parallel and pink, from the test we took when we discovered we were pregnant with Cloud. I remember how it reminded us of a section of road—the single road, straight and relentless, down which we had to walk—and how this road was called *life*. Whenever this image springs to mind, I think about how unexpected it was that the road would fork into two.

One thing I can't do anymore is blame Acek. He truly loved us and took our fear seriously. Who else can we say that about? Was there anyone else who didn't laugh off our concerns or tell us to get over it? Another memory that often surfaces: Gabe holding our child, fresh and wet from the womb, calmly kissing me, his old wife, goodbye.

I know you came to think that Acek didn't care. Is that any consolation—to know that he did?

*

Even as I regained consciousness, I could sense I wasn't in the hospital. The surface beneath me felt lumpy and uneven. The air was thick with a pungent, meaty smell. My eyes opened to a familiar coffee table, a familiar TV set and boom box, familiar stacks of old newspapers and magazines—though it took me a while to figure out where I recognized them from.

It was Acek's apartment. I tried to get up, but my whole groin felt tingly and sore.

"Acek?" I called. "Acek? What happened? Where's the baby?"

I heard him padding over to the sofa. Saw his face come into view as he crouched next to me.

"Shhh, Vivi. Don't worry. It's okay."

Words that only made me more frightened. Despite the pain, I sat up.

"What happened, Acek? Is the baby okay? Where's Gabe?"

"They're fine. Just fine. And you're safe. Everything is okay."

Everything was obviously not okay.

"Acek, please," I begged. "Tell me what happened? Why am I here?"

Tears surged into his eyes. I could tell he was trying to find the words to explain.

"You're safe, Vivi. I saved you. You're all right."

Awkwardly, he seized my hand and squeezed it. Then he left and came back with a bowl of herbal soup.

"To help you recover," he said, pushing it at me. "I got the herb mix from the traditional Chinese medicine shop. Good for healing from wounds. I used real chicken too."

I looked down. I was in an oversized T-shirt and an adult diaper. My belly was still large but squishy. I had given birth, hadn't I? I remembered pushing out the baby. Did Acek put these clothes on me? What was the diaper for?

I glanced up, confused.

Acek blushed. "You're bleeding . . . down there."

Finally, it began to dawn on me, what might have happened. What Acek might have done. But it was impossible, wasn't it? How could he have done it, even if he'd wanted to? I shook my head, the implausibility of it all flooding my brain.

"No," I said. "No, Acek."

But he nodded. "Yes," he assured me. "You're safe."

The bowl in my hands clattered to the carpet, spilling soup everywhere. Shutting my eyes and pressing them into their sockets, I began to wail. Faintly, from behind the wail, I could hear Acek's voice, confused.

"Vivi, isn't this what you wanted? You were so scared, remember? You said you didn't want to die?"

But then he let me go on, sitting beside me in silence. Awkwardly again, he squeezed my hand and padded off to the kitchen. He came back with a cleaning rag and more soup.

"Please, Vivi." He pushed this bowl into my hands too. "You'll feel better after you eat."

I nodded. Then, when he went back to the kitchen, I set the bowl down and tried to leave.

I slipped out through the front door in my bare feet, still sore and throbbing between my legs. I managed to waddle only a few steps down the stairs before he caught up with me.

"Vivi, you can't."

"My baby, Acek," I pleaded. "I have to get him."

His grip on my arm tightened. "You don't understand, Vivi. You can't. *You can't.*"

He said the last words through clenched teeth.

"Vivi. If you go back, they'll dispose of you."

His words stopped me in my tracks. I kept my eyes on the floor, on the threadbare brownish carpet that looked like all the threadbare brownish carpet lining the corridors of every cheap apartment building in Sydney. *Dispose*. I felt his hand shake. Or was it me?

When he spoke again, his voice was gentler.

"Please, Vivi. Please. Let's go back inside."

*

Once we were back in the apartment, he told me how he'd saved me from me. Remember, before he got his electrician's license, he used to do work for the main water company in Sydney—not officially or anything. Whenever they were short of labor, they'd contact an agency who'd contact a guy who'd round up other guys like Acek—typically migrants, cheap and eager for work.

For a time, they were working on a sewer tunnel network on the lower north shore. Acek was assigned to clear the section under a fancy private hospital, with another guy named Hassan.

"A lot of buildup," Acek told me. "Mostly the usual—sand, mud, rocks, that sort of thing. But the stuff from the hospital . . ." He trailed off before resuming, with another list: "Human stuff. You know . . . bits of body. Organ. Bone."

Hassan was an old hand, and he'd done hospitals before. It was waste from the rebirth rooms, he explained. The staff were supposed to clear the bigger chunks away themselves, but if they were too lazy, they'd just pry up the grate and stuff everything down.

What they found gave Acek nightmares for ages. Some parts were decayed to the bone, what was left, blackened and foul. Some were fresher, identifiable: a toe wearing nail polish; a lobe of brain; a lone hand, ragged at the wrist, jagged at the bone.

"Terrible to be a woman," muttered Hassan after they both emerged into one of the rebirth rooms, only for a few minutes, to violently throw up.

Acek had reached for the tap in the corner to clean up the vomit.

"Leave it, Arvin," Hassan had ordered. "A surprise for those fuckers. They should do their job properly. Poor mothers. They give us life, and those fuckers just stuff them down the fucking drain."

As Acek recounted the story, my mind flashed back to the lavender-tiled rebirth room from the maternity-ward tour, Gabe and the other couples walking around admiringly, the woman serving as our guide explaining the strict standards that ensured the room's hygiene. I pictured young Acek and Hassan in their sanitation worker suits, bursting through the grate into our midst.

Acek continued. The idea of rescuing me had occurred to him the day I broke down while working on that foot massager. More specifically, that night—after I'd gone home, and he'd locked up and returned to his flat. He'd taken his dinner alone, as usual, while reading the newspaper, and thought about what I'd said about not wanting to die. He loved me like a daughter. How could he simply stand by and watch me get replaced?

Over the next several weeks, his plan grew flesh. Crucially, I mentioned in passing that I would be delivering at the same hospital whose bowels he'd once crawled through with Hassan. It was too much of a coincidence. The rotting hand he saw that night, snapped off at the wrist—there was no way he would let it become mine. He was meant to rescue me.

Acek admitted what I'd always suspected: he disliked Gabe. "Smooth people always choose the smooth path. But at least," he conceded grudgingly, "he phoned me like you told him to."

Hearing we were heading to the hospital, Acek headed out himself, in an old waste-era van he'd bought from a mate who owned a small moving business. The exemption license was active for a few more weeks, so it could still be driven within the city. He parked near the hospital, clambered down a manhole, and made his way through the tunnels. He'd been doing practice runs for two months. In his waterproof backpack was an extra respirator for me, and a cooler bag packed with raw pig's organs for my hungry new self.

The drains leading to all five rebirth rooms were connected by the same tunnel. Once he reached this tunnel, it was a simple matter of popping his head into each one to check if I was there. I wasn't. Not yet. He ended up waiting for me for seven hours. In the meantime, two other women underwent rebirth. He sat there, squatting in the dark, listening to the sounds of new mothers feasting, the crunch of bones and squelch of flesh. Like the first time, the tunnel was littered with women's parts, and he longed desperately to climb into an empty room, rip off his mask, and wretch violently, like he and Hassan had done back then. But he managed to keep it down. This time, he couldn't risk being caught. I was at stake. From the room at the farthest end of the tunnel, he heard a door open. A light flicked on, shining through the grate—a subterranean sunbeam. He waited till the light flicked off and the door closed again. Then he pushed open the grate and peeked out. It was me. As quietly as possible, he lifted himself into the room. He wasn't as slim or agile as he used to be, but he managed nonetheless.

He unpacked the respirator and the bag of pig's organs and waited, trying to steady his breathing. He'd done his own research at the library too, and knew what came next.

Once my new self had crawled a distance away from me, he sprang into action. Taking me by the arms, he dragged me clear of my small wriggling self, then around in an arc, back to the grate. He strapped the respirator to my face, then lowered himself partway, onto the topmost rungs of the ladder, before clutching my naked body around the waist with one arm and pulling me through. Carefully, he laid me on the drop cloth he had spread out at the ladder's base to keep me dry. Then he climbed back up to dump out the pig's organs: lungs, heart, stomach, liver, kidneys, a mess of intestines, and a spinal column for good measure. Pork of any kind was expensive, of course, but he'd managed to get offal on discount from a mate who worked at a high-end butcher shop. ("You Chinese eat everything," the mate had observed, and Acek had forced a half-grin. "Yeah. Yeah, I suppose we do.")

Before he climbed back down and replaced the grate, he took one last look at my new self. It had already grown considerably, to the size of a child. And that unnerved him.

"Exactly like you when you were little, Vivi. Exactly."

As he recounted it, his face was pale and his gaze on the carpet, as if he could see her there, on his apartment floor.

He was dressing me in a loose-fitting track suit when the sickening sounds of feasting commenced from above. Then, pack on his front, he carried me firefighter-style through the tunnels back to the van.

Once we'd reached the flat, he'd wiped me down and changed me again. And showered and changed himself, of course. And that was that. Now, I should really try to eat. It would help me recover.

He'd served me soupy ryce and chicken before starting his story in another attempt to feed me. I hadn't so much as touched it. I stared at the pale shredded flesh mingling with the white grains. I spotted a dark artery, trailing hose-like in the soup. I ran to the toilet and tried to throw up.

But I couldn't. As nauseous as I felt, as much as I wanted to, nothing came out. After hugging the toilet bowl for a while and having another cry, I emerged and ate some spoonfuls, hunched in silence. Acek had the tact to leave me alone.

*

The next several days were a fog. When I wasn't sleeping, I was crying. When I wasn't crying, I was thinking. The thinking was too much. Stopping the thoughts required falling asleep. Crying was the quickest route to sleeping, so it was just as well that thinking often led to tears. At intervals, I ate, and my body, despite my grief and confusion, hungered for the nutritious meals Acek prepared for me—traditional dishes, warming ones made with vinegar and wine, with ginger and wolfberries and dates. And meat. Not just chicken, but pork too, purchased at the same time he'd bought the offal. He'd even kept a portion of the pig liver for my meals, but my taste buds were too westernized, so he ate it instead.

I tried leaving a few more times. Each time, Acek brought me back—except once, at two in the morning, when I made it as far as two blocks in Acek's flip-flops and came to a halt in the middle of the empty street. I turned around and trudged back to Acek's myself. Who was I kidding—they would never give my baby back. My new self would never let me glimpse him. Gabe would call the police. He definitely didn't want me coming round—he'd already kissed me farewell. I would be hauled away and disposed of, biohazardous waste that I was.

But why else had I endured all that fear, if not to hold my baby at the end? How big was he? How did his skin feel? I felt desperate to lay eyes on him, to feel his weight in my arms, to breathe in that baby aroma I remembered from my two nieces and nephew when they were newly born. I regretted all the dread I'd felt: what kind of a mother had I been, to think so much about preserving my own life? What kind of life did I think it would be without him? I didn't deserve him, and this was my punishment.

And yet I still longed. I longed with an ache so unbearable and burning it would break from my throat in a scream. My body yearned too. To my surprise—and Acek's—my milk came in, swelling my breasts hard and tight and red. They leaked. Acek took a trip to the library to consult a book for mothers lactating in the wake of a newborn's death. He bought me some comfortable sleeping bras for support, and I stuffed them with rags to absorb the milk. I used ice packs and ibuprofen to ease the pain. I wondered, why would a mother's old self ever need to produce milk? What was the point? It made me weep.

The birth announcement came in the post, the simple blue card bordered in giraffes and balloons that Gabe and I had picked out months in advance. At the time, we'd had to leave spaces blank. Now the gray rectangle for the photo was filled: a baby with a thick shock of black hair in a giraffe-print swaddle, angelically asleep. My baby. He looked perfect. I scanned the details below the photo. His name was Cloud. Weight: 3.1 kg. Height: 52 cm. I got out a tape measure to see how long that was. I wondered at where the name Cloud came from. Our final candidates had been Arthur, Oliver, and Lucas. Cloud was good, though. I liked it. Didn't seem like Gabe's style, so perhaps new Vivi had picked it out.

By that point, my milk had begun to dry up and my breasts weren't as swollen. Although I felt relieved, I was also upset that my ability to breastfeed was leaving me—the only proof that nature had also given me the right to raise my child.

I had my first outing, not counting the times I'd tried to leave. Acek had closed the shop for several days to take care of me. He had brought home a few jobs, but was missing some crucial tools. He took me along to the shop to pick them up.

He drove. What a luxury. Steeped in grief as I was, I could appreciate it: being conveyed directly to a nearby destination, watching the buildings go by. Not even having to book a time slot or walk to and from a designated car-share parking spot. No wonder Gabe had always wanted a car of his own. Acek was trying to use the van as much as possible before the exemption license expired. By then I knew the bigger plan: to move to the country to avoid detection—and for me, temptation. Even under pain of death, how long would I be able to resist trying to see Cloud if he were so close by?

I tried turning my mind to logistics to avoid thinking too much about my son.

"If the exemption license is expiring," I asked Acek, "can we use this van to move?"

"You can get a temporary permit if you're using a vehicle to leave the city for good," he explained. "It doesn't cost too much. Next week I'll move all the stuff out of the shop to the apartment. We'll save on rent that way. After that, we'll move out of the apartment and drive everything over to the new place."

Acek had already bought a property in the country. By Sydney standards, it was a bargain, but he'd still spent all his savings to do it. It would pay off in the long run, he reasoned. No more paying rent for lodging or the shop, or worrying about rent increases. And as we'd discussed in the past, business had been dwindling. There was more demand for hobblers in regional areas. Money was scarcer there.

Once we were in the shop, I saw that Acek had already begun packing. Some boxes were already filled, and several of the shelves were bare. Bare shelves. I'd never seen such a thing in Acek's shop in all my years. I'd often complained about how cramped it felt. Now, looking at all the blank space, it felt empty and strange.

Acek didn't let me lift a finger, not in my condition. So I sat on my old stool at my old workbench and watched him retrieve what he needed. Even with items half packed away, he knew exactly where everything was. As he plodded around, carefully picking his way here and there, it truly hit me for the first time how much he was doing for my sake and at what great cost. The expense, certainly: all the money he'd blown on the property, the van, the organs, the meat. But also what he was giving up: the shop, his home, the network in Sydney he'd spent years building up. Here, when he needed something, Acek always had "a mate" to ask. There, he—we—would be striking out pretty much on our own. Despite my misery, I felt suddenly grateful —and loved.

When we were back in the van, waiting at a traffic light, I turned to him.

"Acek?"

"Hmm?"

"Thank you."

"It was nothing, Vivi." There was the slightest quaver in his voice. "Your mother would have wanted me to. It was nothing at all."

*

That was how I came to know the full story. Not that it had ever been a secret. It was simply one of so many facts, so many details about the past that had occurred to neither Pa nor Acek to ever talk about. The past: a heap of people, events, places, objects—any memories of them made painful and irrelevant by time and distance. With neither Acek nor Pa being great talkers, what occasion had there been to ever bring them up?

I had always assumed that Acek was Pa's friend from childhood. This was almost accurate, but it wasn't exactly the case. Sure, they'd known each other since they were kids. But the real friendship had been between Acek and Ma.

Acek and Ma—Ahong and Ahun—were next-door neighbors in one of Medan's predominantly Chinese districts. They'd been inseparable since childhood. While the other boys were off playing marbles, hunting frogs, and engaging in mock battles, Acek didn't mind jumping rope or running a pretend restaurant or playing dolls, as long as it was with Ma. They stayed friends growing up—just friends. Neither was interested in the other *that* way. Eventually, Ma got a boyfriend, a longtime classmate of theirs—Akiong, that is, Pa. Despite being a teenager, Acek showed no interest in girls at all, which inevitably led to rumors that he was "off" somehow.

Ma and Pa got married. They helped Ma's parents run their record shop. Acek continued working at his family's restaurant. His older brother got married and had two sons, which took some pressure off him to do the same. Ma and Acek remained friends, though it was harder with Pa in the picture. There was the matter of propriety to consider. It was strange for a married woman and an unmarried man to be close friends and nothing else. All three of them—Ma, Pa, and Acek—were aware of this, and though Pa had nothing against Acek personally, he was wary of the relationship between his wife and his wife's friend. At the same time, he and Acek didn't get along well enough to establish a direct friendship of their own. So, Ma and Acek were careful to keep their visits casual and publicly visible enough so that no one would talk. In this case, the fact that people thought Acek was "different" helped.

Then Ma got pregnant with Vera. Ma and Pa became a ma and pa. Ma had been looking forward to having a baby. Surprisingly, it was what came afterwards that hit Ma hard.

Like all new mothers, Ma was in great shape: strong, full of energy, perfectly in tune with her new child. But now she was sad. It didn't affect her day-to-day functioning, and no one noticed but Acek, so Acek was the only one she spoke to about it.

She brought the baby to his parents' restaurant one late afternoon. The lunch rush was over, so Acek sat at an empty table with her, drinking iced tea.

"How are you feeling?" he asked, giving Vera's chubby arm an affectionate squeeze.

"The same," she answered.

"Any idea why?"

Ma was quiet for a while.

When she spoke, it was to say the strangest thing. She couldn't stop thinking about rebirth. How she was an entirely different person now. How the old her was dead.

"Not just dead. Murdered, Ahong."

Acek had never thought about it like that.

"And not just anyone," she continued. "Me. I ate *me.*" She let out a weird laugh. "Ahong, I ate your best friend. How do you feel about that?"

Acek felt uncomfortable. "Don't say that, Ahun. *You're* my best friend. You're still you."

"Yeah. I know," she replied, though she fell silent again.

This time, when she spoke, it was to point to her sandaled foot.

"Remember when we were little and we were chasing that cat? And I fell and cut myself on that broken flowerpot? Remember how it left a scar?"

Acek remembered. He looked at where it was supposed to be, but it wasn't there.

"Was that part of the process?" he asked.

"Most of the scars and marks get passed on, but not always."

"You used to complain how ugly it was," he observed.

"Yeah, I did, didn't I?" She tried to laugh. "Well, I miss it now."

It took Ma the better part of a year to get back to "normal," though she did in the end. She had even seemed all right when she got pregnant again some years later—with me.

"Didn't Pa notice?" I asked Acek as he continued the story while we were in the kitchen. He was boiling yet more herbal soup. "Didn't he realize that Ma was . . . sad?"

Acek reflected. "Your Pa really loved your Ma. Practically worshipped her. You probably don't remember. But I'm not sure if he noticed such things."

I felt it made sense. I thought of Pa's recent fixation on the motherland. It was easier to idolize something if you didn't see it for what it really was.

Giving birth to me went smoothly, and afterwards, Ma was sad again. But this time, she was back to herself in a matter of weeks.

"What choice do I have?" asked Ma when Acek brought it up, trying to be a good friend. "It's just part of life, I guess."

Then she added, "I shouldn't think too much about it. I have two girls to raise now. I can't afford to be so depressed again."

Strangely enough, it was Acek's turn to be sad. Her attitude was pragmatic, no doubt, but this time, he really did feel like a part of his friend had disappeared, or a version of her. He thought about how, technically speaking, this Ahun had replaced the previous Ahun, who had replaced the Ahun he had grown up with. And the more he thought about it, the more he understood what Ahun Number Two had been trying to articulate after the birth of child one, when she'd pointed to her absent scar. Although his friend had moved on, he hadn't. Couldn't. He remained affected thereafter by what that past version of his friend had said. So, you see, in some sense, our breakdown in the shop that day was something that Acek had been looking out for all along.

When Acek got the news about Ma's death, he'd just moved to Australia, and he couldn't afford to come back for the funeral. But, lying on his lumpy mattress in his crummy shared room in his crummy migrant-quality shared flat, facing the wall for privacy, he'd cried and swore solemnly to Ahun, of whom no versions existed anymore, that he would take care of her daughters as best he could.

Vera and I were half her—the closest she would come to living and breathing on this earth again. He established contact with Pa to lay the groundwork for taking care of us later on. Communication with Pa caused him to worry—Akiong obviously wasn't taking his wife's death well. Then, one day, out of the blue, Pa expressed the desire to leave Medan. He couldn't take the memories anymore, needed a fresh start. Acek saw his chance to watch over Ahun's girls properly. He suggested Pa and his daughters join him in Sydney. Grief drove Pa to extremes, and he said yes.

Everything had fallen into place for Acek to watch over Vera and me. And relatively quickly, it became apparent that Vera would be all right, but I needed him more. He was struck by how closely my mannerisms resembled Ma's. And my personality. I was prone to living life in my head, assessing, processing, contemplating, overthinking. After a while, Vera didn't want Acek's help, which was fine. He was happy for her. But he was also happy that I chose to remain at his side.

Eventually, I married Gabriel, whom he didn't particularly like, but who seemed to take care of me well. I (we) told him we were pregnant. He remembered when we broke the news—how it reminded him of Ma's pregnancy. This memory triggered other memories: Ma's horror at having murdered her old self,

Ma missing her absent scar. He would keep an eye on me, just in case. You and I had no idea, did we—that even before the breakdown, we were under observation all the while?

I had the strong sense that Acek had been wanting to speak to me about my mother for a very long time. Just talking about her made him happier and lighter than I'd ever seen. It was close to midnight when he finished, and he was obviously exhausted, but the youthful flush in his cheeks lingered for a while yet—the gentle afterglow of a lightbulb after switching off a lamp.

Only then did it occur to me to ask. He'd focused on my mother's story, but left his in shadows. It had always seemed disrespectful to ask him, but it felt like a good time now.

"*Are* you gay, Acek?"

I felt myself blush. He did as well. It wasn't the sort of thing you brought up with an older person. But he did answer.

"Vivi, I don't know what I am."

He seemed to reflect on this. Then he added, "Sometimes, we just are what we are."

*

You know, I often wonder how things would have turned out if you hadn't called Acek. Or if you'd only phoned to say hello, to merely check in rather than suggest meeting up in person, in that park. By the time you called, I had already begun to make peace with the unexpected turn my life had taken, the extension granted it. I wasn't there completely, by any means, but I'd say I was on my way.

I would remind myself that the alternative to my present state—Alive with No Baby—wasn't Alive with Baby. It was Babyless and Dead. And whether I was dead or alive, Cloud wasn't mine but yours. I would wonder at the fact that I didn't miss Gabe one bit. Maybe I'd always known deep down that I was a pebble he'd picked up and pocketed on a whim. I was experiencing the release of being discarded at long last. You were a far better fit for him: strong, energetic, efficient, sharp. I belonged here, with Acek. Sometimes we just are what we are.

Oh, but you did call. Acek's surprise was visible. And audible.

"Vivi?" I heard the shock in it from my end of the sofa, saw his hand almost drop the phone. Until that point, I don't think he truly registered what it meant for us both to exist at the same time—for you to be you and for me to be me. Weeks and weeks back, he'd called your and Gabe's apartment to leave a congratulatory message, solely for the purpose of avoiding suspicion. He knew it would seem strange not to contact you at all. But up to that point—and don't take offense—I don't think he gave you all that much thought. As in, it was I who was Vivi, not you. And I was with him every day.

So, perhaps that added to his surprise at how apologetic you were for not having phoned earlier. For not updating him or calling to see how he was.

"It's all right," he managed, pale. I could hear your voice only faintly, and could already tell how unsettled he was by how it was mine. "I know you've been busy. How's the baby?"

I leaned in to listen, but couldn't make anything out.

When he hung up, I pounced.

"What is it? How's Cloud? Is he all right?"

He blinked at me, as if he wanted to make sure I was real. After all, he and I had just gotten off the phone.

"The baby is all right," he murmured in a faraway voice. "She wants to meet up. So I can see him."

"When?"

"Sunday. At eleven. At a park."

I wanted to go. It was my chance to see Cloud. Perhaps my only one ever. At first, Acek refused. The risk was too great. He was absolutely right.

I burst into tears.

"I won't let her see me," I pleaded. "I promise. I just want to say goodbye."

I want you to know I really meant that. You won't believe me, but I genuinely meant to say goodbye.

iii.

The rain falls in a steady drizzle as I cycle to meet Aie Ing Lan. I called her eldest daughter, Gwek Hwa, several days ago to arrange it. Aie's eighty-six and, until recently, has been in pretty good health. But last year, she had a bad fall on the stairs, and it's been up and down since. Gwek Hwa suggested we confirm again the morning of, so I phoned two hours ago, and she gave it the go-ahead.

"Mama even asked if you were still coming when she woke up. She seems to be having a good day."

So, despite the wet weather, there's a lightness in my body as I ride through the streets. It all depends on how you define it: what a "bad" or "good" day is.

It usually takes about half an hour to get there, but I've made a small detour to buy a box of pastel tahu from my favorite bakery. It sits in the crate behind me, my rain mantle draped over it, its gentle heat warming my back.

The box is still warm after I park and chain my bike. I greet Gwek Hwa's brother, who has time to greet me back. The morning crowd has receded and, except for a few retirees lingering over toast and half-boiled eggs, the shop has emptied out. He calls

Gwek Hwa over, and I pass her the pastel. She says thank you, I shouldn't have, et cetera. We make the usual friendly chitchat.

Gwek Hwa takes me upstairs to the second floor. Her father—Aie Ing Lan's husband, who founded the coffee shop—passed away more than a decade ago. When that happened, Gwek Hwa and her husband moved in with her mother so she wouldn't be alone. I wait at the dining table while she goes to fetch her mother, whom she helps to the seat opposite mine. I stand to greet her. Just one glance tells me what Gwek Hwa's already said: she is indeed having a good day. Her eyes are bright and alert, and there's a smile on her face as she lowers herself carefully into her chair.

"You too," she replies when I tell her how well she looks today.

I laugh. "Is that so, Aie?"

She gives a single nod, full of vigor. "Yes. You look peaceful. Relaxed."

Gwek Hwa leaves us, and a few minutes later, her son comes up bearing coffee, srikaya toast, and two of the pastel I brought. He looks older than Cloud, but not by much. Once he's set the tray down, Aie Ing Lan takes her grandson's hand in hers and gives it a pat.

"This one has the most interest in running the coffee shop someday. He's already helping out."

He grins and ducks his head modestly before beating a retreat.

"What about your son? What are his plans?" she asks, lifting her cup, shakily, to her lips.

She knows Iwan is graduating from high school. Her body may be failing, but her memory is excellent.

I name the place and program he's gotten into. She raises an eyebrow.

"So he's not going to help you with the shop?"

I shake my head.

"You're all right with that?"

"It was my idea. I want to give him the freedom to choose."

She sighs. "Yes, I suppose it's this way with the younger generation."

Then she says something that I don't catch. It sounds like a proverb, by the rhythm of it. My Hokkien is still far from perfect. I merely nod, pretending to understand.

She points at the snacks and urges me to eat—a gesture of care, as is the comment that follows.

"You know, it's not safe where you are. You really should move."

Almost every time I've visited recently, she finds a way to tell me this.

"Don't worry, Aie. The neighbor and I pay a security fee."

By which I mean we pay the local gangsters to not damage or loot our shops. A lot of Chinese-owned businesses are "offered" this "service"—most likely, her coffee shop too.

"Yes, but if anything happens, you're too far away from us. There's strength in numbers."

By "us," Aie Ing Lan is referring not just to her family but other Chinese. My shophouse row sits outside the main Chinese areas. I can understand the logic: when the May 1998 riots happened, everyone in the Chinese areas banded together to set up barricades and defend themselves. If something similar happened where I was, Shirly, Iwan, and I would more or less be on our own.

Aie Ing Lan speaks from bitter experience. Her brother's tailoring supplies shop got torched in '98. And before that, she lost her father and uncle in the mass killings of '65 and '66 when the family was living in Riau. That was when they were massacring all the communists. If you were Chinese, they had extra cause to suspect you of being one. Often, that was reason enough. Her father and uncle happened to be in the wrong place at the wrong time and got rounded up. They were never seen again.

Over the years, Aie Ing Lan has shared these stories with me. As I've said, her recall is exceptional. I suspect she has a photographic memory, though she doesn't call it that. She can recite in detail all the medications and treatments her late husband was on during his last days in the hospital. She remembers what she ate for breakfast the morning they received news that her father and uncle had been taken away. She can tell me about every single person who's lived on this stretch of street—their names and nicknames, who sold what, who married whom. Whether they're alive or dead, still here or moved away, she'll remember something about them, including Acek and Ma.

What she doesn't know because it exists outside the bounds of any memory: that Ma is my Ma. I have a cousin in Australia, you see. A second cousin, specifically. Her name is Vivian. As far as Aie Ing Lan and her family are concerned, Ma is her mum. Several years ago, Vivian felt the urge to find out more about her mother. Since I live in Medan now, I said I'd be happy to help.

Which is how Gwek Hwa found me wandering up and down the street that day, obviously searching for something. And how she introduced me to her mother. And how, over time, I have gained their trust.

You of all people should know how good I am at gaining trust.

*

You'll never guess where the inspiration for your gift came from. The Tjong A Fie Mansion in Kesawan. It's been around since 1900, though Tjong A Fie's grandkids only opened it to the public about thirty years ago, in 2009. Iwan was nine when I took him. He was supposed to go with his school, but on the day of the field trip he got sick and had to stay home. To make up for it, I brought him the following weekend. I'd never have gone otherwise. Once you live somewhere, some things just become too touristy for you to do.

We even got assigned a guide. He took us round the whole grand place: the wood-paneled hall for receiving guests; the open courtyard linking Heaven and Earth; the ballroom and family temple on the second story; and a whole host of minor rooms—for sleeping, for dining, for sitting around. And of course, photos and placards with reams of information about the man himself, Tjong A Fie, who migrated from Guangdong to join his brother during Dutch colonial times. They grew an empire here, built on tobacco and rubber, palm oil and sugar, tea and railroads, mining and banking. At one point, the Dutch appointed him Majoor der Chineezen—Mayor of the Chinese. Chief Chinaman. He built the mansion for his third wife, but he also funded a lot of projects for the public good: mosques, churches, Hindu and Buddhist temples, hospitals, schools, the big clock for the town hall. "He built them all, paying no attention to religion or race." The tour guide rattled off his prepared script with an admirable amount of enthusiasm. "Tjong A Fie was generous with his wealth, and the whole society benefited from it."

It only struck me afterwards, when I took Iwan for moorkop and horen at the TipTop nearby (another throwback to colonial days): intentionally or not, the mansion was basically a PR campaign for the Chinese. Especially in Medan, where bad stereotypes about the Chinese run strong. Insular, cunning, money-minded. Even the Chinese in other parts of Indonesia are wary of the ones from Medan.

But look at Tjong A Fie! Here was a Medan-Chinese tycoon who spread the wealth, who maintained good relations with people of all races, who was even best buds with the local sultan at the time. Was that the lesson? Follow in Tjong A Fie's footsteps and scatter your enormous fortune, and no one will hate you?

"What was your favorite part, Iwan?"

I zipped the pouch of all these thoughts shut and smiled brightly at my son licking yellow cream from his fingers. He'd seized the horen by the horn.

He thought for a bit. "I liked the butterflies and flowers painted on the ceilings."

I nodded. So did I.

As I watched him eat—one of life's greatest satisfactions is to watch children eat—I couldn't help but think of you. I remembered what a picky eater he was when he was little, the lengths you went through to get him to consume something besides plain pasta, ryce, or white bread. Nowadays he ate everything with the gusto you'd expect of a growing boy. But you weren't here to enjoy it, or any of the other things he could do now. Reading and writing. The cute remarks he made. The interesting questions he asked. I'd robbed you of all that.

One day you would find us. And when you did, how could I make amends? I thought of Tjong A Fie. How would I scatter the enormous fortune I had stolen from you? How could I give any of it back?

That was where the idea for the gift came from. In a few days, Acek and I were due to have our usual phone call. Acek being Acek, and international calls costing what they did, our conversations never lasted very long. The spoken reason was to keep the other updated on important life details. The unspoken reason was to make sure the other wasn't dead—by your hand or anything else. This time, I asked him for the location of the record shop my mother's parents owned. The seconds ticked by as he mulled over this request.

"Don't do anything rash," he said when he finally spoke.

"What would I do? You said my family doesn't live here anymore. Neither do yours."

"So why do you need to know?"

"I just want to see where we used to live, that's all."

"What if someone recognizes you? And she uses it to find you?"

Hadn't I thought of the same thing? Wasn't it why I'd been staying away?

Then again, wasn't I planning the gift in anticipation of Vivi coming for me?

I didn't tell Acek my idea, of course. All I said was "If she really wants to find me, she will."

In the wall of silence that followed, I sensed a weak spot.

"Please, Acek?"

He relented and told me the address.

I went the very next day, while Iwan was at school. The weather was blistering hot. I'd brought my camera. My plan was modest back then. I would find the shop—whoever owned it now, and whatever it sold—and I would take a few photos. In the album I intended to make for you, the page would be labeled, *Where we lived when we were little. Where Ma grew up.* The rest of the book would be memories of our son: photos, recorded milestones, happy moments, cute things he said. This was my fortune: our child and a glimpse of the Ma we never knew. And this was how I would share it with you.

The problem was, despite the address, I had trouble finding the exact place. I narrowed it down to two shops next door to each other—one selling sporting goods, the other shut and locked. My own memory was hazy. All I could remember for certain was a pale-green exterior, but both shopfronts were a dingy white.

I felt suddenly ashamed. Hadn't I lived here till I was seven? Wasn't it bad enough that I had no recollection of Ma?

I wandered inside the sporting goods shop under the pretense of browsing to see if anything could jog my memory. Then I lingered outside, sauntering back and forth, examining every corner and cornice. The young shop owner asked me if I needed help, then if I was lost. I asked about the vacant space next door. They had sold picture frames, he said. But they had moved, and there was no new tenant yet. I asked if anyone else had been there before the picture frame shop, but he didn't know. He himself had only moved in last year.

I decided to take a photo of both shopfronts. I got out my camera and was just about to cross the street when a woman about my age, a dishcloth slung over her shoulder, came over with a cup of old-fashioned coffee—the kopitiam kind—which she passed to the shop owner.

"Thanks, Ci," he said, accepting the coffee, though he looked young enough to be more the latte/cappuccino type.

She addressed me. "You lost? What are you looking for?"

The shop owner cut in. "Ci, do you know who used to occupy

the lot next door? Before the picture frame shop? She wants to know."

The woman cocked her head, one eyebrow raised. "Is that so? Why?"

"Better ask her."

She turned to me, expectant. I felt my face turn hot.

"My cousin," I stammered. "She used to live here. But she moved to Australia. She wanted me to take photos. For old time's sake. She gave me her old address, but I can't find it."

I told the woman the address, and she raised an eyebrow.

"Your cousin, huh? What's her name?"

I should have given Vera's, but I was already too nervous.

"Vivian. Her parents owned a shop here."

I gave Ma and Pa's full Chinese names: Tan Eng Hun and Ng Kim Kiong.

She shrugged. "I wouldn't remember, but tell you what. My mother's memory is first class, and she's lived on this street her whole life."

As I crossed the road with her to the coffee shop, I felt giddy. Gone was my fear that you would use my indiscretion to track me, displaced by curiosity and hope. She brought me to a table in the back where an elderly woman sat, a cup of tea at her elbow.

"This is my mother, Lie Ing Lan."

"Hello, Aie," I greeted.

"And your name?" asked the daughter.

Still too flustered to do a good job of lying, I introduced myself by the Chinese name I now go by. "Bie Eng. Lim Bie Eng."

"She's helping her cousin," explained the daughter. "Her cousin's parents had a shop here." Then to me: "What were their names again?"

"Tan Eng Hun and Ng Kim Kiong."

There was a glimmer of recognition in the old woman's eyes. She came to life.

"Ahun and Akiong?" she asked, sitting up straighter. "The Ahun whose family owned the record shop?"

It was all I could do to keep my lie straight. "Yes, that's her," I said, my throat catching unexpectedly. "Ahun. Eng Hun. My aunt."

*

How long have I been visiting Aie Ing Lan? Ten years? Not often, but often enough. I've kept my visits regular but low in frequency so as not to wear out my welcome, and to avoid too many questions about my own personal history. When asked, I try to keep the details simple and as close to real life as possible. Like my cousin, I was born in Medan but grew up in Australia. My Australian husband died when our son was little. The memories were too much for me, and I decided to move back here, leaving my parents and sister over there.

By and large, I have been successful in keeping the focus on Aie Ing Lan and her past, including whatever she can remember of my cousin's mother. I sense she enjoys having a reason to put her incredible memory to use, and to have someone listen to her recollect.

Today, I have exciting news to share: my cousin is planning to visit. I've been making a scrapbook for her, of all the information about her mother that I've gathered from these chats.

Aie Ing Lan scoffs. "From our chats? There's not enough to fill a whole book, surely."

I show her the thick notebook I've brought with me every visit, flipping through all the pages filled with text.

"It adds up, Aie. I have enough, thanks to you."

Aie Ing Lan modestly waves my thanks away, but there is an air of satisfaction in her smile.

"If you don't mind my asking, is there anything else you think I should include, besides what you've already told me?"

It turns out that she's been waiting for this question. Her eyes sparkle and her smile broadens in the most mysterious way.

She motions to the cabinet behind me, to the column of three drawers on the right. "The top drawer," she directs. "There's an envelope. Bring it here."

I follow her instructions. Slowly and shakily, she takes out a black-and-white photo, which she places on the table between us.

"This is for your cousin."

A mixed group of teenagers and kids clustered in front of a black car in the street.

Aie Ing Lan points at one of the teenage girls. "That's me." Then, at the little girl standing in front of her. "And that's your cousin's mother."

I almost can't believe my ears. I stare at her, at Ma. She looks around six or seven. She's in a shift dress, sporting a bowl-cut bob. Her arm is draped jauntily around the shoulders of the boy next to her, who looks about the same age.

"Who's that?" I ask, pointing at him, though I've already guessed.

"That's Ahong. I've told you about him. He and Ahun were inseparable. Even after they grew up." She chuckles. "Everyone thought they were sure to get married, they were so close. Until we realized he was . . . different. Good kid, though. Never got into trouble. Helped out his folks, though they sure gave him a hard time."

She sighs. This last remark seems to trigger a troubling memory. Or a few. She frowns.

"Poor fellow. Anyway, he was the first to move to Australia. Can't blame him. I think he even helped your cousins and their father, Ahun's husband, move there too. You can ask her more about that."

I stare at the boy. Crew cut. Big grin. Scrawny limbs sticking out of his collared shirt and shorts. Puberty hasn't yet brought in his square jaw, or his "differences." Together, he and my mother look so happy. So carefree. Like the whole earth is theirs to roam.

"I think I told you," says Aie Ing Lan, "his folks moved to Jakarta in 2005. To join their other son, Ahong's older brother. The normal one."

"Whose car was it?" I ask, changing the subject, pointing at the photo.

She chuckles. "My older brother was getting married. His future in-laws hired it for the wedding. Boy, were we excited! A big, flashy car!" She chuckles again as she observes, "Though, I suppose, cars are a big deal again nowadays."

She tells me the names of the others in the photo. I write everything down in my trusty notebook. She carefully places the photo back in the crinkled envelope and hands it to me.

I know my manners well enough to attempt refusal.

"You should keep it, Aie."

Gently, she pushes my hand away. "I have other photos. I can spare this one."

I thank her profusely. Vivian will truly appreciate it, I assure her. It's true: I do, and you will. We've never seen Ma as a kid. With reverence, I place it in my notebook, so it won't get folded or bent.

If this were a TV drama, now would be the time to end the scene. A picturesque way to close: this unexpected glimpse into Ma's childhood. Little Ma and Acek happy in their innocence. The photo itself, a crowning addition, making your gift complete.

But not quite. There's still something missing. An absence that even this photo doesn't fill. It's why I'm making this final visit—not just to ask Aie Ing Lan what else she thinks she needs to tell me, but to ask her specifically for what I know she hasn't.

"Aie," I begin delicately. I imagine broken traces on a circuit board—tiny sections of exposed track. I visualize precision tweezers carefully guiding the thinnest of copper wire into place. "I understand you don't want to talk about it. And you've been so helpful. But I think my cousin needs to know."

She shakes her head.

"Please, Aie."

"There's nothing to tell. And anyway, what would be the point?"

I'm silent. She's right. There would be no point.

"Tell your cousin her mother had a whole life. The way it ended was an accident. Better not to dwell on it."

I don't contradict her. I don't protest. I simply listen and nod—then nudge. It's my last time here. I can't come away empty handed.

"Please, Aie," I repeat.

Again a sigh.

"All right. But like I said, there's nothing to tell."

Like good days and bad days, it's all relative. What's nothing to her is something to us. At long last, after all these visits, I learn the details of how our mother's body was found—in the middle of the night, lying to one side of the road, legs tangled in her bicycle, just two streets from our home. She'd gone to deliver medicine to a sick aunt not too far away and had been cycling back. The cause of death was obvious—a bloody wound matting her hair, marking where the rock had struck her skull.

Aie Ing Lan knows all this because she heard it straight from the man who found her. He had raised a cry, and word spread. Everyone came out. Someone went to fetch Pa and keep Vera and me at home.

The way Pa keened. Unearthly. It went on and on. Like a mother dog protecting her pups, he wouldn't let anyone get near. As if all she needed was time. As if holding her in his arms could bring her back to life. They never caught who did it, not that they investigated—probably some hoodlums who'd drunk too much and were having some fun, who saw a Chinese riding her bike late at night and thought it would be funny to pelt her with a rock.

"An accident," Aie Ing Lan says sadly. "Who knows if they meant to kill her. At least they didn't—"

She stops, but I hear the words she hasn't said. I think of the stories I've heard about 1998 and 1965, and I fill in the rest: *at least they didn't beat her. At least they didn't rape her. At least they didn't hack her to death or burn her alive.* I hear the words like they're out loud. Is this what's called a mercy? That our mother died the year before all of that happened, in a quick accident instead of in terror and pain? I think about whether you can call an accident an accident if it happens because conditions make it likely to occur. I think also, fleetingly, about the quick deaths my mother experienced even before being hit by a rock—quick painless deaths that all mothers undergo.

We sit in silence for a while.

"There," she says. "That's it. I told you. Nothing much."

We're both blinking back tears.

"Thank you, Aie," I croak. "Really, my cousin will be grateful. Thank you so much."

A moment passes. She speaks again, more to herself than me.

"A good memory is a gift. But sometimes you just want to forget."

We chat a little longer, and when I say goodbye, she suggests bringing my cousin when she comes to visit.

"I haven't seen Amui since she was little," she says. "Maybe she'll have questions about the information I've shared. Bring the book you're making for her. I'd like to see it too."

I lie to Aie Ing Lan for the last time. "That's a good idea. We'll stop by."

"I can't even imagine her grown up. She was such a small thing when I saw her last."

I nod. "It's been a long time since I've seen her in person myself. We used to look similar. But when we were older, that changed."

iv.

Acek and I agreed that he should go to the park first, and I'd follow later. He left early, to be in place well before Vivi and the baby arrived. He took a bag of stale leftover rolls to feed the pigeons. To make us both less nervous, I made a remark.

"Remember when I told you not to feed the pigeons bread?"

He broke into a gray-toothed grin. "You said it wasn't healthy. I should feed them peas and seeds."

"And you said, 'No one likes health food. Pigeons have it tough enough.'"

He chuckled. "And I said, 'How would you like it, Vivi, if I took away your KFC?'"

We both shared a laugh then, and when he zipped up his backpack, I noticed his hands weren't shaking anymore.

Once he left, I assembled my disguise. I'd bought some lipstick from a pharmacy and now I applied it, coating my lips a dramatic purple-brown. The last time I'd worn makeup was when Gabe and I got married. Anything to avoid the possibility that people would notice she and I looked the same.

The baseball cap I wore was Acek's, though the sunglasses were mine—a decent pair from the op shop where we'd bought my new wardrobe. I took a deep breath as I stepped out the door, and again as I stepped out onto the street. A breeze was blowing. Though I wore the sunglasses all through the train ride, I kept my eyes on the floor.

The park was a straight shot from the station entrance, and as I walked, I maintained a forward and faraway stare, fixed on a distant point beyond the reach of my vision, where I imagined my baby to be. Do we remember the time we took apart the TV? When Acek taught us how the cathode-ray tube worked? That was the image in my head as I walked toward the park: my eyes shooting electrons in a steady beam, lighting up a point on a pitch-black screen.

I confess, I was so intent on seeing Cloud that I didn't spare much thought for you. Up to that point, insofar as you'd crossed my mind at all, it was purely in terms of your impact on me. You had supplanted me, made me obsolete, and now my life and child were yours. After all that reading I'd done to prepare for the pregnancy, you'd think I'd remember: the fact of my survival affected you too.

This realization only hit when I saw you. Acek was still waiting when I got there, looking around and checking his watch. He spied me, but looked away almost immediately, and I myself tried to look like I was ignoring him. I sat on a low wall under a tree a good distance away and cursed myself for not bringing something to make myself look busy—a magazine or newspaper, one of those rolls that Acek was breaking up and throwing to the birds. I checked the time myself. Had Acek heard wrong? Had you forgotten? It was then that you came into view, out of breath, baby in arms. I wasn't prepared for the hunch in your shoulders, or your drawn, colorless face, or the dark circles under your eyes. I recalled our sister each time after she'd given birth—radiating energy and vigor, broad-shouldered and strong. Forget looking like a new mother; you didn't even look like you were in normal health. You barely even looked like me. Even from that distance, I could see that Acek was also shocked.

Once you attained the bench, you dropped your diaper bag like a sack of bricks. For a moment, I worried the baby would follow. But you managed to keep your hold on him as you lowered yourself carefully next to Acek. How tiny he was. And perfect, from what I could see. I yearned to come in for a closer look but didn't dare. In the birth announcement photo, his eyes were shut. Now, they were open, staring at Acek from where he sat in your lap, propped up against your middle. Acek put his finger in Cloud's hand, and I felt a stab of envy. I would have given anything to feel Cloud's grasp, to feel the weight of his little body on my lap and against my stomach. The absence of it was so painful, it felt like hunger. It was all I could do to remain where I was.

Hello, my dearest, my little one, I said silently. Behind my sunglasses, I let the tears trickle down my cheeks. *Goodbye*, I willed myself to think as well, but couldn't. The word would form, but not as a message, just an object, unpropelled by intent. A word like any other word. Sky. Bread. Pigeon. Goodbye.

Then, too soon, it was over. Before I knew it, Acek was getting up, patting you on the shoulder, walking away. He wasn't abrupt about it, but from the look on your face, it was obvious that he was the one who had ended the conversation, not you. You looked dazed, disappointed, as if you'd been hoping for a longer chat. The daylight made you look washed out and weary, and this made me feel even sorrier for you. Then, I saw you slide over to your diaper bag and, resting Cloud belly-up along your thighs, take out a thermos and various plastic containers. To my horror, I realized what you were doing. I'd only ever seen baby animals being given bottles—ones who'd lost their mothers. And here was our son, with two mothers living, being fed like an orphaned calf. My stomach churned with revulsion and pity—then, increasingly, anger, rising like a morning sun. I thought of my breasts just a few weeks ago, swollen with milk. I could have given him what you couldn't. My son wasn't yours. He was mine.

It wasn't the first time I'd thought that, but now it rang in my brain like a command. You couldn't take care of him properly. I could.

A whisper at my ear made me jump in surprise. It was Acek. He'd quietly circled back for me, worried what I might do if left alone.

"Vivi—" he started, then faltered, his eyes on the other Vivi we were peering at in profile beyond the hedge.

"Vivi," he began again, pulling himself together. "Let's go."

*

We didn't speak the whole way home. I thought I was the one lost in thought. But back at the apartment, when I saw Acek bent over the kitchen sink, drinking water and splashing some on his face, I came out of myself enough to see the extent of his distress.

"What have I done?" he murmured, staggering to the sofa. "I didn't think you'd end up—"

He dragged his hands over his features, then up again, as if he were trying to wipe his whole face off.

It was my turn to be strong.

"Acek. Look at me."

He didn't move.

"Look at me, Acek."

Gently but firmly, I pulled his hands apart.

"Acek, it's me. Vivi. *I'm* Vivi. Not her, me."

His eyes refocused. He nodded.

I'd never seen Acek like that—stolid, monotonic Acek. I made him lie down while I fixed us dinner: ryce, stir-fried gai lan, and baked beans. All the meat had run out by that point—soup bones, too—but thanks to all the rest and Acek's care, I was pretty much back to full health.

Over dinner, I grilled him about their conversation. He told me what she'd said about her condition and that she was seeing a specialist soon. He'd told her he was relocating to the country and moving in with his late brother's daughter.

I nodded. That was the plan: once there, we would live as uncle and niece.

I asked him whether she'd mentioned Gabe at all. Only in passing, he said. Gabriel was confident her health issues could be solved. Gabriel had taken on a new role at work in anticipation of the new-mother energy she would bring to domestic duties, so now he was stressed about having to help around the house and with Cloud.

Like the time Acek told me the logistics of how he had rescued me, his contempt for Gabe was more open than ever before. I understood why Acek had attempted to conceal it—I would have found the fact that he didn't like my husband upsetting. Now I found it freeing. Maybe I'd never liked Gabe much either. I must have confused his liking me with my liking him. I even felt pity for my old self—you—stuck with Gabe. I could imagine him chiding you in his on-the-surface good-humored way: for leaving dishes in the sink, for not putting things away, for not eating nutritiously or cooking well, for failing to function as well as he did, which was how everyone should.

And then, like before, anger grew: why should Gabe get to have our son—the son that I, with my own body, carried and bore? The body that Gabe couldn't wait to kiss goodbye? It served him right to get a worse version of me instead of the souped-up model he'd been looking forward to.

Again, that conviction, slightly more evolved but in essence the same: my son wasn't his, or yours. He was mine. And again, the sense that I should act on that conviction.

I think that was where the germ of the idea started, though it was some time before I persuaded myself and Acek to put it into action. In case you wanted to know.

*

In the meantime, believe it or not, I was too busy to come up with any evil plans. We were preparing for our move to the country, and I was busy committing the details of my new identity to heart. I helped Acek vacate the shop—at night, to avoid any of our neighbors seeing me. The morning he was due to turn in the keys, Acek went round to say his goodbyes. I wished I could have, too. Though I barely ever stepped out of the shop on workdays, there's a certain connection that comes from working alongside each other, day in and day out, on the same block. Acek told me that Fred the barber had even got all teary eyed.

"The smell was finally too much for you, eh, Arvin?" he joked. "Maybe I'll come visit and bring it with me."

When Acek told me this, I sat up. "He wouldn't, would he?" I asked. "Visit?"

"Unlikely," said Acek. "It's a fair drive. And even longer by train."

But he understood my worry. No matter how careful we were, someone was bound to recognize me someday. And word might get back to my old self, or Gabe, or Vera. I'd already started wearing light makeup, not just lipstick, in an effort to disguise my features. Acek borrowed books from the library, and I learned how to apply eyeliner, how to contour and highlight, how to pluck and pencil my eyebrows. It was unsettling, the difference it could make.

I might not even have gone so far as to get the procedure if it hadn't been for an incident that really rattled me. I ran into one of my old classmates at the supermarket.

"Vivian?"

I'd been contemplating the instant noodles. I shouldn't have turned, but it was too late.

There she was. Ellie. To be more specific, since there had been two Ellies in my class, Ellie J. She had a daughter of maybe eight or nine with her who stood to one side, fidgeting and looking bored.

"Vivian? Is that you? I almost didn't recognize you. You look great!"

I blinked. "Sorry?" I asked.

"Vivian?" she repeated. "It's Ellie Jensen. From school?"

I maintained my politely blank stare, and her certainty crumbled.

"Oh, I'm sorry! I thought you were someone else."

Poor Ellie J. It was always easy to make her blush. There was one year when some mean girls even took to calling her Tomato Face before they lost interest and found someone else to torment. As she turned and trundled her trolley away, her daughter trailing behind, I glimpsed a scarlet cheek through the strands of her hair as she glanced back for another look.

Once she was out of sight, I abandoned my groceries and hurried straight home.

Home. I was already calling Acek's apartment that, even though Acek had already given notice and set a move-out date. The place was crammed with boxes and junk we'd moved from the shop. In a few weeks, we'd be driving north to the new property.

When I blew in, Acek looked up from the workbench he'd set up between the lounge area and dining table. He'd been hard at work finishing some final jobs before the move.

"Someone recognized me," I panted. "Someone from school."

He listened calmly as I told him the whole story and gave a heavy sigh when I was done.

"I was worried about this," he muttered before meeting my gaze. "I have an idea. But maybe it's too extreme."

It was. But as the days passed, my uneasiness only grew. I asked Acek to make the phone call.

The plastic surgeon was, who else, an old mate of Acek's—though this time, Acek wouldn't say from where. The clinic interior was white and clean, though in a low three-story building that had seen better days. Acek came with me. We shared the waiting room with two young men, one with a crooked nose and a nasty scar down the length of his cheek. They were called in first.

"What kind of place is this, Acek?" I couldn't help but whisper.

"I've known him for ages," Acek reassured me. "He's top of the line."

When it was our turn, the doctor came out all smiles—a man about Acek's age, burly and bald, a back tattoo sprouting from the collar of his shirt, winding up the thick folds of his neck. They clasped each other's arms, clapped each other on the back, asked how the other was doing before referencing mutual friends from the old days.

"Hear from Mikey much?"

"Not at all. Get the news about Chin?"

"Yeah. Jace told me."

"How's Jace doing?"

"Still in it, believe it or not."

Acek's friend whistled. I still didn't know his name, or the name of the clinic. No signs anywhere. He ushered us into his office, and we all sat down.

"Related?" he asked. It was unclear whether he was addressing me or Acek, but Acek gave me a nudge.

"I'm Nina, his niece."

I'd spent the last few days memorizing the details of my new identity, but this was the first time I'd said my new name out loud. Contrary to what I expected, it made me feel confident. Bold. Like going out in public to show off a brand-new pair of trainers for the first time.

"What are you looking to get done?"

This was the part where I faltered. "Eyelids . . ." I began. "Maybe nose?"

We both turned to Acek, me for help, him for clarity.

Acek cleared his throat. "It's like this. She wants a fresh start. Thought a new face might help."

Acek's friend turned to me. "Look, darl. We don't need reasons, but you do have to know what you want."

What *did* I want? When was the last time I'd been presented with a chance to freely choose my future rather than simply go with the flow? Was it pregnancy? I had wanted a baby, but I didn't remember ever making the decision between having one and not. Same with marriage. Yes, I had wanted to marry Gabe. But when a guy is down on bended knee in a park under a hand-painted *MARRY ME* sign taped to a tree trunk while your brother-in-law takes photos, how can you refuse? Here, now, it was different: there was no path of least resistance. Eyelids, nose, cheekbones, jaw, chin—Acek and his friend were leaving it entirely up to me.

"A strong jaw," I said finally, nodding in Acek's direction. "Like my uncle's. But for women. And a slimmer nose."

Acek looked surprised, but his friend chuckled. "Now we're talking, darl."

Nine days later, I was biding my time in Acek's apartment, face wrapped in bandages, waiting to heal. In addition to the nose and jaw, I'd gotten my eyelids done too. Talk about mate's rates—speed-wise *and* fee-wise. When Acek told me the bill, I was stunned. Even with my lack of knowledge about going rates for cosmetic surgery, I knew Acek's friend had done it for cheap.

"What'd you do, save his life?"

Acek shrugged. "Something like that."

I was under doctor's orders to avoid strenuous activity during the healing process. Unfortunately, this meant saddling Acek with the bulk of the packing, loading, and cleaning in preparation for our big move. I felt guilty, but it couldn't be helped. Once the bandages were off and the sutures removed, I started going for walks, to keep from getting underfoot; Acek's apartment wasn't big enough for two. The swelling and bruising were still pretty bad—but I didn't mind. They made me unrecognizable. Sunglasses put too much weight on my face, but I still wore my baseball cap. The first morning, I started out with the intention of keeping to the area, but I soon found myself on a train bound for the station near the park where I'd first seen my son.

I sat on the bench where you'd fed Cloud a bottle, and the memory got me all upset again. Before I knew it, my feet were taking me to your place—once my place. I stood opposite and stared up the wall of glossy glass at the approximate spot where your apartment was. I checked my watch: ten in the morning. I walked away, only to return and sit on a discreet, sheltered ledge outside the building opposite yours. I'd never really noticed it before then. Funny, isn't it, how you can live somewhere, yet fail to notice all the little things?

I didn't intend to stay for long, but it was easier to stay than to go. An hour passed, then two. I wondered if you and my son had gone out already, or if you both were still inside. I got my answer when I spotted you down the street, carrying Cloud. You were heading home from something that had evidently exhausted you. You looked even worse than that day in the park, and Cloud looked more radiant by comparison—plump and healthy and happy. What was a girl like you doing with a baby like that? As you searched for the keys to let you in the front door, you turned your back to me completely, and I waved at my son. I thought I could see him contemplating me.

After you took Cloud in, I left. But I came back in the days following—the days I had left in this city. I returned at different times. Once to catch Gabe coming home from work. Since I was leaving, I thought I should say my goodbyes, for my own sense of closure if for nothing else. I was surprised to see how weary he looked, a far cry from his usual well-rested self. But other than that, I felt nothing else. I even spent some time rummaging inside me for emotions—love, longing, desire, et cetera. I tried to recall specific moments from my life with him: us sharing laughs, us going places, us eating dinner, us bickering, us having sex. When I recalled them, it was like watching a movie about someone else. It disturbed me, how removed I felt, as if I wasn't the same person anymore—though I was. More so, ironically, than if Acek hadn't intervened. I was more truly me than the defective version of me that was you; yet I was sure I felt less like the old me than you did. I had broken away, could forge my own path. You, on the other hand, were no better than a train, bound to follow the tracks that had been laid.

I saw you and my son only twice more—both times as you were leaving, rushing, obviously late for wherever you were going. The second time, I saw that you'd purchased a baby carrier to hold Cloud in; it was the model that Gabe and I had viewed in the baby shop when we were still pregnant. I felt okay with this. I would need a similar thing if I took my son back. Though I was in better shape than you, it wasn't as if I had any new-mother strength myself.

Like a good daughter and little sister, I did go round to Vera's. I didn't dare linger for fear of attracting the neighbors' attention—you remember from our sister's stories how nosy they were. But I stood outside our sister's gate and said goodbye in my head. It was evening and I could see the lights on inside. I pictured the whole family around the dining table: Vera, James, my nephew and nieces, and maybe, if they'd managed to drag him away from his TV, Pa. As with Gabe, it surprised me: how removed I felt, how unregretful. I felt relieved to be let go. Now that they had you, I could finally drift away.

*

All the space. That was the easiest thing to get used to out in the country. The house wasn't huge by house standards, but it felt massive after the cramped conditions of Acek's place. And it was certainly bigger than Gabe's apartment, which had been luxurious but compact. Regarding size and other features, Acek's house bore many similarities to the one that Vera and James owned—single-story, drafty, creaky timber floors. A key difference, though, was the price. I knew what my sister and brother-in-law were still paying off: triple what Acek had already paid in full. And where Vera and James had two small rectangles of lawn—out front and in back—Acek's house sat in the middle of a plot of land more expansive than anything I'd ever imagined myself living on. But the main reason behind Acek's choice hadn't been the house or even the size of the property. There was an enormous industrial shed out back, a little bigger than the house itself and practically new. The previous owner had erected it as a gift to himself in his retirement years, when he would finally have the time to tinker with old automobiles to his heart's content. Except it turned out he hadn't had any time left. He got diagnosed with stage-four terminal lung cancer. Within a few months he was dead.

This was the story the real estate agent had told Acek. The man's widow was a nice woman—had only wanted "a fair price," which, at country levels, Acek was happy to pay. Prices in the area, unfortunately for her, had plummeted ever since the new petrol regulations doubled driving times for waste-era vehicles. And, unfortunately, the property wasn't well-situated enough to lure any wealthy eco-car owners on the lookout for a holiday home.

For an extra five hundred, the widow even threw in an old sedan. It ran okay, but her late husband had been meaning to fix it up even more—"He always said it had potential," the widow told us when she handed over the keys. She'd wanted to meet us personally. She even showed us around the property. By then, with the aid of light makeup, I could go around in public with Acek without people wondering if I'd been beaten up and if he was to blame.

She really was a nice woman. She put her hand on Acek's shoulder and said, "I just want you to know. Barry always liked the Chinese. Good, hardworking people. He always thought Australia should establish better relations with your nation."

Acek nodded solemnly. "Thank you. It means a lot."

As we watched her son drive her away—he'd stayed in the car—I thought about what she'd said about what her late husband had said: about the old sedan having potential. The same could be said for me: I had potential. Always did. Now I was fulfilling it. I strolled round the edges of the whole property, then in and out of the shed. I felt like a pet dog in the park when the owner lets them go off-leash and they break into a mad dash, round and round, tongue flapping in the wind. This was the life. My life. A life that would have ended if Acek hadn't come to the rescue. I was meant to be alive. I surveyed the house on my right and the shed on my left, hands on hips, and took a deep breath of fresh country air. All I lacked was my son. The son that rightfully belonged to me. You were married to Gabe—you could always have more. Another rebirth would do your health good, anyway. I, on the other hand, wasn't planning to get married or pregnant again. I would remain myself, so Cloud was to be my only child.

Getting rid of you wasn't in the equation at all. Not at that stage. Only later did it become an unavoidable part of the plan. You know how it is. You start working on a microwave, thinking it's the HV diode, but it turns out to be the magnetron. So you open up the magnetron, optimistic that it'll be a straightforward filament issue, but it's just too compromised, so you end up having to throw it out and replace the whole thing.

One thing always leads to another. Acek and I should have anticipated that.

I eventually brought the idea up to Acek one evening. After several days, we'd finally finished cleaning out and wiring the shed.

"Let there be light," I announced, flicking the main switch, setting all the LED strips aglow.

"You going to say that every time you turn them on?" Acek joked.

Insects swarmed into the barn, hovering and clustering around the lights—moths, some beetles, and all kinds of flies. We plunked down in the pair of splintery rocking chairs Acek had salvaged the other day, opened two tinnies, and sat rocking in the wide-open doorway, peering out into the night. Bundled up in our nearly identical thick hoodies, jackets, and beanies, we were barely distinguishable, except for our faces.

Acek regarded mine. "I think I'm getting used to it," he said in a complimentary kind of way.

"Yeah, me too," I replied. I'd made it a practice to stare into the mirror a lot, to accustom myself. My nose was narrower, my eyes were rounder, and with the stronger chin and chiseled jaw, I felt leaner and meaner than ever before.

I felt it was a good time to raise the matter, or at least, test the waters. I'd waited so long because I was worried about how he'd react. After all, my new self was still me in a sense; if I weren't alive, you'd be the only me around. Now I was proposing that we take away your child. If Acek had cared enough about me to save my life, it would be only natural for him to still care about you—at least, enough not to hurt or distress you in any way.

"Thank you again, Acek," I began, carefully. "For rescuing me."

He gave a dismissive, embarrassed humph and kept his gaze on the dark outside.

I decided to come at it sideways. Draw him out first to get a better idea of where things stood.

"Do you regret any of it, Acek?"

"Regret what?"

"Saving me."

He regarded me, brow furrowed. "What kind of a silly question is that?"

"It's not," I protested. "What I mean is . . . Look, you saw her that day. How sick she was—and weak. She wouldn't be like that if rebirth had gone properly. If she'd eaten me, she'd be stronger than either of us. It's because I'm alive that she's like this."

He took a slow sip of beer. "Yeah," he assented at last. "Yeah, I know."

As the silence settled, I calculated my next move. To my surprise, he spoke first.

"You know, I've been thinking about it. What I'd do differently if I could do it over."

"What would you do differently?"

His gaze remained outward, into the trees, into the night.

"I would have killed her and taken the body away. And I'd have left you in the room."

He nodded slowly as he replayed the improved plan in his mind.

"Yeah, that's what I would have done. She wouldn't be in this bad state. You'd still have your old life. You'd get to be with your baby. Win-win-win."

His words should have pleased me—a clear sign that his allegiance lay with me, not you. Instead, I shivered.

I even found myself protesting. "I don't know, Acek. To be

honest, I'm kind of glad I'm not in my old life anymore. Besides, I don't have new-mother strength either. If you'd left me there, I might have ended up in the same condition as her."

I thought of Vera—of trying to do all she did without any of the strength or stamina or focus. I thought of how I'd have managed without all the rest Acek let me have and the nourishing meals he'd cooked for me. The answer: probably not well at all.

Remembering myself, I stepped out of your shoes and back into mine. "No, I don't miss my old life," I reflected. "But I do wish I could have taken the baby with me. I wish he were here with me now."

I let this sentiment hang in the air for a while. Then, as if something had just occurred to me, I turned to him. He was still staring out into the trees, rocking contemplatively back and forth.

"Hey, Acek?"

"Hmm?"

"Do you think it's too late?"

"What's too late?"

"Getting to be with my baby. You mentioned it just now."

He was silent for a while, as if trying to grasp the question. When he replied, his tone was gentle.

"I think so. I think so, Nina. I'm sorry, again."

It was a reply filled with spaces. Between the first and second "I think so"—a thoughtful pause, as if double-checking to confirm the impossibility of what I'd suggested. Before "Nina"—a recollecting pause, because we'd agreed that it was the name he should call me all the time now, just to be safe, and it still didn't quite roll off his tongue. Before the closing apology—a pause to give me space to absorb the sad but inalterable fact that I would never get back the baby I'd carried and birthed.

Before pregnancy, the uterus is no bigger than an orange. Even the smallest spaces provide room for things to grow.

"I wonder," I said after a pause of my own, "if she would find it a relief. As you said, she's not in a good state. Maybe it would be better to take the baby off her hands."

Acek's chair stopped rocking. "Kidnapping?"

"Not kidnapping," I reasoned. "He's my child, right?"

I shared my justifications: how you and Gabe could always have another child, but how I couldn't—not if I wanted to remain me. How having another child and going through rebirth again, properly, would restore your health.

He didn't respond. But he didn't object either.

Above us, the bugs were really going crazy, fluttering and zooming around those LEDs. As Acek and I sat quietly side by side, I felt it must be the same for the thoughts in our heads.

*

That became the intention. Not to kill you. Not to hurt you. To help you, in a way. Ironically, if that had stayed our plan, who knows whether we would have attempted to carry it out. Our distance from the city made it difficult to do any proper reconnaissance. Neither of us had any idea about your schedule nowadays, or Gabe's. Even if, ethically speaking, taking Cloud for my own was now permissible. Logistically speaking, the risk of failure was too great.

In the meantime, to Acek's relief, other things kept us busy. We officially opened for business—we needed the income badly after all the expense of relocating and saving my life. We had business flyers made and distributed, leaving them in letter boxes, posting them on telephone poles and community boards. Acek even had us going door-to-door, to shops and offices, asking to speak with whoever was in charge. He'd introduce us: Arvin and his niece Nina. We'd just relocated our hobbling business from Sydney and were new to the area.

"If you ever need repairs done, let us know. Here's our info. We'd appreciate the business very much."

I'd never seen Acek so affable. He always acted politely toward customers—but never as friendly as this.

"Where's the real Acek Arvin? What have you done with him?" I joked in a low voice as we walked out of one office.

He made a face. "You do what you have to," he mumbled, adjusting his polo-shirt collar and pasting on a pleasant smile before leading the way through the next door.

You do, I reflected later as we ate our packed lunches in the sedan. I thought about how hard it must have been for him when he first came to this country. How hard even Pa must have found it, and Vera, and little me too—though I didn't register it back then. My thoughts wandered even further up the line, to our great- or however-many-great-grandparents boarding the boats to Sumatra from Fujian. I even thought about Gabe's parents, coming here from New Guinea and India, and their forebears arriving in those places from wherever they'd originated in China. I thought of an electrical current—of electrons, like streams of people, repelled from negative to positive situations.

In the late afternoons, Acek taught me to drive. We had two cars now: the van and the sedan. Conveniently enough, the fake ID Acek managed to get for me was a driver's license, so I didn't have to sit a real test, just be good enough not to get pulled over. Not that my fake identity would ever let me take a real driving test, or access any government service ever again.

I still remember my favorite stretch of road—long, with no intersection or interruption, flanked on either side by trees and trees and trees. And to all appearances, flat, till the small rise followed by the sudden dip—a tiny roller-coaster–like plummet, if I gunned it right, that always sent my stomach fluttering and made me smile. I'd never imagined being able to drive myself someday. It was a skill Gabe took for granted, having grown up in a country town. But it had never occurred to me to envy him until now. I never realized what it would feel like, to be behind the wheel myself.

Eventually, we got customers. A trickle at first, of the usual jobs. TVs. Microwaves. Fridges. The odd DVD or CD player. Then, suddenly, the heavens opened, and business rained down.

Our door-to-door visits to random offices had paid off. Local businesses didn't have the budget to spend on expensive RDC equipment. And there was no stigma surrounding hobbled items here. A local gym chain asked us to supply their changing rooms with hobbled hairdryers. A law firm called us in to fix a 1990s Xerox photocopier, a job we pulled off by the skin of our teeth. Add to that the number of individuals who had household items that they'd been waiting for Billy's Boys—the other hobbler in the area—to get around to, and we had nearly triple the amount of work we had back in Sydney.

There was only one problem: we couldn't handle it all. If we wanted to keep up with customer demand, Acek would have to hire more employees. An unprecedented event for Arvin's Hobbling Services, but it seemed a shame to let our limited working capacity put a ceiling on our income.

I was also worried about what having extra employees around meant for getting Cloud back. We discussed it over breakfast one morning. Plain porridge. Not even the congee kind. Rather, the oat variety championed by health nuts. (While unpacking, I'd stumbled across an old blood test Acek had taken years ago, indicating he had high cholesterol. I'd asked Acek if he'd done anything about it, and he'd said yes, he hadn't gone to the doctor since.)

"If we do hire more people, it'll make things difficult," I remarked. "They're sure to ask questions if a baby turns up."

Acek sighed. "It's already difficult as it is. We still haven't come up with a plan. And that has nothing to do with having extra employees or not."

I supposed he was right, but I still felt uneasy about creating a situation that could be used as an excuse to never get Cloud back. With each passing week, I could feel him—the possibility of having him, holding him—slipping further and further away. At night, in the privacy of my bedroom, I would sit upright in bed or walk the room holding a bundle in my arms, pretending it was him. The bundle was a rolled-up scarf, which I swapped out for a rolled-up jumper as the weeks continued to slide by—my estimate of how big he was now. And he was growing every day.

But with the passage of time, I could also feel how my hunger for him was becoming increasingly artificial—a conscious attempt to recreate what I had felt on waking up in Acek's apartment and what had been reactivated upon seeing Cloud for the first time. It wasn't that my love for him was fading—that was untouchable, existing on another plane. It was my conviction that he belonged with me that was beginning to recede. He had you and Gabe, after all. And though you were in bad shape, I could tell how much you loved him, even from afar.

I did end up agreeing to more employees. It was clear we needed the help. Acek put up an ad at the local Chinese grocery, and wouldn't you know it, we got eight candidates calling before the week was out. We took three. One full-timer—a woman older than me but younger than Acek who had extensive experience in electronics repair—and two TAFE students looking for part-time work.

Having others around was strange at first. I began wearing makeup every day, taking refuge in the security of disguise. You could tell Acek wasn't used to additional company either, but over time, we grew used to their presence. Luckily, the new employees were hardworking and conscientious. Sometimes I wished the older woman, Lina, were more easygoing. But her primness and propriety helped lend the working environment a more serious air and kept the younger ones in check. If Acek, as their boss, was the uncle figure, then Lina, though younger than Acek, played the role of aunt.

I'd never worked in a group environment before, and I found it interesting to see everyone assume certain roles according to their individual personalities and quirks. Zoe was the cheerful, playful one. Libby who was white, was quirky, with a bit of punk-rebel thrown in.

Maybe it was this new community that encouraged my new identity as Nina to develop further, honing it into something sharper and more distinct than it would have otherwise been. Not that my new role was entirely unlike me—but it was more pronounced, an exaggerated version of myself. I had always been quiet. But in the context of this new "work family" I became "the quiet one." In group settings, I'd always tended to hang back rather than participate, but now I was "reserved"—though not "standoffish," to my relief.

Because everyone believed Acek was my biological uncle, they tended to see my traits as a version of his. And because of the backstory Acek had come up with for me—the same one he'd told you that day on the park bench—I cut a tragic figure, suddenly orphaned, except for my uncle, all alone in the world.

Initially, it surprised me to see how I appeared in the eyes of others. As a business, we got a tax break for providing carpool services to employees, and I remember driving one morning, Lina next to me and Zoe in the back, when Lina turned and asked me in her direct way, "Was it difficult to drive again after your parents died in that car crash?"

"Lina!" exclaimed Zoe from the back seat.

"What? If that happened to me, I'd be too scared to set foot in a car again!"

I remember feeling flustered—but funnily enough, not for the reasons they thought. Where I felt as if they were on the verge of uncovering my lie, they thought the question was too personal, too insensitive. It made me realize that it wasn't me they saw, but the skin I was inhabiting. Tragic, reserved Nina.

"Yes," I said. "But I don't want to talk about it."

It was as easy as that.

What a revelation—that I now had an outer layer, not *not* me, exactly, but not entirely me either. Like a hoodie. Thick and padded, but only given form by the body inside. Looking back now, it was eerily fortunate that I would have developed a unique persona, separate from you, before you and Cloud arrived.

I remember the evening Acek told me the news. It was approaching summer, and the days were growing longer again. I was in the lounge room putting up some curtains I'd found in an op shop two weekends before. They were threadbare—their previous owner must have washed them regularly—but they were such a pretty shade of pale blue. When I looked at them, I felt as if the sky were coming in through my eyes.

He told me you'd called him earlier in the day.

"How's Cloud?" was the first question out of my mouth.

"She didn't say. But I didn't ask."

I was standing on a stepladder at the time and had just lofted the pole bearing the new curtains into place. I knew Acek well enough to know that he had more to say if I gave him time. He cleared his throat.

"She asked if she could come here. With the baby. She wants her old job back. She and Gabe are getting divorced."

I nearly fell off the stepladder. But I regained my footing.

"What happened?" I asked, hopping down.

"I don't know exactly. But she said Gabe can't take her condition anymore."

Though it was no longer my blow to bear, I felt it, the breath knocked out of my lungs. And then the fury and disbelief. How dare he. First he'd kissed me goodbye, and now he was doing the same to you.

"So, what did you say?" I asked, still trying to process what Acek had just told me.

"I said yes, of course, she and the baby could come."

This was still more to process. I sat down on the stepladder. He sat down on the sofa. We listened to the crickets chirping outside.

He broke the silence. "With them here, it'll be easier. For you to get Cloud back."

"I know," I replied.

Still, neither of us spoke or moved. For me, it was the shock. In the span of a few seconds, what I had wanted so badly and was so out of reach had drifted once again into my grasp. But there was also the tragedy of it. We were two hunters who had laid a snare. But the creature limping into it was already trailing blood.

"So they couldn't fix what's wrong with her?"

"I guess not."

"How did she sound?"

He looked even more troubled than before.

"Hopeful," he said. "It made her really happy when I said she and the baby could come."

"So . . . when will they arrive?" I couldn't help but ask. It was important. Even if we didn't have the heart to do it in the end, we had to be ready.

"A few weeks, she reckons. She hasn't even told her—I mean, your—sister and father. And there'll be legal stuff. Who knows how long that'll take."

Her—your—. Understandable—everything was collapsing in again, Vivi and Nina colliding. What was yours was mine.

"If she's here," I observed, "taking Cloud will be easier, but also harder. What will happen after we take him? She'll be here too."

He nodded like his head was made of lead.

"We'd have to do something about her, if you want to take Cloud and keep him. She can't stay around."

The gravity of what he meant sank into me, and suddenly, I too felt weighed down.

"No, Acek." I shook my head. "No, no. We can't do that."

Wearily, he leaned forward over his paunch, resting his forearms on his knees, and looked me in the eye.

"Nina," he said. And the way he said it was deliberate. Nina over Vivi.

"Nina," he repeated. "We wouldn't have a choice."

V.

You ended up taking two months to arrive. As you provided Acek with updates, Acek, in turn, would update me. Gabe wanted to leave you, and you wanted to leave Gabe, but that didn't make it easy. Gabe suggested marriage counseling, in case it was possible to reconcile—about what exactly, you still wouldn't say. All you said was that a counselor would only try to pressure you into changing your mind, and you didn't want your mind changed. Plus, everyone was already trying to convince you to stay: Vera; James, as mobilized by Vera; not Pa, of course—Pa remained in his own world, swaddled in blankets, sitting in his room, watching Chinese palace dramas. But even Gabe's family made an effort. You hadn't seen his mother since the wedding, but she made the sixteen-hour train trip interstate and showed up at your door. I recalled her as a plump, jovial woman with merry eyes. I imagined them darkened by sadness, or maybe even anger. She, too, had begged you to change your mind, insisting on how much her son loved you, entreating you to think of the baby, at which you retreated and locked yourself and Cloud in the bedroom. You refused to come out or let Gabe in until his mother had left. You thought of moving out right away, but what little savings you had would be drained by even the cheapest of hotels. And you didn't want to stay with Vera and have her try to talk you out of it every day.

You and Gabe agreed to a truce of sorts. He would stop trying to get you to change your mind as long as you stayed in Sydney long enough to finalize the paperwork for the divorce—it would be easier that way. He moved into the room that was meant to be Cloud's once he got older. He requested to spend more time with Cloud before you left and took him away. He offered to cook dinner for as long as you stayed. A model husband and father to the end.

One could almost forget that he was the one who wanted the divorce, not you. That, for everyone's focus on getting you to change your mind about what he wanted you to change your mind about, no one thought once of asking him to change his—because his request was seen as reasonable, and your refusal of it wasn't. You vented but still wouldn't tell Acek the exact issue, as if, for all your rage, you were nonetheless ashamed.

Acek let you talk. What choice did he have? He couldn't hang up. But I know it made him uneasy, listening to you speak for so long—you, the false me. Hearing your story made him sympathize, which was what he didn't want to do. It made what we were planning even harder than it already was. But it was clear that you were desperate for moral support.

I listened in, my ear close to Acek's, and felt bad for you. But not bad enough to hope you wouldn't walk into our trap. Eventually, everything was settled. You set a date for your arrival—you and Cloud would be taking the train. Acek and I would pick you up from the station and take you to your new home.

Acek had found a place for you to rent—a small, cheap house

near a useful bus route, but still a fair way off from any of the towns. Gabe had offered financial support, but you'd refused. I understood. You didn't want to feel indebted. It was exactly what I would have done. The house was isolated enough that there were barely any neighbors to speak of. A peaceful area hemmed in by trees. I once watched a program on TV about slaughtering cattle—how cows were calmed by enclosed spaces because it simulated the protection of a herd. How the humane way to kill a cow was to lead it down a narrow tunnel and have a machine give it a big hug before another machine put a bolt through its brain.

And for all my heart bled for you, when we met you at the train station, I only had eyes for Cloud. He was strapped to your front as you carried your backpack on your back, both arms rolling two big suitcases, a car seat balanced on one of them. Unlike last time, he was facing out, not in toward your chest. He really had grown. His head eclipsed the bottom half of yours. As Acek and I walked over to help you with the luggage, I wanted to ask if he could talk yet, or walk. He was nearly one. But I kept my mouth shut. I didn't even dare look at you, though I was wearing full makeup and sunglasses. What if you recognized me? All would be lost.

When you turned to Acek to tell him something, I darted my hand out and gave Cloud a quick stroke on the head. His hair was so soft. His head was so little. It was like stroking a rabbit or bird. He stared at me with wide eyes, and I wondered if he sensed who I was—if he knew I was his real mother, the one who had carried him and given him birth.

I helped lug the suitcases up the porch steps, then waited in the van while Acek took you inside. The last person who lived there had died there—it had been his house—and the son had asked if we wanted to keep any of the old stuff. I'd helped Acek throw out the bed and buy you and Cloud a new mattress, but the rest of the stuff wasn't bad. Prior to your arrival, we'd outfitted you with everything: hobbled stove, fridge, microwave, washing machine, phone. We'd even bought you supplies—groceries and the like, to get you started in your new home. At the time, it felt like we were furnishing a dollhouse, and as I watched the three of you enter, I thought of you as the doll and me as the girl.

Acek came out soon after.

"That didn't take long," I observed.

He looked dazed, like he had that day, months ago, when he'd met you in the park. But he tried to shake it off.

"I didn't want to . . ." he mumbled. But his explanation trailed off as he reversed out onto the road and drove us back home.

I didn't press him. I was feeling stunned myself. Had you really come? Had you really brought me my son? Were we really going to do what we had to, so Cloud would be mine?

When we arrived back at the house, Acek turned the engine off and finished what he had started to say.

"I didn't want to forget that you're you."

Then, to my surprise, he broke down sobbing. In my whole life, I'd never seen Acek like that. He cried for a long time. Whenever it seemed like the tears were about to subside, another wave would come, and he would start again. It reminded me of vomiting—when you stay at the toilet bowl, trying to force yourself to vomit more to get it all out, so you won't have to come back later and do it again. And I rubbed his back like I would if he were being sick, up and down, the palm of my hand consoling him. *There, there.*

I don't know how long we stayed in the van, but eventually he was done. He wiped his face on his jacket sleeve. Then he looked at me full in the face.

"Nina," he said, his eyes still red, his nose still running, his face still puffy, "tell me the truth. Do you still want Cloud back?"

If he'd phrased it any other way.

But he was exhorting me to be truthful. "Yes, Acek, I want him back."

But I also felt sorry for him. How could I force him to commit such a deed?

"Acek," I said gently, though I didn't want to give Cloud up. "It's okay. Let's forget about it."

He shook his head. "No, it's my fault," he murmured. "You didn't ask for this. What was I thinking, separating you from your child?"

"Acek. You did your best. If it weren't for you, I'd be dead."

But he shook his head again. "I'm responsible for this situation. I have to finish what I began."

Then he took a deep breath and got out of the van.

I followed, frightened yet grateful. Frightened by the magnitude of what we were about to embark on. Grateful that Acek was determined to go ahead. I wouldn't have done such a thing without Acek's help. It would have been impossible. But I knew Acek, and I sensed that he wouldn't turn back. And I knew that if he didn't turn back, I wouldn't either. Our course was set.

By the time we reached the house, you could hardly tell he'd shed a tear. And as the rest of the afternoon progressed, he seemed to harden. By dinnertime, he was made of stone.

*

It was this stone face that you'll remember, I'm sure. I'd watch whenever he turned it to you, and feel your heart break afresh each time, almost as if it were mine. Acek had already taken pains to be on his guard when interacting with you, but that afternoon marked a definite turning point. He'd flicked a switch and gone cold.

The sad thing was, over time, after your initial confusion, you seemed to adapt. You gradually stopped seeking any warmth from him, then tried to act aloof as well. That was the strangest thing about watching you—feeling as if I knew what was going on inside, witnessing me endure circumstances that I would never have been able to bear.

I also watched as your initial optimism and determination began to dwindle to an alarming degree. On your first day at work, you had the air of a hopeful, fresh-faced employee, even when Acek assigned Lina the task of showing you around instead of doing it himself.

"This is Vivian. She's new here. And this is her son."

That was the whole of Acek's introduction, and I saw your face fall even as you worked hard to maintain your smile.

I remained at my workstation, my gaze following you discreetly as Lina gave you a tour, showing you where we kept everything, making the rounds to introduce you to everyone. After visiting Libby's bench, you stopped at mine.

"Nina, this is Vivian. She just started working here. And this is her son, Cloud."

I took a deep breath and looked up at you, holding my child.

"We met the other day," I said in the low monotone I'd been using since moving here. Now, in your presence, it rang artificial in my ears. My heart began to race.

"I helped my uncle pick her up from the station," I explained to Lina. Then I reached out to tickle my son's foot.

"Nice name—Cloud," I remarked casually. "How'd you come up with it?"

I cursed myself for talking so much. You'd find me out for sure.

"Thanks. I was looking out the hospital window while holding him for the first time. And I saw a single cloud in the sky. It just felt right somehow, didn't it?" you asked Cloud.

He didn't answer, of course, or even look at you. He was just a baby after all. But the strangest thing was that I felt this somehow disappointed you—another snub from someone to whom you believed you were close. I noticed a twinge of discomfort cross your face as you shifted your hold on him.

You noticed I noticed. You turned away in embarrassment.

"Let me show you the bathroom," said Lina, leading you away. "We just use the one in the house, but if you need to clean off beforehand, there's a tap outside."

As the three of you left the shed, I exhaled in relief and glanced over at Acek, who was working on a set of vintage lamps. Our eyes met briefly, and he nodded. We had passed the first test.

Since it was your first day, Acek drove you and Cloud back home on the earlier side. He had driven you here too, but starting tomorrow, you and Cloud would take the carpool with Lina and Zoe, driven by me.

Once you were gone, the whole shed took an unofficial tea break, gathering in the kitchen corner—a folding table with a hobbled kettle and microwave—to chat about you.

"What's wrong with her? Do you know?" asked Lina. "Didn't she just have a baby?"

"Rebirth complications," I said.

"I didn't even know that was a thing," breathed Zoe, aghast.

Libby looked equally shocked. I tried not to be annoyed. It wasn't their fault they didn't know, just as it hadn't been mine.

"It's very rare. Hardly ever happens," Lina reassured them before remembering to be sympathetic. "Poor woman," she added hastily.

Then she probed further. "She mentioned she used to work for Arvin back in Sydney."

I nodded.

"Does she have a husband? Did the baby's father move up here too?"

"I think he left her," I said.

Lina shook her head in solidarity. She, too, had an ex.

"What a dick," Libby remarked.

"Where's her family?" asked Zoe. "Doesn't she have anyone to take care of her and the baby?"

How innocent her question was. And the way she asked it—wide-eyed, as if she couldn't imagine family not helping one of their own.

"I guess not," I said. And when the words were out, even I felt bad for my former self.

When the water in the kettle finally boiled, the conversation had moved on.

*

Months passed. More time than either Acek or I had intended, but a disappearance and kidnapping was hardly something we wanted to rush. At night, we worked on soundproofing the spare room in preparation for holding Cloud there. It was at the far end of the house, well away from the kitchen and bathroom, which Acek allowed employees to use. Nonetheless, we always kept it locked.

Soundproofing took longer than anticipated. Proper supplies

took a while to arrive. There were other arrangements that had to be made too: Acek had to find someone trustworthy to help Cloud and me obtain the right documents once we reached Medan.

Medan made the most sense, logistically. Acek still had some connections there, and documents would be easier to obtain. But the idea of moving back still felt strange.

"It's like regressing or something," I joked one night as we worked on the spare room. "You took so much trouble to move Pa and us here, and now I'm going back."

"Makes sense when you think about it," remarked Acek after a time. "The old you going back to the old place."

"Yeah," I laughed—the laugh I'd laugh if we were discussing *the plan*, as we came to call it. A half-hearted chuckle. An attempt to set my conscience at ease. Laughter. The best medicine.

At least it was a part of the plan I could chuckle about. There was one part that was no laughing matter. Late one night, I was to show up at your house and drug you. Then I was to drown you—fill the bathtub, place your head in, leave you be. The easiest, most bloodless way. In order to reach that step, I had to gain your trust. Again and always, that image: that road, and the steps required to reach its end. I'd merely swapped one path for another. No, not even swapped. Ironically, this road would lead me back to the old road—a winding detour returning to a version of the original route laid out for me. *Motherhood, here I come.*

More months passed. Even after everything was in place and ready, inertia set in. Or reluctance. Whatever you want to call it. To swing a hammer, you have to raise it first. You were still struggling, that much was clear, but despite that, you and Cloud seemed to be building a new life here—and no matter how much time went by, it seemed too soon to smash it into smithereens.

The presence of a baby lent the shed a homelike feel, and the other employees' attitudes grew more familial as well. About a week after you started work, Zoe brought in a used dog playpen. She'd been over at a classmate's house and spied it lying disassembled in the corner of the garage. The classmate's father had once bred beagles, and the pen had kept the puppies contained.

"Don't get offended," Zoe warned you as she brought it out of the boot. I'd just done the carpool run, and we were all getting out. "I know it's for dogs, but when I used to watch my little brothers and sisters, I wished I had something like this. It's still in good condition. We can disinfect it too."

Lina, ever sensitive, scoffed. "Don't be ridiculous, Zoe. What kind of new mother needs a cage to keep their kid safe?"

The answer, of course, was you. I saw you redden and say you'd think about it. That was the day Cloud tried to grab an uninsulated wire and nearly electrocuted himself. We set up the pen right after.

That was the start of it. Everyone began chipping in. Zoe brought in a playmat from a classmate's sister. Libby found a play kitchen on the curb with *TAKE* taped to the wooden fridge door. Whenever someone visited an op shop, they'd scour the toy section for anything good.

Up to that point, I'd only ever risked stealing moments. Small ones. Stroking his head on the first day. Tickling his foot when you stopped by my desk. Pulling a face and making him smile. Waving at him. Reaching for his hand and giving it a little bob. They were few enough to count. I was too worried you'd see it—the way my whole being hungered for him, and then, the resemblance between my being and yours. I stayed away, observing from afar, keeping my gaze transitory or indifferent, all the while burning inside.

Zoe was the one who began offering to watch Cloud whenever she happened to be between tasks and saw you needed some help. I took the idea from her. I suggested to Acek that he offer to watch you sometimes, so he could pass Cloud to me. I still didn't dare to offer to care for him myself.

I still remember being alone with Cloud for the first time. By alone, I mean away from you. The part-timers weren't there that day. You were working to a deadline—a bakery needed their stand mixer repaired by tomorrow, and Cloud was having *that kind of day*. That's what our sister used to call it, remember? During Terry and Matt's toddler years, when the most absurd thing would send them into a rage? We'd go over for dinner as usual, and Terry would be screaming about how the tofu cubes were the wrong size. Or Matt would be on the floor, kicking and punching the air because his favorite set of pajamas was in the wash. And our sister could quiet them in an instant—as new mothers were capable of doing, effortlessly, as nature intended. *This is the nth time I've done this today*, she'd laugh lightly. Just part and parcel of motherhood. But slightly different for you, given your inability to effectively calm.

You were sitting in the playpen rocking Cloud, trying to soothe him. I remember seeing you lift your head to look at the enormous mixer requiring your attention, and I felt the yearning in your gaze. How you longed to be there, completing a task you were proficient at, instead of where you were, helpless despite all your effort. I understood all too well—and yet, again, I felt that same spark of anger as whenever I witnessed your incompetence in caring for our son. I was just about to go get Acek, to ask if now was the time to offer help. But he was ahead of me. I saw him approach you and, after a short discussion, he exited the playpen with Cloud in his arms. As you returned eagerly to the mixer, he carried Cloud out of the shed. I let a few minutes tick by before making my own casual exit. On the shaded side of the shed, he handed our son to me. My son. I pressed him to me. How small and warm he was. I never wanted to let him go.

But of course, I had to. I spent five minutes with him before Acek brought him into the house to eat biscuits in the kitchen. I returned to the shed and resumed working on a stained-glass lamp as if nothing had happened at all. I counted twenty-two minutes until Acek came back in with Cloud, who was crying for you. And, secretly, I bemoaned the extra time I probably could have stolen without you being aware.

Acek and I grew better at finding ways to sneak me more time with Cloud. He came back from WholeSale the following weekend with two massive jars of jellybeans. He would slip them to Cloud one at a time, and soon, Cloud didn't hesitate to cast himself into his arms. One Saturday, at a fundraising sale in the local community center, I came across a windfall of old kids' DVDs. With their help, keeping Cloud entertained was a piece of cake.

He was growing up so fast. Since you'd joined us, Cloud had learned how to walk and talk. You were worried he was developing on the slower side, but I was simply in awe of how he could speak or walk at all.

I still remember one sunny day when I was watching him outdoors. By that time, I'd grown bolder, stopped worrying that spending any time with Cloud was suspicious. On occasion, I offered to babysit him too. It was prime dandelion season, and Acek's property had broken out in yellow flowers and white puffs. Who'd have thought, but Cloud preferred the flowers. With my help, he was making a bouquet.

I spotted a cheerful colony of them.

"Look! So many!" I cried, running over to lead the way.

I don't think I'd ever seen anyone look so happy. As if it were the first time anyone in the universe had smiled. All joy in the history of the world paled in comparison to his.

From where he'd been squatting, he wobbled to his feet, the flowers he'd already collected clutched securely in a chubby fist.

"You can make it!" I cheered.

The distance hadn't seemed an especially great one, but as I watched our son teeter through the long grass, I realized it was no small feat for him.

I kept up the encouragement.

"Almost there!" I exclaimed, stretching out my hands.

When he reached my fingertips, I leaned forward and pulled him the rest of the way into my embrace. I even kissed his cheek.

"Good job!"

We beheaded all the blossoms. I carried him back into the shed so he could present them to you.

*

Then, out of nowhere, a year had passed. Summer had rolled around again—the same time last year when we'd gone to the train station to pick you up. Acek was the one who called attention to it. He was sitting at the dining table studying the calendar we'd got from the Chinese supermarket. They gave them out free with minimum $88 purchases toward the end of every Western calendar year.

Acek lay a broad finger on a square in early February and tapped.

"Sincia's coming up," he observed. "Last year, it fell earlier. In late Jan."

I'd been wiping the kitchen counters. Rag in hand, I looked up.

"Guess so," I said.

He paused before he spoke. "Vivi and the baby came up about that time. A little after."

I was silent.

He continued. "Cloud's getting bigger. Not a baby anymore."

"He's not even two," I replied, trying to keep my tone light.

"He's two next month," countered Acek. Then more quietly. "The older he gets, the more difficult it will be."

"Yeah," I acknowledged at last. "Yeah, I know."

Up to that point, I'd been keeping a certain distance from you. Not an unfriendly one, but we barely spoke or interacted. This was made easier by the fact that, by that point, you were far from friendly yourself. Your health and mood seemed to have grown steadily worse over the course of the year—the toll of caring for a spirited toddler in your condition, all by yourself. In fact, forgive me for saying so, but you'd become withdrawn and irritable. The worst part was watching you take Cloud for granted. Sometimes you even lost your patience with him, which was shocking to witness. Who'd ever heard of a new mother getting angry at her own child?

I mustered all the maternal indignation I could as I sat looking at the calendar with Acek, and we set a date to put the plan's final stage in motion: the first day of Lunar New Year. Acek had been thinking of hosting a New Year's Eve dinner for all of us—a way of celebrating more than a year in business. If he did, then he'd give everyone the following day off. I would find an excuse to spend the day with you and Cloud, and begin the long-delayed task of gaining your trust. Fortunately, a few days before New Year's Eve, a man in Kempsey called, saying he had some spare parts we might like to look at. He described a few of them.

If they were as he said, they'd be worth the trip. And it provided the perfect excuse to lure you out.

I was so nervous on the drive up that I barely opened my mouth. As if I hadn't driven you to and from work five days a week for the past year. But this time was different: we were alone, and you were sitting next to me instead of in the back. I remember thinking I didn't need to talk your ear off, but I certainly should make an effort. I even scolded myself at one point: *What's wrong with you? Don't you want your son back?*

At a red traffic light close to Kempsey, I craned my neck to look at Cloud's sleeping form in the rearview mirror. I did want him. I did. I took a deep breath and pulled myself together. My son was at stake.

The transaction went smoothly. We found the place easily. As you and I sorted and priced, I marveled at how eerily in sync we were—clear evidence that our minds had once been one and the same. After the haggling was done, the man turned friendlier. Gave Cloud his dead daughter's plush lion and got teary, which nearly broke my heart. Turned out he was Aboriginal—Wiradjuri—and heading back to country. His father didn't have long to live.

To my surprise, he looked at me and asked, "Ever think of going back?"

"To Indonesia?" you added.

My heart stopped. I really thought the game was up. How did you know—how did he know—that the plan was for me to take Cloud back to Medan?

But then you and he continued talking, and I realized that I'd misunderstood. That wasn't what either of you meant. It was all I could do to keep from laughing in relief.

My confidence grew at the beach, bolstered by getting to play with Cloud in full sight of you. I raced the waves with him. I swung him and spun him and dipped him as you trailed behind us and watched. I won't lie about how triumphant I felt, the sea wind whipping through my hair, the salt-sticky clutch of his hands in mine. You and I had done battle, and I had won, and Cloud was my rightful prize to parade around. I was confident enough to make better conversation over lunch, keeping in character all the while. Acek's niece, quiet and tragic. Though at one point, I accidentally hit a nerve while trying to sound sympathetic, which sent you into silence for a long time.

After the beach, I drove us to a playground teeming with new mothers. The contrast between you and them was startling. I got to take a few turns on the slide with Cloud in my lap, and I got to push him a bit on the swing. But the victory I'd felt at the beach was gone, replaced by pure pity for you. I watched another mother help you by picking Cloud up and carrying him to the top of the slide, and how you took the gesture like a blow to the head. I watched another mother nearly make you cry at the swings, and it was too much to bear. I scooped Cloud off the swing and herded us away to safety. I bought us ice cream. As we sat on a bench, safely away from the mothers, I felt strangely protective. Like a sheepdog. Like a father—a storybook one—protecting his family, keeping danger at bay. The feeling stayed all through the drive back, and even when you invited me in. *Enough for today*, I thought, alarm bells ringing. *Don't get drawn in too much.*

But after a brief inward tussle, my lips formed their reply anyway: "Sure."

This was the first time I'd stepped foot inside your house. It was good for me to be there, I reasoned. I could familiarize myself with the layout. It would prove useful when I came back to drown you and take our child. But even as I used my end-goal of killing you to rationalize my presence, I tried to push it out of my mind. Yes, that would happen—the unthinkable—but not right now. Not in this moment, which had its own timeline, its own self-contained present and future—you, me, our child under one roof, happily existing in one space. I sat on the sofa in your messy lounge room and played happily with our son as you pottered around the kitchen making afternoon tea. And I had that feeling again—of squinting at a blurry photo—an image developing, but never fully—of waiting for colors to deepen, lines to sharpen, a world to come into clear view.

You broke the spell.

"You're good with kids. Have you thought about having any yourself?"

I remember blinking. What were you talking about? We did have one. He was right here.

I blinked again.

The image resolved, with startling clarity—but a different one, not the image I'd been craning to see. Not a new world but this one. I recalled myself and the part I had to play. In my fluster to avoid suspicion, I blurted the first lie that came to mind.

"I can't have children."

I don't know why I said it. As your eyes widened and you apologized for asking, I cursed myself for creating yet another lie to keep track of. I left as soon as I could, my breath hard in my mouth. Driving back, I nearly hit a kangaroo. It bounded out from the trees, and I swerved hard to avoid it. If there had been any oncoming traffic, I'd probably be dead. Like my pretend parents. I pulled over to the shoulder of the road and came to a stop. The driver behind me got out of his van to see if I was okay.

"You're not supposed to swerve," he scolded after making sure I was unharmed. "You'll cause a big accident. If a roo's in the road, better brake or slow down."

"I know," I said shakily. "I just forgot."

I thanked him. With a parting look of disapproval, he got back in his van and drove on.

I was fully gathered by the time I got home. Acek came out of the shed at the sound of me pulling in. I wondered if any of us had actually taken the day off.

"How did it go?" asked Acek.

"Good," I said, before updating him about the new lie. We'd agreed long before that it was crucial we keep our stories in sync. For some reason, I didn't feel like mentioning the roo. But I'd think about it again, on and off, over the next several days.

More specifically, what that guy said. Which is what every driver in Australia's supposed to know when it comes to kangaroos. You're not supposed to swerve.

Don't swerve, I'd tell myself whenever I thought I was getting cold feet again.

*

What had changed?

On some level, nothing. I still wanted Cloud—more than ever, in fact. Now that I saw him, touched him, spoke with him on an almost daily basis, I was addicted. I couldn't imagine him not being part of my life or me not being part of his. I woke up on Saturdays leaning toward Monday like a plant stretching for the sun. I remembered how I used to bundle up clothing and cradle it as if it were him. How silly. It was impossible to ever go back to that.

On some level, everything. Because even as I still wanted Cloud, I found that I also wanted you to live, to heal, to thrive. For a year, I'd remained aloof in order to avoid detection. Now I knew there was another reason, whether or not I'd been conscious of it: that I might get too close, that I'd feel too sorry for you, even though I knew you would have killed, eaten, and replaced me without any remorse.

But that wasn't your fault. Remorse comes with awareness, with memory. You wouldn't have recalled anything. Me, on the other hand—I would remember. I was aware. Could I live with what I was about to do?

On the other hand, could I live without doing it? Could I live knowing that I'd given up my child?

I stayed on script. As intended, our day out had kindled familiarity between us—even more than I'd originally planned. All I had to do was keep it going. So I offered help when you looked like you needed it. I asked how you were. I responded amiably when you did the same. When I was making coffee or tea, I asked if you wanted some as well. If you seemed to be having a difficult time with Cloud, I offered to take him off your hands for a while. You even began to request my assistance when it came to taking care of him. Could I watch him while you used the bathroom? Would I mind getting the wipes out of your backpack? Could I see if Cloud had left Ion in the sedan?

"Things seem to be going well," observed Acek one day as he stopped by my bench. I was fixing an electric fan, but I knew he wasn't talking about that.

"Yeah," I murmured, spotting the severed wires. The stator needed to be replaced.

Out of the corner of my eye, I saw him linger, then walk away.

Later, I'd wonder whether I would have sensed what was wrong if only I'd glanced up. Or heard the breathlessness in his voice. Or noticed the slowness in his gait. Five, ten minutes later, I heard a dull clatter. I looked up to see Acek crumpled in a heap on the floor, his trusty thermal mug leaking coffee, on its side.

"Shit! Arvin's dead!" yelled Lina, racing over—along with the rest of us.

Perhaps out of annoyance, he stirred and groaned.

"I'll call Triple 0," piped Zoe.

"No, no," mumbled Acek, struggling to get to his feet. He got as far as his knees. "I'm not paying the ambulance charge."

"I'll drive him," I said, lifting his arm over my shoulder. "Help me load him into the sedan."

Soon, he and I were speeding to the hospital, Acek groaning and bathed in sweat, the car engine rattling in protest whenever the speedometer indicator ticked above 45.

"Don't," wheezed Acek. "You'll damage the engine."

Teeth gritted in frustration, I stopped trying to make the car go faster than it could.

Acek began to mutter. Soon I realized they were instructions: the name of the drug to slip in your drink; the dosage; where he kept the key to the room for Cloud.

"Tell me later, Acek," I said.

His words were labored when they came. "Maybe. There's no. Later."

"Don't say that. We're almost there."

As I sat in the waiting area, hoping someone would come out and give me news, I gave myself permission to throw hope out the window. What if Acek was right? What if he died?

Then my next, selfish, thought: would I be able to carry out the plan myself? I already knew the answer. It would be impossible. Losing Acek would mean surrendering Cloud. Simple as that.

Eventually, a man in scrubs called for me: "Family of Arvin? Arvin Ja-putt-ra?"

"Ya-poot-ra," I corrected, absentmindedly.

"Your relative has a major blockage in his aorta. He needs stents. We're waiting on the surgeon for an emergency angioplasty."

"Will he be okay? What are his chances?"

He eyed me cautiously. Was I the type who could handle more information, or should he keep it vague?

"It's never a hundred percent, but these types of situations usually turn out. We just ran some tests, and there doesn't seem to be any immediate danger. After this surgery, he may have to return for another one, but most likely, he'll be all right."

I shut my eyes and thanked the universe for saving Acek's life.

The nurse said they were going to admit him for the surgery. Did I want to see him beforehand? The answer was obviously yes. When we reached the examination room, the mere sight of him made me burst into tears of relief. He was sitting in a chair, still hunched in pain and coated with sweat.

I squeezed his hand. "They said you'll be okay, Acek."

"I know," he panted, squeezing back. "I know."

At the nurse's request, I moved the sedan to the main car park. While walking to the canteen, where I'd agreed to meet you all, relief washed over me again. In light of his near death, Acek saving my life took on new significance. He had sacrificed a great deal to rescue me and help reclaim my child. It would be unthinkable to let that go to waste.

I was filled with new purpose. The world had never looked so vivid. What I had to do never seemed so clear. When I updated you all about Acek, I felt Cloud's presence, bright and warm as fire, as you held him and listened, though I kept my gaze away. The others left, but you insisted on staying. I could tell how worried you were about Acek—even more than I was in that moment. Ironic, given what Acek and I were planning to do to you. But your distress made it difficult for me to refuse you. What was the harm, I thought. I soon found out.

How pale you turned as we walked through the hospital to the waiting area where the nurse had told me to go. I couldn't help but ask if you were all right, and eventually you told me: bad memories from all the time you spent in hospitals and clinics after Cloud was born. The doctors had been concerned about him, given your condition. And they'd tried to piece together what had happened. I confess, for a split second, I was alarmed, but the diagnosis turned out to be wrong.

"Malabsorption," you said.

I shifted uneasily as you explained it. I don't think you noticed my discomfort. You were so eager to tell me, as if you'd been dying for a friend to talk to all this time. How could I tell you I wasn't that friend? How could I tell you that I was, in fact, the very meal you had failed to digest?

I steered you away.

"If you don't mind my asking, what happened with your husband?"

To be honest, I only expected to hear what I already knew: Gabe had left you because of your condition. But you hesitated. I glanced down and saw your index finger worrying your thumb, rubbing the knuckle—and I saw my own hand was doing the same. Hastily, I wedged my hand under my thigh to stop it, grateful you hadn't noticed. It was a tendency of mine, whenever

I felt shame or guilt. Like I was feeling now, meaning you were feeling the same.

It turned out that there had been a cure—and you had refused. When you told me what it involved, I understood why.

"It's basically rebirth, but without the pregnancy."

As you described the procedure, I recalled the intense and constant fear that had plagued me—and you. Fear no one had understood or taken seriously. And now, to have the very thing we so feared offered as a cure . . .

The same thought popped into my head as that day on the hospital tour when we were standing in the rebirth room. What a joke. An enormous, cosmic joke.

You began to cry. I gave you tissues. I forget what I murmured in response. Something sympathetic—insufficiently so, whatever it was. There wasn't enough sympathy in the world for what you'd had to endure. I was genuinely thinking all this in earnest when it struck me. I was in on it, this awful, deadly prank. Not just in on it—wheeling it to its end. But because it was you, the victim was me. For an instant, our selves collapsed into one another. I was thrown into sudden panic, frantic to find the seam that joined us, where you ended and I began.

Cloud began to fuss. I willed my breath to steady as I focused my gaze on him. My son, whom I loved. And from that anchor point, I regained my hold on myself as separate from you. I suggested you take him out for air. With you gone, my head felt lighter, clearer. I had space to myself once again.

The clarity of vision that I'd experienced after learning that Acek was going to be okay—it returned now. And I understood the issue and knew what I had to do. The problem was that I was standing in your shoes as if they were mine—which they were, once. But no longer. I had to sever us completely if I were to do what needed to be done. There was no other way. I recalled the day Acek turned to stone. I understood that I must do the same. If I continued on like this, I would be incapable altogether of carrying out the plan.

By the time you returned with Cloud, my heart had hardened into diamond. Unchippable. Unscratchable. I had placed you on one planet and me on another—I would never confuse us again. You were obviously upset, but I maintained my emotional distance and merely observed you. After the doctor told us that Acek's operation was over, I offered to take you and Cloud home, and you agreed. After I dropped you back at yours, I stopped at a petrol station to fill up and buy Coke and chips. When I returned to the hospital, Acek was already awake, though still prone.

"How do you feel?" I asked, leaning over him.

He grimaced and responded with great effort. "Tired."

I nodded sympathetically.

"The others went back," I said. "Vivi stayed longer. But Cloud was getting restless, so I took them home."

He stared at the ceiling. I supposed he had little choice as to his view.

"I can't be friendly with her anymore, Acek. I know it will make it more difficult. But I can't."

Acek blinked. "I understand."

He had to stay overnight. I kept him company but caught a few hours' sleep in the back seat of the sedan.

VI.

"Ma, don't worry. I'll be fine."

Iwan gives me an affectionate nudge with his shoulder. He assumes I'm anxious about his trip to Bangkok with his friends. It's not an illogical assumption: it's the longest he'll have ever been away from home. But it's your arrival I'm worrying about, not his departure. Where are you? Your present was ready last week, our son is leaving, and you still haven't shown up.

I smile and pat his hand.

"I know," I say, and resume staring out the train window. Beneath a dull gray sky, green foliage whips past, made monotonous and featureless by our speed. We're on a new express service that runs between Medan and the port at Belawan—part of the improvements they've been making to public transport in the ongoing effort to reduce carbon emissions and attract tourism and business. Though the train is "express," if you look out the other window, you can see sleek, black Greenlites on the parallel toll road, zipping past. Riding inside are people who can afford to be environmentally aware without foregoing the convenience of a private car.

Iwan's reading his Bangkok guidebook—the latest edition,

updated for this year, a gift from one of the friends he'll be traveling with. The same friend, Indra, is paying for the hotel suite the three of them will be sharing. Indra's father heads a successful RDC-tech company, so basically, he and I are in the same industry, but on opposite ends. Iwan believes that even though Indra acts like a jerk, he's essentially good at heart. I've met Indra a few times and have my doubts, but he's always polite to me. Another Greenlite zips past. I'm pretty sure Indra's in one of those.

But enough about Indra and Greenlites and other trivialities. I clear space in my mind so I can fully enjoy these last moments with Iwan. I lean my head on his shoulder and reach up to ruffle his hair. I close my eyes and savor his body's warmth. Each previous time I have held him, at every age, is contained in this moment: the absent-minded resting of his sixteen-year-old shoulder against mine as we sat in the cinema watching *Star Wars XXV*; us lying in his bed, his flushed eight-year-old face breathing hot in my ear as he slept off his fever; his little head burying into my neck, wetting it with tears, when he skinned his knee at five; these memories and more—stretching back all the way to the first time he called me Mama. Me. On the deck of the ship we took to get here from Sydney, I was still looking over my shoulder every minute, expecting your vengeance, your wrath.

"Awter!" he exclaimed, pointing at the horizon. "Big Awter!"

"Yes, big water!" I affirmed. It was the happiest he'd been since waking up in a strange windowless room, never to see you again.

I lifted him—easily, which you could never do—and pressed him to me, my cheek sinking into the cushion of his.

"Say 'Mama,'" I urged for the hundredth, thousandth, millionth time.

A pause. Then, compliantly, "Mama."

How my heart melted. And how it broke because yours was breaking somewhere, and your heart had been mine.

All of those moments, and everything in between, nest within this here and now. My eyes fill with tears of gratitude. I'm so thankful for all the time you've let me spend with him—for the privilege of raising him to the cusp of adulthood. He's a good boy, smart and levelheaded. He doesn't need me anymore.

"Ma, don't cry. I'll be back soon. You won't even notice I'm gone."

I wipe my eyes and smile.

"I know," I say for the second time.

Our farewell at the port is rushed. The passenger terminal is swarming with people, and it takes a long time to find his friends. The boarding announcement blares over the speakers. His hug is fierce and brief.

"I love you," I say.

"Me too," he replies. He means it, but he's also eager to break away and join the queue.

There's a fenced area on the dock where people can wave loved ones goodbye as ships set sail. I stand there and wave. My eyes scan the tiny figures on deck in search of you, but without success.

The next train back to Medan isn't for two hours. I treat myself to a leisurely coffee and cake. On the ride home, I gaze at the empty seat beside me and wistfully fill it with Iwan's imaginary form. My mind turns to wondering what you might look like now—how seventeen years may have weathered and recast your features, whether I'll recognize you immediately or need a few seconds for things to click. I try to recall what you looked like on that last day.

Like a ghost roaming a set of rooms, my mind drifts through the events of that evening, circling the edges, lingering in places, pacing their length. I remember stopping by Acek's room as you and Lina packed up for the day and got ready to head home.

"Sorry," I said, apologizing for the fact that you'd managed to slip in earlier. "I had Cloud on my lap. Before I could do anything, she'd already picked up the tray."

Acek didn't reply, just heaved himself out of bed and padded to the bathroom, returning with a red silk pouch—the kind Chinese people everywhere keep jewelry in.

"The pills. There are three, just in case, but you only need one."

He stared, almost in a daze, at the pouch before finally handing it to me. I stuffed it into the back pocket of my jeans.

"She asked me why," he said abruptly, startling me. "Just now. When she came in."

"What did you say?"

His eyes searched my face, wary, almost as if he were worried it was you he would find.

"I said sorry."

We stood in silence for a while.

"I'd better get going," I said at last.

He grunted in agreement. "Be careful."

"You too. Get some rest."

After dropping you and Cloud off, then Lina, I drove to buy the beer. In the car park, I forced myself to eat the sandwich I'd packed—to absorb the alcohol. The last thing I wanted to do was to get tipsy enough to slip up. It began to rain. I drove back to your house and knocked on the door, six-pack in hand. Faintly, I could hear Cloud crying. I waited patiently as you tended to him. The sounds died away, and I tried knocking again.

"It's Nina!" I shouted to dispel any fear that I was a dangerous stranger. Not to worry. No strangers here.

The door swung open to you, holding a teary Cloud, the expression on your face so wide-eyed and fearful I almost wondered if you'd guessed why I was here. I stammered the excuse I'd prepared and apologized for the way I'd acted at the hospital. I asked if I could come in.

I held my breath. You pulled Cloud closer to you, as if to protect him. For an instant, I thought you knew. For an instant.

"Sure," you said softly, wearily. You stepped aside, and I took off my shoes.

The whole place was so messy, it took me a while to register the spilled milk, the scattered food, the bowl and cup overturned on the floor.

You tried to clean it up, but Cloud was still hiccupping tears, so you didn't want to put him down. And I didn't want you to. You should have your time with him. I let you feed Cloud dinner, and yourself too, as I wiped up the spill and swept the floor. I even washed the dishes in the sink. You merely let me. Cloud must have had some tantrum, I reflected, stealing a sideways glance at your tired face. Not just tired—troubled. Pity stole once again into my heart, but this time it worked in my favor. Maybe it was better to put you out of your misery once and for all. To let you rest.

While you put Cloud to bed, I prepared the drinks. The cutting board and knife were still out. I wiped them dry and chopped up one of the pills, scooping the powder onto the flat of the blade and emptying it into your bottle. Then I ripped the corner of the back label so I could tell it was yours. I put all the bottles in the fridge to keep them cold. From the sound of it, you were brushing Cloud's teeth in the bathroom. I set to work clearing and washing the remaining dishes, then giving the dining table and floor a proper wipe. When that was done, you still hadn't come back. I crept to your bedroom. The door was ajar. From where I stood, I could partly see you, lying with your back toward me. Though you hid him from view, I knew Cloud was beside you. I was worried you'd nodded off next to him, but then I glimpsed the slight movement of your arm, and knew you were stroking him to sleep. I crept back to the lounge area, and to keep my mind from thinking too much, I looked around for another task. I began cleaning up all the toys. By the time you emerged from the room, I was nearly done.

I got out our beers. We drank. It was strange, how ordinary it all felt. I found myself doubting the reality of what I was doing: maybe the pills were fakes; maybe there were no pills; maybe we were just hanging out and I'd pick you up tomorrow as usual. Everything would go on exactly as before.

But then I saw it, the way your body began to relax and slacken. My pulse quickened. There was no denying the reality of the situation any longer. It occurred to me that I should say something to ease you out. Words of comfort, closure. I tried to speak, but my voice wouldn't come. I cleared my throat and tried again.

"I really am sorry."

You blinked, puzzled.

I continued. "Not just about that day at the hospital. I know how Acek's been acting towards you. It can't be easy. Since you were so close to him."

I wanted to keep going. To assure you that Acek did care about you. But where would I have gone from there? How could I tell you he cared about you so much that he was helping you kill your replacement and take back your child?

Again, you blinked. More slowly this time. Were you already slipping away? Did you understand what I'd just said? The words fell from your lips, clumsy and heavy.

"It's not your fault."

Oh, but it was.

The sound of your voice unsettled you. I could tell you were processing what it meant. You declared you were going to make toast.

"D'you want some?" you mumbled.

I put on a pleasant smile—the kind that indicated that nothing was wrong, that everything was as it should be.

"Sure," I said.

I even managed to maintain the expression when you tried to stand, and failed. When the look in your eyes turned from confusion to terror, before your eyes rolled back in their sockets and your head flopped forward. I lowered you gently until you were resting on your side.

"I'll take good care of Cloud," I whispered in your ear. "I promise. I'll take good care of our son."

Something made me look up sharply. I half-expected to find Cloud standing there, watching me do away with his mother. But there was no one. Leaving you on the sofa, I crept over to your room.

I went in. I lay on the bed, where I'd seen you lie, in the exact same position. I stroked Cloud's forehead and kissed his cheek. He exhaled deeply and shifted, but slumbered on. I hovered my nose close to his, to breathe in his scent. *My son*, I thought. Now truly mine. I let the minutes pass before rising to my feet. It wasn't over. I had to finish the job.

Finding your ID was easy enough, but it took me some time to locate the passports and other documents I needed to get Cloud and myself out of the country. I discovered them in a folder, in a drawer with the album of Cloud's holosonogram. I took that, too, and some other photos. I noticed there weren't any of Gabe. I packed two bags full of Cloud's stuff: nappies and nappy-related items, clothes, toiletries, assorted books, and some toys, including Ion. The room Acek and I had prepared was already stocked with some items, so I didn't need to bring very much.

Next, I called Lina. Using your voice, I told her there was a family emergency. Could she please tell Acek and the others? Cloud and I had to go to Darwin and wouldn't be back for at least a few weeks. Then I called our sister. At the sound of her hello, I broke into a sweat.

"Ci?"

"Vi?? Is that you?"

She didn't even wait for me to answer in the affirmative before scolding me.

"I was so worried after you hung up on me! I left messages! Did you get them? Why didn't you return my calls?"

I was surprised at how happy it made me to hear her voice, maternal and anxious. I didn't miss her exactly, but I still cared about her on some level. The same with Pa. Speaking of which: "How's Pa?"

The usual reply: "He's fine."

I took a deep breath. "I just wanted to let you know some big news. I'm moving to Darwin," I told her. "I got offered a job there."

"*Darwin*?" she exclaimed. "That's so far away! What kind of job? Vi, be careful. It might be a scam."

I couldn't help but chuckle to myself. For a split second, I was lifted out of the present and dropped back in the past—little Vivi once again, being mother-henned by her big sis. It didn't last long.

"Did something happen with Acek? Is that why you want to move?" Vera demanded to know.

Acek. Suddenly, I remembered he was waiting for us—Cloud and me. I poked my head out of the kitchen and saw you lying limp on the sofa. The horror of the situation, this act, came rushing back.

"No," I managed to answer. "It's not anything like that."

Vera sighed. "Vivi, please. Darwin is too far away. You won't have anyone there. Come back here."

I felt a tear trickle down my cheek. I thought I'd spent them all. How could I tell my sister that I still wouldn't have anyone, even if I did go back? That I never had?

"Vivi," she urged again. "You're being silly. Cloud should grow up around family."

"I'll call you in a few weeks when we get to Darwin," I said.

I would. It would be the last call I'd make before heading for our real destination—Medan.

I resisted the urge to hang up. The whole point of calling Vera was to make sure she didn't suspect anything was wrong. I waited for her to respond, which she did.

"Fine," she sighed. "Don't forget, okay?"

"I won't."

I fell silent, and she hung up first.

I cleared the empty bottles and took them out to the car to throw away later. I loaded the boot with the rest of the stuff. There were only two things left to do. Kill and dispose of you. Take Cloud home.

That was the order I was meant to follow. Originally, Acek was supposed to do the first and I the second. We'd planned for him to drive over once you had passed out. But so soon after the surgery, he wasn't in any condition to help.

I ran the bathtub. As it filled, I fished a wrinkled bedsheet from the washing basket—dirty or clean, it didn't matter—and spread it next to the sofa. As gently as possible, I transferred you onto it and dragged you to the bathroom. As the water rose, I checked to make sure you were completely out. I lifted your leg and dropped it. Then both arms. Then your head, letting it fall back with a *thunk*. I slapped your cheek, soft, then harder. Not a single movement or sound. If I didn't drown you, you'd stay in this state for at least a few hours more. Back pressed against the tub, knees tucked into my chest, I watched you lie there, and that strange feeling crept over me again. The same one I'd had the day of our excursion when picking you up, when sitting on your sofa, of a blurry image, of waiting for the final picture to sharpen into view.

The water was almost at the rim. I turned off the tap and dipped my hand in to test it. I wanted it to be warm.

And then I realized—Cloud was sleeping just across the hall. It didn't seem right, murdering you as he slept just a few meters away. Murdering you in the same house at all. Abruptly, I switched the order. I'd take Cloud home first. Then I'd come back to deal with you.

Cloud grunted a little when I picked him up and ran him to the car, but by the time I'd strapped him in the car seat, he had fallen asleep again. I locked the front door—with your keys. I checked my watch. About twenty minutes home and twenty minutes back. You weren't going anywhere.

When I burst through the door with Cloud, Acek rose from the sofa. He'd been waiting for us.

"The room's unlocked," he said, pointing, as if showing me the way.

"Ssshh. Mama's here," I cooed, placing Cloud on his new bed. Miraculously, he fell back to sleep. Acek was behind me. We both breathed a sigh of relief.

"I have to go back," I whispered.

"What do you mean?"

"I still need to take care of her."

Acek's eyes widened. "You haven't . . ."

I was already hurrying away, back to the car. I'd explain the ethics of my decision later.

The drive back to you was the longest twenty minutes of my life.

And, as you know, by the time I made it there, you had vanished. The back door was ajar. I checked the whole house. I hunted outside with a torch. You were properly gone.

*

Now you're the one hunting me. You've waited all these years, and though I'm grateful, I'm curious why. I'll ask you when you get here, if you give me the chance. It's late afternoon by the time I arrive back at the shop. I take down the sign directing customers next door to Shirly's. Then I head over to Shirly's myself to collect any jobs people have dropped off. They've left names and numbers, and I call each one to confirm safe receipt. Privately, I'm pretty sure I won't get around to them, but I can't just stop taking customers. I've been awaiting your arrival for seventeen years. Life has to go on.

Shirly stops by just as I'm finishing with the last call. She asks how seeing Iwan off went. Do I want to go out for dinner with her? I tell her I feel like staying at home.

"Tomorrow then," she insists. "Otherwise you'll be lonely while Iwan's gone."

"Tomorrow," I promise, fully intending to keep it if I'm still around.

The staircase seems darker and narrower tonight.

"Hello?" I call out when I reach the second story. Silence greets me. Nevertheless, I check each room with care. Once I'm certain you're nowhere to be found, I relax. I make instant noodles for dinner. I bathe and, before going to sleep, reach under my bed to pull out your gift. I take both albums from the box and place them on the bed, side by side.

They look identical—bureaucratic blue with gold trim—but one is devoted to the previous generation, and the other is devoted to the next. There ended up being enough material for two books instead of one. *The Book of Our Mother* reads the first when you open the cover. *The Book of Our Son* reads the second. "Our Son"—common ground, as opposed to "Cloud" or "Iwan."

Not that the new name I chose was unrelated to the name you gave him. *Iwan*, one letter away from *Awan*—Indonesian for "cloud." And when Chinese people here ask for his Chinese name, he has one too: Cie Hun, or affectionately, Ahun. "Hun," like the second half of our mother's name, Eng Hun. Identical in Latin script, though in Hokkien they're different words entirely: 芬 and 雲; *Fragrance* and *Cloud*. Ahun, our mother. Ahun, our son. Cloud. Iwan. Awan. Different editions of the same thing.

I open the second book first precisely because, after seeing him off today, our son is on my mind. Below the handwritten text that reads *The Book of Our Son* is the birth announcement you sent Acek—our son, days old, ruddy cheeked, snugly swaddled, framed in giraffes and balloons and pale blue. I've taken it out often during these past several years to study it, to trace it, fingers hovering over his baby face, so new that it's creased, like a dress shirt fresh out of its packaging. Now the photo is yours.

I flip through the rest of the book slowly, reliving our son's life from womb to now. Here are the holosonogram pictures—the best ones. And here are some other photos I took from your house. Cloud doing tummy time on a baby mat. Vera holding Cloud in one arm, Haze in the other, sitting next to Pa with his usual faraway gaze, Vera leaning in to compensate for Pa's indifference. (I heard from Acek last year that Pa passed away. Is it sad that I wasn't that sad? Somehow, it felt like old news.) Cloud in various poses: crawling in a park; face smeared with orange mash in a high chair; standing barefoot on the grass; sitting on a beach with you—a photo that must have been taken by Gabe. Our son grows before my eyes. The location changes from Australia to here. Iwan stroking a stray cat. Iwan's first day of school. Iwan playing soccer. Him blowing out candles on birthday cake after birthday cake. They're all solely of him, or him and other people. As a courtesy to you, I've omitted myself from the album, but there are five shoeboxes of photos I didn't use. You'll find them in the living room cabinet if you look. Interspersed throughout are various captions, notes, and mementos. Where X shot was taken. A funny thing he said at age Y. A cute story from year Z. Drawings in crayon. Paintings in watercolor. Excerpts from assignments for school. His diplomas from primary, middle, and most recently, high school—all real, no copies. You can lift them off the self-adhesive backing if you need originals.

Lastly, a photo of him at last week's ceremony receiving his high-school diploma, solemn and handsome in red and black batik. My heart swells with pride not just for what he has accomplished, how much he has grown, but for me as the mother who has watched over him all this time, shepherding him through. This is something I can never disclose to you—my satisfaction at a hard job well done. I acknowledge full well that you had it harder; I won't minimize that. But I didn't find it easy, being a single mother, in a mostly unfamiliar country, all alone.

Other matters I'll never divulge—all my mistakes along the way. When I lost him at the market. When I slapped him for stripping an entire coil of high-grade insulated wire. When I left him unsupervised on the workshop floor to dash upstairs to the bathroom, only to run back down when I heard him howl. There was a bright pink mark on his index finger. I had left the soldering iron on. And, of course, all the times I snapped at him when I was tired, or yelled at him over something unimportant. Lapses that caused Shirly to laugh whenever I told her about them—"That's nothing. Let me tell you the time I . . ."—but that filled me with remorse all the same. How could I ever take our son for granted in light of what the privilege of raising him cost you?

Those moments have no place in this album. It's meant to share the happy times with you, which I've otherwise deprived you of. And to prove to you that I took care of our child well.

I set aside the album and turn to the next one, *The Book of Our Mother*. This one is the opposite of its counterpart—text-heavy, photo-poor. It contains three pictures total, which are all I have of her: the one of our third birthday, with Ma lighting the candles; the photo we used for her funeral, which graced the foot of her casket; and the group photo Aie Ing Lan gave me to give to you. The first two, you'll recognize, but I've written a caption for the third. The rest of the album is filled with stories and bits of information, re-organized and written neatly on acid-free letter paper. They're mostly based on the notes I took when speaking with Aie Ing Lan, but I've also included all the things Acek told me about Ma. Everything I've learned about our mother, you will too.

I wonder how you'll react when you find out that rebirth also troubled her, if only after the fact. We're not alone, you and I. Even though it felt like it, it wasn't just us.

I close the second album, then put them both back in the box. Then I take it to Iwan's room and leave it on his bed. *For Vivi* reads the envelope taped to the lid. There. Even if you don't give me the chance to present it to you myself, you can't miss it.

*

I live long enough to eat dinner with Shirly. She invites me to come with her to a church event the evening after, and looks anxious when I decline. She can't keep me company the next couple of nights, either: she's having dinner with her brother's family, then with an old high-school classmate.

"Don't you have other friends?" she asks, concerned.

I smile and reassure her. "I don't mind being alone."

Three more days pass. Doubt begins to set in, weakening my faith in your arrival.

Finally, one late afternoon, as I'm fixing a clothes iron, you walk through the door like an ordinary customer. I recognize you at once. I've been waiting for this moment. Yet I'm at a loss about what to do. You head right for me. Fear glues me in place.

I brace myself for what comes next, but you do nothing—just stand there, studying me, as if I'm some sort of exhibit. So I study you back.

Our appearances have diverged even more over the past seventeen years. I used to be the fatter one; now you're plumper. But my wrinkles are deeper, and I have more dark spots than you. I don't wear makeup anymore, but I notice you've done your eyebrows and are wearing lipstick. Your hair is short and dyed black. Mine is pulled back with a claw clip and shot through with white strands. I stand up. Your posture is better.

"Thermal switch?"

That's the first thing you say. You're looking at the clothes iron I'm repairing.

"No, the switch is fine," I say hoarsely, finding my voice. "It's the heating element."

"Ah," you say. "I'm rusty after all these years."

"Cloud's not here," I blurt, to get the disappointing news over with. "But he'll be back in a few days."

You merely adjust the large purse over your shoulder.

"Yes, I know. He went to Bangkok with friends."

It takes a few seconds for me to register what you've just said.

"But how?" I stammer. "How do you know?"

Suddenly, you look tired. You sigh.

"Can I have a cup of tea?" you ask.

It's getting late anyway, so I close the shop and take you upstairs.

*

As the tea leaves steep, you wait in the kitchen with me. I suppose I don't blame you, given what happened the last time you let me give you something to drink. We don't talk. I eye your purse and wonder what kind of weapon would fit inside. Your gaze wanders and settles on the calendar. I see you note the dashes I've marked.

"This is when I thought you'd arrive," I say, running my finger from the second dash to the third. Then I point to the first dash. "That's when Acek told me you'd broken into the house."

You nod. "Yes, I listen in on your and Acek's conversations. That's how I know Cloud is in Bangkok."

I try to process what you've just told me. "You listen? But how?"

"I work at the telephone exchange that handles Acek's line. It was easy to set up. We sometimes get orders from the police, too, to tap suspects."

"You listen in on all his phone calls?"

"I record them," you clarify. "But not all of them. You speak with him on the last day of every month, so I usually set the tap for then. But I knew he'd call after I broke in, so I set one for that time as well."

You check your watch and pour the tea: a cup for me and a cup for you. You hand me mine and wait for me to sip before you drink from yours. I'm too dumbstruck by all this new information to be a good host. You open a jar of cashews on the counter and help yourself.

"You've known all this time . . ." I murmur.

"Not everything. Just what you've told Acek. Which isn't that much. But it's been good to know how our son is doing."

You call him "our son" too. I'd assumed you were coming here to take vengeance. Now I'm not so sure, and I can't bear the suspense.

"Are you going to kill me?"

Your forehead creases and your lips twitch upward.

"No," you say at last.

"Then why are you here? And why only now? If you've known all this time . . ."

Your eyes fix mine, earnest.

"I wanted to give you the time to raise him. And now I want to thank you for taking care of him."

It turns out that the gift of getting to raise him has been that all along—intentionally and deliberately, a gift.

"That night," you say. "When you took him. Just before you knocked on the door, something happened. I got angry at him. Really upset." You shake your head. I can tell you're still ashamed because I see your index finger rubbing the knuckle of your thumb. I still do that too.

"I almost hurt him," you say. "I could have hurt him, or maybe worse. I wasn't in my right mind. But you know, I never really was, back then."

You continue. "When I woke up in the bathroom, I barely knew what was going on, though I did know who you were. I made the connection just before I blacked out. I crawled to Cloud's room, but it was too late. You'd taken him. I still couldn't stand that well, but I managed to drag myself out the back door. It was still raining. I hid behind a rock and watched you search the house and the yard. You almost found me, you know. You came within a few meters of me, but then you went back inside.

"I passed out again. It was morning when I woke up muddy and soaking wet. You'd locked the back door as well as the front, so I went over to the neighbor's property. No one was home. I snuck through the garden gate and through the back door. I was going to use their phone to call the police, or Vera, or anyone. I even picked up the receiver. But, you know, I kept thinking about it—how I'd almost hurt him. How I didn't deserve to have him. How he should be with someone else. And who better than you?"

You pour yourself more tea. "Wasn't that what I'd wanted anyway, I thought to myself. To not go through rebirth? You were the true me—you'd survived somehow. Shouldn't I be happy for you? And how could I even pretend to deserve Cloud after what I'd done? I replaced the receiver. I ate and drank a bit and changed into dry clothes. I hitched a ride and ended up in Armidale. There was a women's shelter there. I stayed for a while. I didn't trust myself to keep away from Cloud if I came back, but when I did, it turned out you'd already left the country."

"When did you start working at the telephone exchange?" I ask.

You calculate. "About two years after that night? Two years and a bit? I did some odd work here and there before that. Had to save up for a new identity. They don't come cheap."

You're about to say something else, but you hesitate. Then you decide to go ahead.

"If I'm honest, it felt like a relief, kind of. To not be responsible for Cloud anymore, even though I missed him. God, I did miss him. But after I almost hurt him that night, I also knew it was for the best."

You lapse into silence, brow furrowed, as if revisiting the past. You must be thinking about the incident you've mentioned three times now, when you almost hurt Cloud. I feel my own forehead crease into a frown, pitying and curious. Was whatever you did really that unforgiveable? Or did it only become unforgiveable because I took from you the ability to make up for it? I think back on my own errors and wonder how I would view the worst of them if I hadn't had the chance to keep going—to experience all the times I did things right, all the ways in which I was a good mother, all the fruit borne only after years of care and love. I realize that there is something else I stole from you when I took Cloud. And in doing so, I deprived you of the horizon toward which we limp. The future. And the hope that comes from having a future. I'm trying to come up with the words to articulate this when you interrupt.

"Just wondering, how did you keep anyone from looking for Cloud or me? I thought at least our sister would worry."

I explain how I called Vera that night—and again from Darwin. How, a while after that, she did eventually get suspicious and ring the police, but they traced my final phone call and searched for you up there. Acek and the other employees got calls from the police, but told them the same thing: you'd said there was a family emergency and would be away in Darwin for a while.

"What about our son?" you ask. "Where did you keep him until you could leave for Medan?"

I tell you about the soundproof room, but not anything else. I don't want to distress you with how he cried for you on and off for a week; how we resorted to children's anti-allergy meds to make him more sedate.

We continue to fill in the gaps for each other. I tell you how Acek and I spent the first few weeks in terror, certain the police, or you, would show up any time. You tell me Vera and James finally saved enough to renovate their house. You walked past once, just to see if you could find out how they were.

I ask how our nephew and nieces are. You shrug.

"And you know Pa is dead," you say.

I nod.

I ask if you know how Gabe is doing. Every now and then, he comes to mind.

The last and only time you checked on him was ten years ago. "You know Gabe," you snort. "Doing great. Happily married. Four kids at the time."

We both roll our eyes.

You explain the reason you've decided to come while our son isn't here: you didn't want to risk him finding out about you. Have I told him?

"Of course not," I say. "But don't you want to see him?"

Pain crosses your face for an instant, and you close your eyes. "Does it matter?" you ask.

I feel the time has come. I show you upstairs to our son's room. You spot Ion on the bed and smile.

"He still has him," you exclaim, giving his mane a stroke. He's even nubbier and grayer than when the man first gave him to Cloud.

I open the lid of the box and explain the contents, though I'll let you take out the albums yourself. I leave you to it, gently shutting the door behind me. I feel as if something has been released—as if my heart has been bound tight for seventeen years, and now, at last, I'm free.

Once in my room, with the door closed, I sit on the bed. The sun has begun to set, and the call to prayer from the nearby mosque floats in from outside. I say my own prayer to Whoever is listening. For forgiveness for what I have done. For our son to find peace, despite my actions. For your relationship with our son. It's your time to enjoy him now. Hope and a future: I return them to you. For our ancestors, especially our mother, and all our mother's selves, and all her mother's selves, and all her mother's mother's selves, and on and on. I thank them for their sacrifice in making my life possible—the life I now choose to pass on. I pray for strength and resolve to join them now. It was Nature's way, and now I willingly surrender to her path. I kneel beside the bed and take out the other object besides your gift that I have prepared for today. Just in case. I was pretty sure I wouldn't need it, and that you'd do the job.

I run my fingers over the pipe's length, the caps on each end, the battery pack duct-taped to its middle. I check the wire connections, and I finger the detonator. I remind myself how quickly it will be over, as long as I hold it close. I take three deep breaths, and on the third, as my thumb presses the square plastic button, out of the corner of my eye, I see the bedroom door open. I scream no, but it's too late.

III.

IWAN/

AHUN/

阿雲/

CLOUD

Faith told me the weather was nice today—not too hot, not too cloudy, just the right amount of sun, with not a drop of rain. She said this amount of rainfall in general is normal for Singapore's dry season, tracking perfectly with the historical average. It's been like this for the past several years. A good sign, though it's too soon to tell if the climate crisis has been averted. We shouldn't congratulate ourselves yet.

As a meteorologist, Faith keeps close tabs on the weather, which is just as well because I don't have much opportunity to take notice. My own job keeps me busy and indoors. And for the past few years, Project Mothers has consumed all my evenings. I come back from the office; we eat dinner—she cooks, I wash up; I head to my desk and work on the report until bed.

Recently, she's also been working late, which makes me feel less guilty. Her group is in the middle of writing several important papers, plus she's heading the organizing committee for the big climate and health conference that starts tomorrow and runs all week. Climate and health. There are a lot of intersections between Faith's and my respective interests, of course, but they rarely come together like this, in one officially important nine-day event.

Which is why, for the last time, I'm rereading my report. Faith advised me not to—what would I change at this stage? A comma? A word? I've proofread it countless times. It's ready to go. But I can't help myself. I'm presenting it tomorrow. After all this time, it's time. A day that will go down in history if I've done a good enough job.

This is potentially a landmark document, with the ability to effect significant changes in maternal health policy worldwide. I clear my throat. Someone once told me the best way to catch typos is to read something out loud. Because Faith has already gone to bed, I try to keep my voice to a murmur while retaining enough expressiveness to capture the introduction's full rhetorical effect:

> Isaac Newton once famously said, "If I have seen further, it is by standing on the shoulders of giants." We might very well say something similar about our mothers: "If I have seen at all, or done anything, or breathed, or lived, it is because my mother gave me birth." Yet by "mother," we would technically mean not just one woman but two—or, depending on how many siblings each of us has, three, four, or more.
>
> It takes a village to raise a child. And it takes women—plural—to have one. But, by and large, the latter is a fact that has gone ignored. Throughout human history and across cultures and societies, with some exceptions, we allow the woman who carries the child to be barbarically murdered and cannibalized by her new self. We call it Nature's Way and accept her death as collateral damage, necessary even, to ensure the health of her new self and child.
>
> As a race, humankind has accomplished a great many things this past century: the eradication of smallpox, the drastic re-

duction in environmentally calamitous livestock and agricultural practices, and the successful minimization of fossil-fuel and energy usage. However, as this report will demonstrate, there is still much to be done in recognizing the basic human right to existence that every mother possesses, not just the ones who are reborn . . .

I don't read the entire report out loud—it's 189 pages long, excluding appendixes, references, and endnotes. But I read all nine pages of the introduction through to the very end and am satisfied. There's not a single typo in sight. Even Faith, who is thoroughly sick of the report, thanks to my talking about it so much, had to nod in admiration when she read the intro last week. I showed it to her over dinner.

"Very inspiring," she acknowledged. "That's some opening, I must say."

Then the buzzer rang, and I reset the timer. When I began to monopolize too much of our dinner conversation, we negotiated a turns system. Now I get fifteen minutes at most to talk about Project Mothers, and she gets fifteen minutes at least to talk about the most exciting or pressing things going on in her life.

I know all too well how fortunate I am to be married to Faith. It's our sixth anniversary next month. She understands how much this report means to me, even if she finds it difficult to care to the same extent. I get it. Our backgrounds are very different. She came from a happy, traditional family and is perfectly fine with the way things are. But then again, who in the world have I ever come across with a family history like mine?

My high-school friend Indra certainly never let me forget it. It was the first thing he mentioned to Faith when he introduced us to each other at his nightclub's big opening bash. His nightclub was called D-Day, so opening night was called D-Day's D-Day. It was awful. The music was loud, and it was too dark, which is what I expected from a nightclub, but I'd never have gone if Indra hadn't insisted.

"You can't mope around forever," he said. At that point, Ma had been dead two years and a month. I was partway through my degree at USU and hadn't made any new friends. Indra, on the other hand, had made tons of them doing his business degree at the private university he was attending—a degree he was slow-walking because he'd convinced his parents to give him the capital to open this nightclub and run it on the side.

Part of me wished I did have new friends so that I didn't have to keep Indra. Part of me wished Indra would just hang out with his new friends and leave me be. But Indra was loyal, in his own asshole way, and I was still too shattered by what had happened to avoid him. Still, everything happens for the best, I suppose, since it's how Faith and I met.

"This is Faith!" Indra yelled into my ear. "She's at the same university as me, but she's majoring in science! Her mom and my mom are friends!"

Faith waved. "Meteorology," she clarified.

"My friend, Iwan, from high school!" Indra yelled into her ear. "He's at USU. His mom is dead!"

"Did it happen recently?" asked Faith, later, once we had left and could hear each other. We'd stayed for almost an hour trying to talk to each other over the music, but when I said goodbye to Indra, she came up to do the same. She was heading off too. We split a taxi, and she dropped me off at Aie Shirly's. After Ma died, Aie Shirly had insisted I stay with her.

"Two years ago. After I graduated from high school."

Faith looked shocked. "I'm so sorry. May I ask how?"

"An explosion. In our apartment. She and another woman died."

Even that wasn't the whole story, though I did tell her eventually, after we started going out.

"It's not your fault," she would say, once she learned the truth.

I would nod. But in my heart, I knew—I know—it kind of was.

None of it would have happened if she hadn't given birth to me. Not that I had any control over that. And maybe things wouldn't have turned out the same way if I hadn't left her to go to Bangkok. I was such a clueless, careless kid. It never even occurred to me that Ma might have had other reasons for acting strange other than me going on that trip. The farthest I'd ever been was to Jakarta and Yogya. I'd never been outside Indonesia before. I thought she was anxious about my safety, or that I'd get into trouble. After all, all we had was each other—who else would she worry about besides me?

The Bangkok trip with Indra and Daniel had been in the works for a year. It was Indra's idea. His family was loaded. They owned an RDC-tech company and had a huge house, so if we needed to study or hang out, Indra's place was always the logical choice. Naturally, their home was equipped with all the latest gadgetry—unlimited internet, HD streaming, EnviroCool-powered climate control, and walk-in freezer and fridge.

"The initial outlay is high, but the energy savings are enormous," explained Indra as we stood among the ice cream and slabs of meat, shivering. He was giving us a tour of the freezer. "You make the difference back in ten years. And because the food lasts longer, we buy in bulk. Economies of scale. It all makes more financial and ecological sense. No offense to your mom, Iwan."

I shrugged. I was used to Indra saying such things.

Anyway, during our last year in high school, Indra became obsessed with T-pop and T-dramas. Whenever we were at his place, LeJend, sparrow, and G-RRR were always playing in the background. Or, if there was no schoolwork to do, he'd subject us to three or six episodes of whatever show he was watching at the mo'. Once the idea of actually going to Bangkok lodged itself in his brain, it wouldn't shake. "B-town, here we come!" he hollered, when he finally convinced me and Daniel to go. He even said he'd take care of the hotel suite. "What are rich friends for?" he asked, grinning at our surprise.

It was impossible not to be infected by Indra's enthusiasm. As I said, I'd never left the country, and now I was going to Bangkok. *Bangkok*, the Mecca of Glow. To prepare, Daniel and I began consuming T-pop and T-dramas too, via pirated CDs and DVDs. To save money, we'd coordinate between ourselves which ones we were buying, then pass them to the other when we were done.

The weeks leading up to the trip were a blur: besides packing, there was all the stuff to do around graduation—events, activities, goodbyes. It was hard not to get caught up. To my shame, I barely remember my last moments with Ma. She insisted on taking the train with me all the way to the port. I just thought she was being clingy. I remember she cried. I do recall trying to reassure her—"I won't be gone long," I said, or something like that.

We said goodbye in the passenger terminal. I remember hugging her before boarding the ship. I remember intending to go out on deck to wave goodbye to Ma, but Indra convinced me I was being lame. "You'll see her when we get back," he said, distracting us with the T-shirts he'd made for our trip: navy-blue bubble letters, hot-pink background—*Banging in Bangkok!*

From that point on, I didn't think about Ma once. The two and a half days at sea were spent playing cards, eating snacks, engaging in faux-philosophical discussions, and of course, binge-watching on Indra's state-of-the-art portable player. And I certainly spared her no thought when we disembarked at Khlong Toei Port in the late afternoon, before sunset. We took the MRT and glided our suitcases across streets as smooth as silk, down boulevards that illuminated, as if by magic, once the sun was red and low in the sky. Bollards and globes teeming with life—we'd seen them onscreen, but it was another thing entirely to witness in real time, in the flesh. They reminded me of tiny, overcrowded apartment blocks. Thailand: a textbook example of crisis-turned-opportunity, using the global energy-saving measures to make advances in bioluminescent tech. The power-plants reportedly bred millions of GLOWW worms a day.

"Genius, huh?" murmured Daniel in wonder as we stopped by a bollard. "Renewable. Regenerating. Organic. How efficient can you get?"

All those glowing, wriggling bodies, writhing and crawling over each other, pressing up against the glass. I could see a few dead ones being jostled around. Their corpses eventually migrated downward to form a stiff blue layer at the compartment's base. Theoretically, a worm could live for three days, but Bangkok boasted changing them out daily, to ensure the streets never lost their light. All that life. All that death. It boggled the mind.

I shook off my thoughts and caught up with the others. They were getting fried crickets.

"Look at me! I'm Bright Ratakorn in *One Blossom Less*," said Indra, batting his eyes, a cricket between his lips.

"But not hot," laughed Daniel, giving Indra's shoulder a shove.

The news came on our fourth night in Bangkok. We'd gone out to karaoke, and Indra had pushed Daniel too far.

"Lower your volume, bro. Just 'cause you're half-Batak doesn't mean you get to hog the songs."

Indra was always low-key making racist remarks about Daniel's Batak-Chinese background. Just like he was always making fun of me being the wrong kind of Chinese—low-class. But that night, for some reason, Daniel had had enough. He threw a handful of peanuts in Indra's face and stormed out.

"What? What?" protested Indra. "People can't take a joke?"

I jogged out in search of Daniel. Indra's voice followed me down the corridor, a trailing sneer. "Oh, now Ahun's mad. *A-hun, ah! Lu ai khi ta lok?* Yeah. Sure. Go back to the hotel I'm paying for. See if your hobbler mother can foot the bill instead."

Indra was obviously drunk. This was mean, even for him. I couldn't find Daniel either. He'd disappeared into the crowd. I took Indra's advice and went back to the hotel. Slipped under the door was a handwritten message, headed *URGENT:*

For Iwan. Your mother had an accident.

There was an Indonesian phone number. I dialed it. Aie Shirly picked up. There had been an explosion. Ma was dead.

I packed my bags, scribbled an explanation to my friends, and headed for the port. I pleaded with the booking desk to change my ticket for the next ship out, which was in the morning. I slept at the terminal. I spent most of my time on board at the bow, staring at the horizon, willing it to come closer, willing us to go faster. I had to get home to clear it all up. It was a misunderstanding. My mother wasn't dead. An explosion? It was too absurd.

I went straight home. Everything looked normal from the

outside, except for the bright yellow tape stretched across the front. My key didn't work for the entrance, but the back door opened just fine. The shop interior looked the same as it always did, the floor and benches strewn with jobs-in-progress, my mother's desk littered with invoices and forms and notes. *See? Ma is okay.*

I sprinted up the steps. That was when I first caught it—a certain alien quality in the air, hanging about the living room and kitchen, as if strangers had been through, tracking dirt in, sitting on the chairs, touching our things. I raced up to the bedrooms. Plaster and fluff and bits of twisted metal, scattered across the tiles. More yellow tape, stretched across the doorway to Ma's bedroom. I peered in. Splintered wood and shards of glass. What remained of the mattress, charred and black.

I heard someone calling my name. It was Aie Shirly. She'd been on the lookout for my arrival for the past three days. Sobbing, I let her fold me into her arms.

The police requested I come to the mortuary to identify the body. They warned me it might be difficult. Mixed in with my mother's body parts were the other woman's. Same race, same build, as far as they could tell. Right before they lifted the sheet, like a curtain, I felt that same denial rising in me, and in that denial, hope. I felt the possibility of Ma being alive, of there being a colossal mistake made. I would look at the parts presented and see to my relief that none of them belonged to her.

There were two mangled bodies. Fingers. A hand. An ear. I ran outside to retch, head spinning, eyes burning, a searing pain in my chest. They gave me tissues and a glass of water. Eventually, I was able to resume. When I did, I recognized my mother instantly—at least, what was left. Then my gaze fell on the body whose torso had been blown open—a burned, ragged cave—and I realized my mistake: this was my mother, in her favorite green T-shirt and grease-stained jeans. The other body was slightly heavier, in unfamiliar clothes. Yes, this was definitely Ma. The stud in her ear confirmed it—a small silver cloud. I'd given her the earrings for her forty-fifth birthday. Horror vanished, and in its place, the aching urge to touch her. I knew exactly what she would feel like, even as it sickened me to realize that I would never experience the sensation again. The warmth, the density, the contours of her living flesh existed only in memory now. Blinking back tears, I leaned in to stroke her cheek—and saw some of it had peeled away, revealing a clear gel pad.

"What's that?" I asked, my voice coming out strangled and strange.

"It's an implant," explained the coroner. "From a cosmetic procedure."

"What do you mean? My mother never had any procedures done."

The coroner kept silent and the police officer accompanying me cleared her throat. They must have been used to people making surprise discoveries about deceased loved ones.

The police had already explained everything they knew about "the incident," as they termed it. There had been an IED—a pipe bomb—just powerful enough to do severe damage and kill everyone in the room, but not strong enough to destroy anything else. From my identification, they knew now that my mother had been the one holding the bomb, pressed to her chest. The other woman had been standing in the open doorway when it went off. They were still trying to figure out who she was and why she was there.

"You don't recognize her at all?"

"No," I said, feeling dizzy again. They pulled the sheet back over the parts and let me sit down.

"She wasn't carrying any ID?" I ask.

The officer told me they'd found a purse with an Australian's driver's license. But when they had called the Australian police, they were informed that the holder had died twenty years ago.

"So, this other woman . . ." I began, trying to wrap my head around it all. "Maybe she forced my mother to hold the bomb while it went off, and accidentally killed herself too?"

"We can't make that assumption."

"You think my mother committed suicide and took this other woman with her?"

Again, the officer cleared her throat. "We really don't know yet. So far, the only fingerprints we've found on what was left of the bomb match your mother's. But we haven't completed the full analysis."

I felt suddenly indignant. "How can you not know what happened to my mother?"

The officer looked sympathetic. "I'm sorry. We're trying to find out. I know it's hard. Actually, we were hoping you'd be able to clear some things up."

I told her everything I could, which was nothing. Even if they did manage to arrive at a conclusion, what did it matter? Ma was gone. A partial corpse and some appendages. Before I left, they asked how much longer I wanted them to keep Ma's body now that the forensic investigation was done. It was a per-day fee, calculated based on electricity costs. They had more bodies coming through. Freezer space was costly. She didn't say the last two things, but I said them in my head. I paid for another day to get things sorted out.

Aie Shirly offered to let me sleep at her place, in one of her daughters' old rooms, until the police told me I could go back. A policeman guarded Ma's bedroom as I gathered my things—to make sure I didn't tamper with evidence, I suppose. I'd been there unsupervised earlier in the day, not a single guard in sight, but never mind about that.

That's when I saw the blue leather-bound albums on my bed, side by side, and beside them, Ion. There was also a gift box, lying open and empty next to its lid. *For Vivi*, read the envelope taped to it. I tore open the envelope to read the message inside.

Dear Vivi,

Thank you for giving me all this time with our son. I have treasured it and accept that it's over. These two albums are for you. One is about our mother. We always wanted to know her better. The other is about our son. My way of giving back all the years I stole from you.

Nina

Nina. Another unfamiliar name. Ma's name was Rina. Her Chinese name was Bie Eng. But it was Ma's handwriting, make no mistake. I helped out around the shop enough to recognize it from all the invoices and receipts. Her sloping *g*. Her squiggly *m*.

I put the albums and note in the box. I packed Ion and some clothes into a gym bag. My suitcase was already at Aie Shirly's. *I guess this doesn't count as evidence*, I thought, hugging the box to my chest as the policeman escorted me downstairs and off the premises. I knew then, I couldn't hope for any answers from them.

I waited until I could hear Aie Shirly cooking in the kitchen before I closed my room door and opened the albums. The first was filled entirely with photos and notes about me. But was it me? *Announcing the arrival of our baby boy, Cloud!* read the card on the opening page, followed by my birth date. A height. A weight. *With love, Gabriel and Vivian.*

Gabriel was the only name I recognized—my father's. I knew that much about him. But Cloud wasn't my name, and Vivian wasn't Ma. *Vivian, as in Vivi?*

Among the first photos: me, presumably, with another baby in the arms of a strange woman next to an old man; another, again, presumably me, at the beach with a woman who bore faint resemblance to my mother, except for key features—the eyes were all wrong, the nose, the jaw. *The jaw.* I recalled the silicone implant in Ma's ruined face. Gradually, the photos gave way to familiar ones my mother had shown me before. I read all the captions and notes—anecdotes and information about my childhood. They all referred to "our son."

I turned to the second album. It was filled with writing—Ma's best hand in dark blue ink, prefaced by three photos of Ma's Ma, only one of which I'd ever seen—the one of my grandmother alone. *Us on our third birthday, with Ci, Ma and Pa,* read the caption to the photo featuring a family of four around a birthday cake.

Slowly, the truth was coming into focus. I flipped through the pages quickly, my heart racing.

Someone knocked. It was Aie Shirly. Time to eat, she called through the door.

I took a deep breath and closed the book.

"Do you have any relatives you should call?" asked Aie Shirly, scooping rice onto my plate.

Relatives. All those unfamiliar faces in the photos.

"We aren't in contact," I replied. "I don't know how."

A memory: of when I'd learned about family trees in primary school. My teacher had been baffled. She could understand my father being dead, but no grandparents? No aunts or uncles? No cousins?

"Ask your mother when you get home," the teacher urged.

"We had to leave them behind" was Ma's reply. She said it in a faraway voice, with a faraway look, as if the mere act of telling me required her to travel back in time.

"Why?"

She searched for the words to explain.

"They wouldn't have let me take care of you."

Back then, I had used my own reasoning to give her words meaning. My dead father's family must have wanted to raise me. To take me away from Ma. Ridiculous. A child belongs with a mother. Everyone knew that.

As I'd grown older, I'd embellished further: my late father's relatives had not only been unreasonable; Ma's family had been unwilling to stand up for her. Except for one. Not a relative, though. An old friend.

"There is someone," I blurted, startling Aie Shirly. How could I forget?

*

When Akong Arvin told me on the phone that he was coming, I offered to meet him at the port.

"No need," he said.

He showed up on the doorstep on a Thursday morning, two weeks later, as old-looking as I'd expected him to be.

"You can stay here, Akong," I said, taking his ancient rolling suitcase and showing him in.

"Good," he said. I had the impression he'd assumed that would be the case. Then he looked me up and down and up again. He nodded approvingly and grunted, "You've grown."

I showed him upstairs. Even with the handrail, it took him some time.

"I forgot about these shophouses," he panted as we reached the third floor.

The police investigation had concluded long ago. As I'd predicted, they hadn't solved a thing. But Ma's room was still a mess. Most of the wreckage was gone, along with the bed, but I still hadn't replaced the window, and the walls and cupboards were still scorched and shredded.

"So this is where it happened," he said quietly.

He already knew all the details. I'd told him during our first phone call, when I'd informed him that Ma had died. Now he asked for a stool and sat in the middle of the room, staring out through the plastic sheet covering the window, the breeze flapping it gently, open and shut, open and shut.

I let him get settled in my room—I'd sleep downstairs on the sofa. Then we went to visit Ma's grave-tree. Aie Shirly had helped me pick one out. We lit joss sticks and paid our respects. For the first time I'd seen, he cried.

We ate lunch at a place nearby. I felt it was time to ask.

"Akong," I said quietly. "I think I know about Ma and . . . Ma."

He raised one white bushy eyebrow and was silent for a while.

"Is that so?" he said at last.

I told him what I thought I knew, what I'd pieced together after studying the albums, after spending hours turning everything over in my head.

A nod was all it took to confirm the unheard of. Two mothers. A rebirth avoided. But he filled me in as to how.

"Was she really that scared of it?" I asked.

He looked stunned for a moment. Then his gaze turned withering. "Think about it. How would you feel about being killed and eaten?"

"It's different," I protested. "Rebirth's not death. It's the opposite."

Akong shook his head in disgust and continued eating in silence.

With that, something changed between us—and I couldn't change it back. Not even when I showed him the albums.

"It's you and Ma's Ma," I said, pointing to the old black-and-white photo of a bunch of teenagers and kids clustered around a car.

"I can read," he replied.

He was out all day the next day. Visiting relatives or old friends, I supposed. He must have had some around. The same went for Saturday. But by Sunday, he was all packed up to leave.

"You just got here," I objected. "It's what, five days between here and Darwin? Plus the train ride between there and Sydney? And it must have been expensive. Look, I'm sorry for what I said. I'm sorry I don't understand."

This only seemed to piss him off more. "Not everything is about you, you know."

I wondered who else he'd seen while he was here, what disagreements had broken out.

There was no stopping him, but he let me accompany him on the angkot to the train station. I helped with his suitcase. Before he boarded, he stared hard at me.

"Be worth what they went through."

"Huh?"

He repeated himself. Slowly. As if I were hard of hearing. Then he disappeared into the carriage. Shortly afterwards, the train pulled away.

He never called me after that. Or returned my calls. Years later, someone would pick up and I'd get excited: he'd forgiven me at last! But it turned out to be someone else—an employee named Zoe.

"I'm so sorry, Arvin passed on Wednesday."

It was a pulmonary embolism. She told me the funeral was to be held next week. I apologized. It would be impossible for me to make it there in time.

Be worth what they went through.

How often did I think those words then? How many times a day do I repeat them now?

I sometimes wonder how Akong Arvin would react if he knew I was writing this report. Would he be relieved that I'm trying to follow his advice? Every day, I ask myself if Ma would be proud—or the other mother I can't remember, who has no tree, whose remains are who knows where. I'd been so unsure about the truth I'd discovered, I hadn't dared to ask for my other mother's body. By the time I got round to it, the police told me it was too late. They'd disposed of her. So let this report be her memorial. Let this bear witness to them both.

I bind the report with a bulldog clip and center it on my desk. There. All ready to go. Then, because I'm too keyed up to go to bed right away, I prepare my suit for tomorrow, hanging it on the back of the study door. Faith thinks the suit is unnecessary—I'll only be seeing the UN Chief of Maternal Health briefly, after all. But I want to make a good impression so she'll pay full attention to the report when I hand it to her. I can't take any risks.

I'm still too excited to go to sleep, so I spend some time tidying up my books. Or as Faith calls them, affectionately, my "towers." It's an occupational hazard of my day job, bringing home excess books.

To be honest, I never thought I'd end up working as a consolidation technician. Yes, my degree was in library and information sciences, but I always thought I'd be on the front-facing side of things: manning the desk, organizing and shelving materials, assisting patrons. You know what I mean. But upon graduation, Faith got offered a position here. I was so proud. Her parents were too. "Singapore!" they exclaimed. "So-and-so's kid moved there. And who-and-who's kid too. They're so happy. It's clean and safe. Great healthcare. Majority Chinese—you won't have to worry about the race stuff anymore."

As part of her package, Faith negotiated this position for me at their national library, subject to me doing a satisfactory job, of course. No free rides in this country. I've never looked back, though sometimes I miss interacting with people. It's lonely work. I can go a whole day down in the stacks without seeing another soul.

Books take a lot of energy to store. Space. Lights. Climate control. A non-negligible footprint. My job is to peruse our holdings on certain topics and make decisions about which books are no longer necessary to keep. Often the content of older books can be found in newer publications. Or the knowledge they contain has been superseded. We compost these. I understand the reasoning, but I still think it's a shame. Isn't everything unique in some way? Can any individually created object recreate or replace another one? Do true doubles exist? Obviously, my own history leads me to believe no.

I save some of them. "Salvage," Faith calls it. Hence my towers—a good portion of which I've consulted to write my report. The upshot of my current position is that I read widely: fuel for my after-hours work, my meaningful labor. I have often thought of my workplace as a subterranean forest, and me gathering kindling for a fire—this report.

In fact, it was during the course of reading a book, and making a decision about its fate, that I was inspired to embark on this project. I have it here, at the base of Tower P. It was written in the 1970s—part history, part historical anthropology, documenting an "extraordinary birthing practice" practiced among various people groups in medieval Central Asia. In certain communities, so written and oral records attest, it was customary for a mother's reborn self to be separated from the old self in the interests of both selves' safety. Each woman would then be nursed back to full health, and receive assistance from her husband and the wider community in caring for the baby as well. Among the groups where this was practiced, the exact role of the additional mother varied. In some places, the old mother would be accorded a position of respect not dissimilar to a powerful aunt. In other places, the new mother simply became the husband's second wife. In one community, a reborn mother would be offered a choice between becoming her husband's second wife or striking out on her own. In still another, this choice would be offered to the old self. And in another, the husband was removed from the equation entirely, and the old self and new self formed a parental pair—which enlarged to a cluster of three or four "sister-mothers" if any of them underwent pregnancy and rebirth again.

With the advent of modern civilization, of course, such practices were condemned as barbaric and went extinct. *But imagine that*, I thought when I first read the book, and brought it home. My first sa(l)v(ag)ed book. Surely there must have been other societies around the world where similar practices were normal. And I thought of how my mothers felt about rebirth, and how their mothers felt about rebirth. Surely, I thought, they couldn't have been the only ones.

Over the years, in the course of my everyday duties, I gathered my evidence, my twigs and branches to feed the blaze: additional examples of mothers-friendly practices; obscure feminist philosophers lamenting the waste of adult female life; real-life instances, unreported or underreported, where rebirth had gone wrong; studies where women—either reborn but unable to consume the old self, or the depleted old self herself—were nursed back to full health. All of these and more I have compiled in my report, in an accessible and easy-to-digest manner, of course.

I yawn. I'm ready to turn in. It's a little past midnight. I run over tomorrow's schedule in my head again. I'm taking leave so I don't have to report to work. I'll ride the MRT with Faith to the conference venue. As the head organizer, she'll be extremely busy, so I'll take care of myself. I've paid for my registration—though I'm her spouse, I still fall into the category of "member of the public." I'll get a seat up front. The maternal health chief will deliver her keynote. There'll be a short Q&A. When she leaves the stage, I'll hand her the report. Faith has assured me it will be fine—security won't be particularly tight—maternal health isn't a high priority, after all.

I push my chair in and give Ion a pat. He sits on the shelf above my desk these days, watching me as I work.

I get into bed. Faith stirs.

"All set for tomorrow?" she mumbles.

"You're not asleep yet?" I ask.

"Too much on my mind. Organizing this conference is such a

pain. I'm glad it'll be over soon." She sighs. "And the baby's kicking up a storm. I think she's nocturnal. I hardly get any sleep these days."

I nod, though it's dark and she can't see me. I think of the report—I'm always thinking of the report—and suddenly, I feel ashamed.

"You must regret having a lunatic for a husband," I joke.

"Not at all," she replies after a pause. "We all have things that are important to us."

"Do you think the report will make an impact?"

She hesitates. "You've worked very hard on it. And I agree it's an option that mothers should have."

I hear her voice tighten. Just a little. But I hear it only because it's a discussion we've already had.

"It's entirely your choice," I say, reassuring her. "I'm not trying to talk you into anything."

I've tried to persuade her before.

She sighs. "Darling, you know I support you. And I'm so happy you're finally done with the report. But this can't take over our lives anymore. We have to move on."

"Of course."

We kiss goodnight. She resumes trying to fall asleep.

If Faith goes through with her decision, I wonder if I'll miss her. If I'll notice it's not her. Of course, I'll notice, won't I? But the idea of rebirth genuinely doesn't bother her at all.

"What's there to be afraid of? Billions of women have gone through it," she assures me. "I'm sorry about what happened to your mother, darling. But I'm not her."

I know. I know.

I have a memory. A hazy one. So vague that I wonder if it really is a memory, not just my imagination. I'm very young and standing in a field of grass. It's sunny and there's a breeze. I'm walking through the blades, green and high and tickling. Directly in front of me, in the distance, I see my mother, crouched down, arms open. Which mother, I don't know.

I hear her voice. Are you strong enough? Yes you are!

I keep toddling forward, one step after another.

Almost there!

I'm swept into her arms.

Good job!

Her praise is warm and golden. It reverberates in my mind, a gentle, caressing boom. Good job.

The path is infinite. But it only appears so. There is always an end. If I keep going, I'll reach it. I just have to keep walking.

Author's Note and Acknowledgments

This novel grew out of two thoughts I had, in quick succession, when my two children were little, sometime in 2018. My older son was a toddler, and my younger son was an infant. I was pushing them in a massive double stroller, down a shop-lined street, feeling tired and very depressed. I had been feeling that way, on and off, from my second pregnancy onwards. My mood would fall, then stabilize, then fall again, dipping more frequently, and lower each time. On the surface, I continued to function normally, but there was a disconnect between my outer and inner self. On the low days, though I continued going through the motions of life, caring for and playing with my two sons, it felt as if there were another self, deeper down, who could experience no real pleasure or joy. I grew convinced of the complete futility of my actions, and more generally, life.

The two thoughts I had were as follows: (1) my body as an empty, cavernous, flooded house, and myself inside it, tiny and treading water, cut off from the world outside; (2) what if I weren't me? What if I had somehow given birth to another version of myself that had eaten and replaced me, and that was who I was?

*

This project was supported by the Copyright Agency's Cultural Fund. The Create Grant I received in late 2022 enabled me to finally sit down and write this work. Thank you to Jayapriya Vasudevan and Helen Mangham from Jacaranda Literary Agency, and to Daniel Lazar from Writers House for finding this novel a good home. Thank you to Alexa Frank at HarperVia for seeing the worth of this book, and for her thoughtful editorial insight. Another thank-you to Jayapriya, and to her husband Harish, for hosting me for a week in their flat and letting me plonk myself on their living room sofa every day with my notebook and pen. Thus began the first draft.

Thank you to everyone who helped me conduct research on the Chinese community in Medan: Charlotte Setijadi, Grace Tioso, and Zhou Taomo for sharing their contacts and making introductions; my mother's cousin Wim Wirgho, who helped me find my maternal grandfather's childhood address; Sofyan Tan, Finche Kosmanto, and Felix Harjatanaya from Yayasan Perguruan Sultan Iskandar Muda for taking the time to meet with me and giving me a tour of their wonderful school; 陳岷生 and 楊彩莉 for their generosity and kindness in sharing their knowledge with me and showing me around important Chinese cultural sites in Medan, including the Tjong A Fie Mansion, the gallery and grounds at Taman Tjong Yong Hian, the Sekolah Tinggi Bahasa Asing Persahabatan Internasional Asia (亚洲国际友好学院), and the 印華作協蘇北分會; 張舒芸 and 林來榮 from the latter two organizations for their graciousness and time; Meilyana Lidra and Jap Ai Lin for helping me answer questions I had about language, traditions, and day-to-day Medan-Chinese life.

A warm thank-you to Ed Iskandar for his willingness to listen to the challenges I was having structuring the novel and his casually brilliant insight on past and present storylines. And to Norman Erikson Pasaribu for suggesting the protagonist's nickname in 2022. Immeasurable gratitude to fellow writers who were so generous with their friendship and intellectual and emotional encouragement during this project: Grace Tioso and Zhou Taomo again; Jen Wei Ting; Fiona Lee; Clarissa Goenawan; Juliana Chow; Yumna Kassab.

Thank you to my family for always being there: my mother, my father, my siblings, Auntie Mimi and Lian, Justin, and my children. To my best friend from high school, Kathleen Chiu, and my therapist, Suzanne Dang, for helping me crawl out of the pit. Most of all, thank you to God for preserving me through that dark period of my life so I could look back and heal enough to make sense of it. May this book provide a fire for warmth and light, however small or brief its flame, so that other women in the darkness will know they are not alone.

A Note from the Cover Designer

Much of the horror of *But Won't I Miss Me* comes from the casual way its premise is presented. Vivi lives in a typical and ordinary house, she is married to a typical and ordinary man, and when the time comes, she will perform the typical and ordinary task of consuming her prior self.

Rebirth, as seen by Vivi, is both evolution and extinction—motherhood made literal and monstrous. I wanted the cover to capture that disquiet; something soft and luminous that reveals its unease only on closer look.

The photograph, with its translucent veil and interior light, suggests both a womb and a shroud. The pink light evokes life and warmth but also danger—flesh turned alien. The goal was to create a cover that feels beautiful but uneasy, an image that shifts meaning as the reader moves through the novel, asking, as the title does, what remains when the old self is gone.

—Stephanie Shafer

Here ends Tiffany Tsao's
But Won't I Miss Me.

The first edition of this book was printed
and bound at Lakeside Book Company
in Harrisonburg, Virginia, in April 2026.

A NOTE ON THE TYPE

The text of this novel was set in Garamond Premier, a typeface designed by Robert Slimbach over the course of 10 years. Released in 2005, its seeds were planted during Slimbach's development of the Adobe Garamond font family, also based in the work of Claude Garamond (1499–1561) and Robert Granjon (1513–1590). In 1994, a visit to Antwerp, Belgium, served as the catalyst for Slimbach's second interpretation. Garamond Premier differentiates itself from other revivals through its direct basis on the hand-cut models Slimbach studied, faithfully recapturing the elevated grace and clarity of its precursor.

HARPERVIA

An imprint dedicated to publishing international voices,
offering readers a chance to encounter other lives and other
points of view via the language of the imagination.